Final Fire

Other books by the author

Fiction

Support Your Local Vampire Kitty-Cat
An innocent vampire kitty-cat and his human
partner fight for their lives—er, undeadness?—against
the mob and a vigilante vampire-killer gang.

The Hollywood Unmurders
Crimes and dangerous times in La La Land for Patch,
the vampire kitty-cat, and his partner, Meg.

The Summer Boy
A murder mystery wrapped around a
coming-of-age story set in Texas in the 60s.

Gundown
A speculative thriller that explores a
real-world solution for gun violence.

Nonfiction

Mastering the Craft of Compelling Storytelling
Coaching on fiction craft and narrative technique
for writers of all levels.

Final Fire

Rhianna ~ *a story of the Magians*

Ray Rhamey

Ashland, Oregon

The platypus breaks all the rules—it's the only mammal that lays eggs, is venomous, has a duck bill, a beaver tail, and otter feet—and it does just fine, thank you very much.

It can be the same for novels that don't slip tidily into genre pigeonholes. Platypus authors take readers on unique paths to entertainment, truth, and enjoyable reads.

This book is a work of fiction. All characters, organizations, and locales, and all incidents and dialogue, are drawn from the author's imagination and not to be construed as real.

ISBN: 978-0-9909282-9-4

Cover and interior design by Ray Rhamey

To every science fiction and fantasy author that I've ever read, and there are a jillion of you, thank you for fostering in me a mind open to imagining far and wide.

To all of my critique partners and the readers of my blog who gave me helpful comments on openings, you helped me enormously.

To Sarah, wife and partner, who is my first and most important reader.

And to all of us who sometimes feel estranged amidst the tangle of humanity around us.

Embers from the fire of life

1

As I approach the steps to the Chicago Art Institute, the winter wind, called the Hawk by the people of this city, whips the long tails of my coat around my ankles and thrusts icy talons beneath my dress, greedy for my warmth. Last I was here it was a sweet summer breeze; today it is a harbinger of death.

A massive bronze lion, green with verdigris, a snow blanket white upon its back, guards the steps. When I close on the beast, a lean man wearing a black overcoat steps from behind it and eyes me. Then he targets me with a video camera. Fear clutches at me—his camera can see through my disguise.

Instead of the "Annie the tourist" *glamère* that I adopt when among the *lessi*—an illusion of freckles and springy red curls that his natural vision perceives—the camera's mechanical eye will pierce my deception to reveal the true Rhianna, my unblemished skin and straight brown tresses.

I pinch the sides of my hood together to shield my face. Will he tell someone if he perceives my *truself?* Will his tale of seeing two faces ripple outward until someone takes notice? I can't let that happen. Witch hunts have killed so many Magians through the centuries, I cannot risk exposure of the Clans that could spark a new pogrom. Pulling my hood tighter, I trot up the stairsteps past the lean man, paying him no mind as if he were not there.

Please, no trouble.

The lean man's lips move and the wind carries his words to me. "I think I got something."

When I glance at him, he jerks the camera away. Bilious yellow-green threads stream through the aura around his head—his actions are a lie in full bloom. He seeks to hide his purpose.

But it can't have anything to do with me. I cannot be known to him, and I have done him no harm.

Besides, today I die.

Above my head, the Hawk claws at a banner strung across the front of the Institute. It announces a 19th Century American Art exhibit. I need to see a painting there—a portrait of Graeme and me done by the extraordinary John Singer Sargent in ... was it 1874 that we posed for him?

There's no knowing if I will see Graeme on the "other side," or even if there is an other side, but I want to leave life with the image of that happy time in mind. A last comfort for my soul.

My soul.

I have not felt alive in the months since my Graeme was the random victim of a crazed homeless man. I so miss my man's little-boy-lost vulnerability, the hold-me look that made me want to wrap my arms around him.

But Graeme's murder didn't have to happen, did it?

I was there. I was more than there.

If only I had ... if only I had not ... They say the pain of loss diminishes with time, but I can testify that the ache of guilt grows until it eats your life.

Today it gets its last bite of mine. After my final look at Graeme, I will surrender to the winter cold and let the eternal chill that I brought upon my husband be the waiter that serves up my just deserts.

But that's a lie, isn't it? To die is not my punishment, it is my escape.

When I hurry past the lean man, he again trains his camera on me. This time the *lessi* doesn't bother to pretend that I am not the focus of his interest. Burgundy tendrils of hostility join the nasty green of deception in his aura. Why?

A sense of being prey prickles the back of my neck. I rush up the steps. I'm sure he's tracking me with the camera, but I don't think it has caught my face.

Please, no trouble.

~

In the basement level of the Art Institute, a tinny whisper shivers in KB Volmer's earbud. "Hey, you hear me? I think I got something." She steps out of the gallery of art by kids in Ireland. Their stuff didn't look any better than the crap she'd done as a kid that her mom had taped up on the refrigerator.

Speaking just loudly enough for her collar mic to pick up her words, she says, "Again."

The whisper says, "I got a glow."

She snaps into focus. There's only one thing he can be talking about.

The voice murmurs, "It's heading for the entrance."

KB snaps, "It would be helpful if I knew who this was and where you're stationed."

"Schultz, by the lion outside the Michigan Avenue entrance."

There's a quiver in Schultz's voice. Does he shake from the cold or from excitement? His words sure as hell send a thrill through KB. She hopes to be the first of the couple-hundred Homeland Security agents staking out museums across the country to catch one of the homegrown terrorist perps that call themselves the Artisans.

What they demanded just didn't make good sense to KB. That all art should be free? That anyone can take it from museums because art belongs to humanity? Bullshit.

After the second fire bomb went off in the Metropolitan Museum of Art after the one in the National Gallery of Art in DC, Homeland Security deployed thermal imaging cameras to major art museums across the nation. The crude fire bombs the Artisans set—made from flameless ration heaters and lithium-ion batteries—took a while to heat up enough to trigger thermal runaway in the batteries, and spotting them with a thermal camera before they could ignite was KB's mission. Her orders from the Resident Agent in Charge were clear. The RAC had told her, "Secure anything that glows and call the bomb squad."

Anticipation swells in her. Even Schultz sounds tight now; his voice has lost that lame whine—no more bitching about working in the cold.

Terrorists aren't going to start any fires on KB's watch.

KB says, "What do you see? The other bombs were in backpacks."

"Nothing like that. It's a person, a woman. She's walking around like it's a spring day, coat open. Everybody else, including me, is shivering and hurrying to get out of the cold. When I turned the camera on her, compared to other people her infrared output looks like a bonfire. A big person-shaped glow."

"But no bomb? I'm on my way up. What are we looking for?"

"Tall and slender. Wearing a dress and a long black coat with a hood up. The camera just shows the glow, not her actual face."

Oh, man, this has to be it. Reflex sends her hand inside her navy-blue blazer. Just beneath the Art Institute logo, her Walther 9mm semiautomatic waits, snug in its holster. Posing as an Institute security guard is perfect cover, though she hates the skirt—it makes her legs look heavy, and putting one on always feels like a demotion. Damn cold in the winter wind, too.

Her earpiece crackles. Schultz says, "She's going in."

Time to saddle up. KB says, "I'm headed up to the lobby. All stations, be alert for a tall, slender female that lights up your camera."

~

The Institute lobby welcomes me with an expanse of marble that prompts admiration for its grandeur, although I would rather see the meadow that once opened here, cloaked with snow in wintertime, its future a summer of green grass and golden flowers. There was a time I walked a deer path through that meadow to the lake beyond that seemed as vast as an ocean.

Now the meadow is crushed beneath the Institute's massive pile of stone, its future void of life. The lake no longer spills onto a sandy shore but lashes at concrete revetments, its waters the color of metal instead of crystalline blue. My abiding resentment at the unbridled swarming of the *lessi* rises in me—but soon it won't matter to me, will it?

I release the flow of *lledri* that I've kept circulating close to my skin to hold in my warmth. The life energy blends with the *lledri* streaming like golden sparks from people around me, unseen by them, a natural part of life for Magians.

A voice behind me calls out, "Jimmy! Stop!" A boy of about seven zooms past me and glances back, grinning. His foot slips on a spot of melt from tracked-in snow, and I wince at the jagged red-orange burst of pain in his aura when his head slams the marble floor. Oh, poor baby!

Two quick steps and I kneel beside him. His eyes widen, tears spill, and a wail echoes from the marble walls. I cradle his head as I slip my *sight* under his scalp and locate a growing contusion. Gazing into his eyes, I say, "Shhh. The hurt will stop soon, sweet child."

Drawing upon the streams of *lledri* coursing around me, I send my *touch* into the wound, stop the bleeding, and dissolve damaged cells. Soon his pain nerves quiet and the injury is on the way to healing.

I stroke his hair and the boy stops crying just as his mother drops to her knees beside him. She says to him, "Are you okay?"

The boy sniffles, glances up at me—I smile—and he nods. The mother says to me, "Thank you."

"I'm glad I was here." And I am. A moment's respite from my black life feels better than I want to admit. Blame my nature for that, the urge to help and heal that beats at my core.

As the boy gets to his feet, I cannot help but think of my son, Cael, though he is hardly a boy at 110 years old. I picture him, wrinkled and bent with age because he has never found his body's *key* cell that most Magians can trigger to flood their bodies with healing *lledri* and refresh their bodies to limit aging to one day a year.

I know he will miss me, but he will have the care he needs to stay well in Clan Deverell. The clan healer can keep him healthy. He will be fine.

I know my *key*, but this physician can't heal herself.

Still, having seen the boy fall, I instinctively take care on the slippery floor—and then grimace at the irony. What matters a bruise to a corpse?

Making my way to a cashier, I pay my admission and then find a sign for the early American art exhibit that directs me down the long hall that connects to the Institute's other building. And to a past life that was and cannot be more.

~

Heading for the stairs to the main floor, KB aches to break into a trot, but she forces herself to keep to a hurried walk, as close as she can come to the dawdle of a real museum guard. But when she reaches the steps and people can't see her, she charges up two at a time, electric with energy as if she goes into combat.

Who's to say this isn't combat? The war on terrorism is personal with her, and the enemy can be anywhere, is everywhere. She reaches the top and forces herself to put on the brakes when she hits the lobby. Now, if only Schultz is right about this. She scans the first floor like a radar dish hunting for an enemy.

~

Just ahead of me, a thick-bodied female museum guard bursts into the lobby from a stairway to the lower level. I have never seen an Institute guard hurry—they are usually older people who meander, wearing bemused half-smiles at their good fortune to be paid to spend their days surrounded by beauty and treasure.

This guard is younger than the norm. Thirtyish. Broad-shouldered. Short black hair. Like the thin man outside, her aura also radiates the yellow-green of dishonesty. And she too carries a video camera. A museum guard with a video camera? The woman sends her gaze prowling through the lobby.

Is she linked to the man out front? Did he see my *truself* with his camera and report my deception to her? He was talking to someone—

Shaking my head at my paranoia, I aim for the hallway lined with exhibits of medieval armor that look like metal men. My former father-in-law is much like them—short of stature and iron-hard. I wonder if Drago's venom toward me has lessened in the last year. Though why should it? I led his son to his death, did I not?

Taking a deep, cleansing breath, I force myself to narrow my focus to this moment; Drago will have to find some other target for his rage and bitterness, and I'm certain that he will.

~

A tall figure in a long black coat, a hood hanging down the back, strides past KB. Curly red hair, a youngish woman, just like Schultz said, heading down the hall with the knights. KB follows.

She aims her thermal camera. A bright glow flares in the viewfinder. Gotcha! She hustles after her quarry. She wants to run, but doesn't want to alert her target.

KB pulls the sleeve on her left arm up to uncover the tattoo of her brother Jeremy's book cover, *Flying*. Only a few days old, the image of red wings spread in a blue sky is sore. Like her heart has been since terrorists killed him, even though it has been years since ... She narrows her gaze at the woman ahead of her and whispers, "This one's for you, little brother, this one's for you."

When the woman gets close to the end of the hallway, she glances back. Her eyes widen when her gaze catches KB in pursuit. She increases her speed.

So does KB.

~

The guard moves toward me, leaning forward as if she runs even though she walks. Is she after me?

Nonsense, Rhianna. No *lessi* has known of our existence for centuries, and no word has come to me of a breach in our concealment. There will be no return of the persecution that took so many Magian lives.

Unless I am exposed here.

My back tightens between my shoulder blades as if expecting a blow.

A sign directs me through the Sculpture Court to the second level for the art exhibit. I need to thwart the guard's unwanted attention, so after I turn the corner from the hallway and out of her sight, I change my *glamère* from a youthful tourist to the regal dignity of a white-haired society matron I once chatted with in Brussels. Now the museum guard won't know me.

I decide not to change the appearance of my clothing rather than risk an accidental touch revealing that the reality does not match the perception. When my childhood playmates and I practiced our *glamères,* we longed to change our bodies to become real wolves and pumas, or, my favorite, a pony. To our regret, our true forms persisted underneath our deceptions. We were stuck with being human, no matter what our seemingly magical abilities were.

I stroll past a replica of the Abraham Lincoln memorial statue in Washington. It captures the man's strength, but not his wit. How his dark eyes had twinkled, what mischief his quick, playful mind had often devised.

How like the *lessi* to kill the best among them.

~

After the woman disappears around a corner, KB lengthens her stride to close the gap. She says to her collar microphone, "I am in pursuit of a suspect, a real hot spot in my camera. No sign of a backpack or a bomb, but that could be under her coat. Schultz, move inside and guard the Michigan Avenue doors. Use the camera on people leaving." She'll need evidence later. "Did you record her when she was coming in?"

His "damn" answers her question. She says, "Don't forget to record if you see something. Bailey, you on the Columbus Drive exit?"

KB would know Bailey's voice anywhere, deep and full of the rhythms of Chicago's Black south side. She says, "Yeah. I got the doors." A pause, then, "This really it?"

"Looks like. Be on the lookout for a tall, skinny redhead, long hooded coat over a long dress." Might be smart to have backup. "Martinez, where are you?"

He whispers, "Second level, main building. They got a painting with a locomotive steaming out of a fireplace. Weird."

"Get moving to the other side, upper level. I'll locate the subject, then we'll take 'er."

"Okay. Okay. But how do you know—"

"Are you walking or talking?"

"Walking. I'm walking. Jeez."

KB passes a suit of armor and feels a connection with the soldier who had worn the iron uniform. Like him, she's a protector with a mission to stand between evil and her country. She's vowed to do anything to carry it out. She touches her pistol again.

She can't hold back a tight little grin.

~

After I climb the stairs to the exhibit, I look down. The female guard rushes into the Sculpture Court. She peers at the people there.

She can look all she wants, she'll never see the real Rhianna. Now I can visit Graeme in peace. That's all I want—to see his face and then find solace within winter's chill grasp.

~

Movement on the second level catches KB's eye—someone tall in a black coat entering the American art exhibit.

She pounds up the stairs.

2

Inside the art exhibit, a dozen or so visitors wander among the displays. They pay me no mind.

I go to the painting I came to see. Graeme and I pose, *tru-self* of course, otherwise there would have been no reason for a portrait. Life size, he looms in shadows behind me, arms folded, his gaze directed down at me, no doubt thinking about nibbling the back of my neck. He was such a lusty man ...

Oh ...

I swallow against the emotion welling in my throat. I can't attract attention by letting sobs burst out.

If onlyc

In the painting, I gaze out, one hand on a saucily cocked hip. I had dressed for the portrait as if for an outing in those times—a floor-length white linen skirt, a jacket over a pleated blouse, and I hold a straw boater in one hand. The artist captured the golden gleam of my necklace, a delicate thing made of fine strands of woven gold that had once graced the neck of a Celtic ancestor. Other than my clothing, I look much the same now, perhaps a year or so older.

For all I know, the necklace's former owner is still alive, although I doubt it. While Magian bodies seldom fail, our minds eventually do, and then our bodies wither and die. What would the woman think of me, so ready to surrender the life I was taught to value so highly?

I don't have to ask. I feel my ancestor's disdain, even across the centuries.

The stocky guard from downstairs appears at the entrance to the exhibit, her full cheeks flushed, her body tight, clearly on the hunt. Can she, impossibly, be after me?

I sidle closer to a man of my height.

I cannot be discovered. My *glamère* has to work.

~

KB runs her gaze across the visitors browsing the exhibit. The curly-haired woman isn't here. Or is she wearing a disguise? KB eases her thermal camera up.

In her viewfinder, the infrared images of people, so much warmer than their surroundings, are lighter forms against the dark grays of cooler walls and floor, and clear enough to distinguish facial features. She pans the room until she comes to a bright white shape.

She jerks the camera from her eye; where the flare had been three people stand before a humongous painting of an old-time man and woman. There's a skinny, pimply-faced guy; a white-haired, snooty-looking older lady; and a fiftyish blond woman. The guy and the senior citizen wear long black coats.

KB raises the camera, focuses on the glowing spot, and turns down the gain. The glow dims and she zooms in until a woman's profile emerges. She glances KB's way; her face is oval, with delicate features and big eyes like a fashion model. Twenties or thirties, the age of the redhead in the hallway, but not one of the three faces she saw a minute ago. So which one of the three is she?

Okay, maybe there's a way. She turns up the gain until the Artisan's image becomes a bright blur and the two figures next to it show up. The Artisan is between the two normal images.

She lowers the camera. The center person is the white-haired woman. How the hell does she do it?

No matter, KB's got her now. She stifles a rush of delight, but not before tasting it, just a little. There'll be time to celebrate after she has the Artisan in handcuffs. Backing away from the entrance, she whispers into her collar mic. "Martinez! I need you."

"I'm coming. Some old woman wanted to know where the antique paperweight crap is."

"Get your ass in gear. The American art exhibit upstairs. Now!"

KB goes to the top of the stairs and peers into the Sculpture Court. She doesn't see Martinez's bow-legged stride. She paces and then returns to the exhibit entrance. She'll explode if she waits for Martinez. Maybe she can talk the Artisan out of the room and separate her from regular visitors. She has never met a female she couldn't handle. Or a male either, for that matter.

She slips the camera strap over her shoulder, slides a hand under her blazer to make sure her weapon moves easily in the holster, and enters.

~

I'm lost in the painting, reliving that sweet day with Graeme—we had gone on a picnic in the afternoon—when a woman's voice comes from behind me. "Excuse me, ma'am?" There is a sharp edge to her tone. I ignore it.

A heavy tap on my shoulder. "Ma'am?" The voice is tighter. "I need to speak with you outside."

I turn to her, my heart thrumming and a hollowness in my belly. It's the heavy-set female guard. I've never been accosted in this way by a *lessi*. I look down at thick black brows that almost meet in the center of the woman's frown. How can she still be after me? Her persistence is inexplicable. Long ago I perfected the art of avoiding entanglement with the *lessi*, yet the guard is certainly after me.

Who is this woman? *What* is she? How did she know to follow me through a change of *glamères?* Is she a half-breed, an *elessi* ignorant of her heritage but with enough Magian blood to see my *truface?* I search the guard's aura for colors emitted by the unique cerebral mutation that produces our ability to control *lledri*—can she tap the life energy that I use to warm myself, to project a *glamère,* or to *touch* inside someone to heal? The mystery only deepens; the guard's brain is as mundane as most.

Whatever her means of perception, she has to be dealt with. I give her a smile and imitate the accent of the woman from Brussels. "Yes, my dear?"

Her eyes widen and the blue-white of surprise shoots through her aura, perhaps at my regal manner. The woman hides her emotion with a smile as taut as her voice. I also *see* the guard's aura flood with the bloody red of battle. I hold my smile, hoping not to fuel her ire.

The guard says, "If you will step outside, I have a few, ah, questions for you."

I understand; she doesn't want to do anything in front of these people. "Of course, dear, perhaps after I finish the exhibit? It's fascinating, don't you think?"

The guard pulls her blazer away from her body just enough to reveal a holstered pistol. A museum guard with a concealed weapon? She narrows her eyes at me. "I'm afraid I have to insist on now."

The young man next to me says to the guard, "You need any help?"

She shakes her head. "No, I have backup on the way."

His eyes widen at that. "Backup?" He retreats a pace. "Is this a bust?"

"Just a question or two for the lady."

I put my hands on my hips and loom over the guard to deliver a question with all the manner of an outraged aristocrat, drawing out the words. "What is the meaning of this?"

Faces turn our way. The guard notices and clenches her teeth. She slips her hand inside her coat where she wears her gun. "Step outside?"

A Magian would *see* my aura flare with the acid yellow of fear. I cannot let the Clans be discovered else the *lessi* rekindle the persecution we survived so narrowly centuries ago. I will not panic. I turn to the young man who stands between the entrance and me. Giving him my warmest matronly smile as if this were an everyday pleasure, I say, "If you would excuse me?"

He smiles back at me, steps aside, and I move past him, the guard only a pace behind me, radiating menace like a hot wind. I grab the man's sleeve and pull. As he topples toward me, I gather sparks of *lledri* that swirl in the room, emanated by the people here. Focusing the energy into a tight, strong stream, I *push* the man and propel him at the guard. He stumbles into her, tumbling her backward. They fall in a heap, the man on top.

A quick glance at his aura assures me that I have not injured him, his aura's color is all astonishment. I don't care about her.

I run out the doorway and then stop a few paces from the stairs. No one is looking my way, so I change my *glamère* to a Minnesota farmer I met in the 1920s. This time, I include the appearance of my clothes in the illusion, changing it to the worn jeans, red flannel shirt, and the patched green parka he had worn. I calm myself with a deep breath, turn and amble back toward the Celtic exhibit, hands in pockets, just lookin' around. The guard will be after someone running away.

My pursuer charges from the exhibit to find a beefy blond farmer strolling her way, his cheeks permanently flushed from long winters. The guard sees nothing resembling a woman in a long black coat and silk dress.

Disguise is behavior as well as appearance, so I pitch my voice low and say, "Hey! Where's the Men's?"

~

With KB's quarry out of sight, the last thing she needs is some rube who has to pee. She says, "I don't know" and dodges around the guy, heading for the stairs. The Artisan must have moved incredibly fast to get out of sight so quickly.

The hick calls after her, "I'll-be-go-to-Jesus! Whut kinda guard are you, don't know where the Men's is at?"

KB says into her collar mic, "Alert! Suspect fleeing. Tall, white-haired woman."

Bailey says, "I thought you said she was a redhead."

Martinez comes on. "What the hell are you doin'? You got no backup."

"And whose fault is that?" She reaches the stairs. Nobody going down. Martinez hurries through the Sculpture Court below. Has she blown her big chance? She turns and shouts at the hick. "You see a tall woman, white hair?"

The guy snorts. "Oh, you want me to do yore job now?"

KB holds back a retort. "Please. This is an emergency."

He shrugs and points toward the Museum Shop to the left of the exhibit. "Mighta been somebody headed thataway."

She runs past him.

He calls after her. "A thank-you woulda been nice."

Adrenaline quickens her pulse as she slows and approaches the shop entrance. Gripping her gun inside her blazer, she steps through the doorway.

A half-dozen people browse books, toys, and gifts. Nobody in a black coat, but the Artisan could've ditched it. Nobody white-haired, but the perp has changed her appearance before.

KB pans the room with her thermal imaging camera. No glow appears. She wonders ...

She darts out and reaches the head of the stairs just as Martinez hits the top step. She says, "You see a big farmer-type on your way here?"

"Yeah." He points down the stairs. "Asked for the Men's room."

"That has to be her!" She shoulders past Martinez. "Come on!"

He follows her. "Her? All I saw was a guy."

She barks into her mic, "Suspect keeps changing appearance. Now looks like a big blond man. Schultz, you see anybody?"

"Nobody in a hurry on the Michigan side."

"Bailey, you inside or outside?"

"Outside, freezin' my ass off."

"You better get your ass ready." She nears the bottom. The only reason people run is because they are up to no good. She's had enough pussyfooting—she pulls out her gun.

~

I increase my pace as I cross the Sculpture Court, trying to hurry without seeming to. My farmer *glamère* fooled the female guard, but I suspect that won't last. I know a pit bull when I see one; the woman will pursue. Ahead is the exit to Columbus Drive. I have to escape.

I glance back and see the pit bull enter the Sculpture Court. With her is the brown man in the security uniform I passed on the stairs. Oh, chaos, the woman holds her gun! I have no defense against the damage a bullet does. She points at me and they break into a run toward me.

The irony of running for a life I don't want strikes me. But I'm not certain I can withstand torture should I be captured, and the existence of the Clans will come out. Yes, I could destroy myself with Final Fire, but here the explosion of energy cannot be concealed, and revealing the power of *lledri* will focus even more attention on the Clans. No, I have to get away.

I flee toward the exit doors, panic jolting through me, wanting to burst into a scream.

~

When KB sees the big farmer on the other side of the sculptures, she lunges into a sprint and snaps a warning into her collar mic. "I think it's coming your way, Bailey." She wonders if she should unmuzzle the dogs. The dude hasn't pulled a weapon, but he - she used force against her. The Artisan could be armed. For all she knows, she/he could have a bomb strapped around their middle. She orders, "Team Cobra, lock and load!"

Bailey's voice comes. "Goddam!"

Gaining on the farmer, KB shouts, "Halt!"

Her prey glances back and plunges around a corner. Oh, no you don't. You're not getting away from KB Volmer, nossir. She cranks up her speed.

~

Not caring if anyone notices, as I plunge into the crowd I shift into my Rosa *glamère,* the likeness of a young prostitute I met in Reynosa, Mexico in the 1950s. Though Rosa's fine features had a sultry beauty, she was only fourteen. People who glance at me will see a teenage girl in a faux leopard jacket and tight turquoise pants instead of a burly farmer in plaid and denim.

I burst out an exit door. Down the long flight of steps, a yellow school bus unloads a crowd of students about Rosa's age. I will mix with them and then—

"Freeze!" A uniformed Black woman, a gun gripped in front of her body with both hands, aims at me.

I squeal—it takes no acting to sound panicked. Imitating Rosa's heavy Mexican accent, I point at the door and cry out, "There's a beeg man with a gun!"

Uncertainty flickers across the woman's face, then she turns her gun toward the doors. "Behind me!"

I dash behind her but don't stop there. Cutting through the milling crowd of teenage *lessi* being shepherded toward the entrance, I run toward the school bus. The driver steps out the door and yells "Hey!" at me, but I keep going until I round the bus and lean against the rear door. Out of sight of the Institute entrance, I work to catch my breath and my thoughts.

The driver appears. He frowns and says, "You need to join the class."

I shake my head and speak as the little prostitute would, her English broken at best. "I not one of them, *Señor.*"

He says, "C'mon, you can sneak a cigarette later." He steps toward me and reaches.

I can't let him handle me; he'll feel the wool of my real coat, not the fake-fur *glamère* he sees. I step back and hold out my arms to keep him away. "Don' touch me, I scream."

That stops him. He raises a hand. "Whoa." He steps back a pace. "The group's about to go in."

I shake my head. *"Mi madre* cook in the restaurant. I not one of those boys and girls."

He studies me and then shrugs. "Yeah, I guess I'd remember that coat. Sorry."

Ahead, across Monroe Street, is Millennium Park. I'm grateful that the *lessi* feel an occasional need for dirt and grass in their cities. Under this patch they put an underground parking lot. I focus on a trio of small fir trees that huddle in the snow; perhaps, hidden within them, I can use a shadow *glamère* to get free of my pursuit and surrender to my fate.

Peering around the corner of the bus, I see no one coming my way. Yet. I head for the park. The cold strikes, and I hold my warmth close to my body with *lledri*. For now.

3

Gabe River scowls down at the Art Institute across the street from the conference room. Like his mind, the banner that touts the 19th century American art exhibit strains at its bindings.

At the Institute, creative minds rule, free to express what they see and feel. Until today, he has managed to feel that way, creating ads and commercials that he thought were best for his advertising clients. But today he is being chivvied into what he sees as creative prostitution. It does not sit well.

He turns to the wall next to him where the good, the other good, and the ugly sit propped on a waist-high oak rail. Storyboards for three Allied Hardware TV campaigns await presentation to the client, each big black rectangle containing a half-dozen pictures captioned with copy or lyrics. Gabe feels good about his "mini-sitcom" where the Allied Hardware star gets laughs along with delivering the message, and he loves the "mini-musical" campaign dreamed up by Lily, his associate creative director.

And then there's the third spot, Allied's pet celebrity reciting selling points. Lawrence, the agency's executive creative director and Gabe's boss, calls his commercial "Straight Talk." It's straight dull, a close second to watching moss think about paint drying. And now Lawrence has anointed it as the agency's recommendation. And ordered Gabe to do the dirty work of presenting it.

Lawrence sits on the edge of the fifteen-foot conference table, swinging his skinny legs, a lit cigarette between two fingers—he ignores the agency's no-smoking rules, and no one has the guts to stop him. He works at being slender and sports a deep tan in the middle of winter. The unreality of the tan is ridiculous, but Gabe admits that Lawrence looks sharp in his habitual three-piece suit. Gabe is happy to be comfortable in jeans and his navy-blue blazer over a black sweater.

Though Lawrence is fifty-something to Gabe's thirty-whatever and Gabe has a beard, people say they look a lot alike. Yeah, they're both tall, slim, black-haired, and blue-eyed, but Gabe doesn't see it. And he does not consider it a compliment.

One last try. Maybe there's still a chance to talk Lawrence out of it. Gabe goes to the storyboard for Lawrence's commercial. Working to keep his manner calm and reasonable, he says, "What worries me, Lawrence, is that this is just a talking head. There's no branding, no sell."

Lawrence glowers, a look Gabe is pretty sure he practices in a mirror because it always starts with a hesitation as if he has to remember how to adjust his features. Lawrence says, "I told you when I hired you that the only way to do Allied Hardware is the way *I've* been doing Allied. For seven years." He aims a long finger at the storyboard. "And that's it."

How can the man be so stupid? It's time to stand up. Gabe unclenches his fists and wishes his stomach didn't hurt at the thought of speaking truth to power. But it's the right thing to do. "I have to be honest with our client, Lawrence. And, as creative director on the account, I don't think it's right to recommend it."

Beaming the shit-eating grin Gabe has grown to hate, Lawrence says, "As *executive* creative director on the account, I think it's *exactly* right." He sucks on his cigarette and sends a cloud Gabe's way. Gabe is pretty sure Lawrence knows how much he dislikes cigarette smoke. Lawrence says, "Not because I wrote it, but because it's the best thing we have."

Gabe sees nasty yellow-green streaks rise from Lawrence's head as if the air has color, a sure sign that Lawrence is lying. So he doesn't believe his crappy ad is the best of the bunch and yet he's going to recommend it?

Gabe has never found a word for what he sees when people lie. Aura? But it isn't a glow so much as streaming sparks of translucent, luminescent color. He's never heard of anyone else seeing them. People would probably think it was a good thing, being able to tell when people lie. But he hates it. He's felt *outside* since he was seven and perceiving the color of a lie in action cost him his best friend.

Lawrence tells him, "You will present all the campaigns with all of your considerable charm and talent, and then you will heartily recommend Straight Talk."

Gabe itches to grab Lawrence's smirk and rip it off his face.

But he clenches his teeth instead—the job market is subterranean, and he has a family to support and a mortgage to pay. He has to do it the way Lawrence says. Not sure he can control himself if he keeps watching Lawrence's expression, he stares at the hounds-tooth pattern in the carpet. "You're the boss."

"Damn straight."

Lily pops into the doorway. "Client's here." She tilts her head toward the hallway behind her. "Got a second?"

Gabe always has a second for Lily. What he likes best about her is that her brains exceed her looks. She has her own unique beauty—not exactly pretty, but with enormous eyes, a smile that makes you feel good, and great legs. Right now she's making a pin-striped gray suit look hot.

He steps into the hall and she whispers, "Well?" She, of course, wants her campaign to be the recommendation. At least she believes in it.

Embarrassed for what he has to say, he tells her, "We're going with Lawrence's thing."

Her eyebrows shoot up, and then she frowns. "Damn. You were right." She shakes her head. "Why, for God's sake?"

Gabe shrugs. "He says it's best."

"Is he that big an idiot?"

"He's that big a liar."

"You think he's lying?"

"I know it."

Her eyebrows rise again, this time as if she doubts him.

Gabe says, "Tell me something about Tuesday when you went to the dentist."

Her smile drops away. "What?"

"How did the interview go?" A flinch in her gaze tells him he nailed it.

Wide eyes try for innocence. "Uh, interview?" Flickers of yellow-green in the air around her head clash with her red hair.

He shakes his head. "Lilllll ..."

She sighs. "Okay, this headhunter's been begging to talk to me, but I swear I'm not looking." The green tendrils fade away; that's the truth. She frowns. "How can you ... that's weird."

He laughs. "I'm just good at picking up on body language. But if you get an offer, I want a chance to counter. I like what you do."

Her smile gives Gabe a lift and he returns to the conference room. As he arranges storyboards and runs through the pitch in his mind, the reality of what he is about to do sinks in. He has to lie to his client. He has to sell him on the wrong thing.

What a whore he is.

~

In the big lobby outside the Sculpture Court, KB forces herself to scan and rescan the crowd milling this way and that.

The farmer has vanished. She uses her collar mic. "Bailey, anybody come out?"

Bailey's voice rushes into KB's earpiece. "Just a skinny Mexican girl, scared shitless. She says there's a big guy with a gun. I'm ready."

KB scans the lobby. There is no farmer, and no commotion stirred up by a man running around with a gun. Another change? "Did you use your camera on the girl?"

"No, but you said—"

"Shit, I bet that was the Artisan."

Bailey says, "That's impossible."

"The hell it is." Martinez close behind her, KB hurries toward the doors. Just as she gets there, teenagers flood in, plugging the doorways, forcing KB back. She tries to shove her way through, but the kids don't push easy.

Finally outside, she finds Bailey in position, a tall, broadshouldered woman with gun in hand. Even though she's older, maybe in her forties with little bits of gray in her black curls, she's strong and fit. KB likes that about her. "Where?"

The question gets a blank look. "What?"

"The girl."

Bailey searches and then points up the sidewalk at a small figure walking away.

KB's vision narrows; it's as though she looks through a rifle scope. She centers on long black hair, scrawny legs, leopard coat and awful pants. How can it possibly be the Artisan? It's a kid playing hooky from a field trip. But there's nobody else in sight.

Like a hawk above its quarry, her instincts tell her she's right. She yells, "HALT!"

The girl walks faster.

The hawk stoops; KB lifts her pistol and squeezes off a warning shot, aiming to send a bullet past the teenager or whatever it really is.

The slender trunk of a sapling explodes three feet from the girl's head. She startles, her feet slip in the slush, and she falls on her back. She rolls and struggles to a crouch. Her eyes widen when she zeroes in on KB.

KB yells, "Halt!"

The girl sprints away, stooping low. KB aims again.

Martinez grabs KB's arm and pushes her weapon up. "You nuts? That's a little girl!"

KB tears away from Martinez's grip. She flashes on an image she'll never get rid of—American Airlines Flight 11 slamming into the World Trade Center, her brother on board. Old rage explodes and she turns on Martinez. "You got a problem with stopping terrorists?" Martinez flinches back, and she realizes that she's way too much in his face. "Sorry, Martinez. But this whatever-it-is assaulted me and then ran for it. Sound like normal behavior to you?"

He looks to Bailey for support, but she stands quiet. He shakes his head. "No, I guess not." He points at the girl running away. "But you don't know that little girl is the one you had trouble with."

"Look at her run."

"Well, shit, you just shot at her."

Doubt pricks her, but all her instincts say that's the Artisan. The girl is across the street, nearing the underground parking entrance. She says, "Bailey, your camera!"

Bailey lifts the thermal camera to her eye. "Goddam! You're right! Glows like a lightning bug."

Damn right she's right. KB snaps another shot, but the bullet ricochets off a concrete wall beyond the fugitive. The "girl" darts onto the ramp leading down into the parking garage.

KB breaks into a run and shouts, "Follow me!"

She dashes across the street and calls into her microphone, "Schultz, it went into the underground parking entrance on Monroe. Get over here!"

~

I run to the bottom of the ramp and into the first level of the parking lot. I need to go to ground quickly, before the woman is upon me.

Rows of cars fill the dank space. Even though brightly lit, it seems gloomy—the naked concrete floor, ceiling, and pillars all an ugly, unfinished gray. My breath puffs in little clouds of vapor. If only I can slip into a vehicle and lie on the floor.

I trot between cars, trying doors as I go. All are locked! Why are the *lessi* so consumed with things to possess and things to steal? I answer my own question—because they are human, no more or less so than Magians.

I grab at the door handle of a hulking SUV with dark-tinted windows and break a fingernail. I ease *lledri* into the door lock, hoping I can deduce how to open it by pushing on tumblers. But it's electrical, and I can't figure it out.

Tires squeal down the ramp into the garage. I have to find a hiding place, now! A sense of sanctuary calls to me from a far corner. A light is out there, and in the dimness sits a black pickup truck. Perhaps I can use a shadow *glamère* to hide me in it.

I run to the truck and find a bale of hay and a hundred-pound sack in the bed. I lean closer—oats, by the smell. The dry, sweet scent is like a warm, sunny day from my childhood, when my family settled on a farm for a time. A hint of *lledri* radiates from the burlap sack—maybe my luck has turned. This is why the truck felt like a refuge—the only way for dead organic material to absorb *lledri* is from someone who has use of it. A Magian, or an *elessi*.

I climb into the truck bed and then shift the bale and the sack to make a hollow in a corner behind the cab. Stretching my legs between the wall of the truck bed and the hay bale and then huddling behind the oats, I cast a shadow *glamère*. The truck's metal is cold, and I shiver. I warm myself by circulating just enough *lledri* over my skin to retain my body heat and stop trembling. I should be invisible to a *lessi* as close as a foot away. They will have to lay hands on me to discover my presence.

What if they somehow do? Can I kill them? Oh, I *can* easily enough, but will I take a life?

Take a life in order to save one that I am eager to quit?

~

KB leads Bailey and Martinez to the underground parking entrance, their guns out, ready. The rectangular concrete hole in the earth tempts her to rush in. It's quiet now, no cars in the lanes, no gates going up or down. The guy in the booth who collects money gives them a bored glance. She'll search all the levels if she has to. She's not leaving without the Artisan, no way. Trouble is, there are three exits.

Schultz jogs toward them down Monroe Street. KB says into her mic, "Schultz, head over to the Michigan Avenue parking exit. Use your camera on everybody and get the license numbers of vehicles that leave the garage. Call the second you see a glow." Schultz wheels and heads away.

She points at the exit across Columbus and aims the next order at Bailey. "You do the same there. Martinez, take this one."

Bailey says, "Where you gonna be?"

KB smiles. "Hunting."

Between puffs, Schultz's voice comes. "You take ... all the ... damn fun."

He's a two-pack-a-day ex-cop. She says, "This is over, Schultz, you're getting some nicotine patches and hitting the treadmill."

"Yeah ... right."

Bailey says, "What we watchin' for?"

Good question. "Well, so far the Artisan has looked like a tall redheaded woman, an old society broad, a big hick, and a teenage Chicana. You see any of those, stop 'em and call me." She raises her thermal camera. "And use your cams."

Martinez says "Roger" and takes up a position by the exit lane.

Bailey says, "Why don't we just barricade the exits, check everybody out?"

While KB believes Homeland Security has the power to do whatever it damn well thinks it needs to do in the interests of national security, her by-the-book, tight-ass Resident Agent in Charge thinks there are limits. She nods. "Good idea, Bailey, but we don't have the clout. And we don't need a bunch of pissed-off citizens complaining." Especially not to the RAC.

Bailey nods. "You got that right." She turns away, then turns back. "They's somethin' weird 'bout that girl. You know how she fell on the sidewalk?"

"Yeah. So?"

"Those blue pants of hers oughta been soakin' wet with a big dark spot, you know? But they were the same when she got up."

Damn. "Good eye, Bailey." But what does it mean?

Bailey nods and strides across the street to her post.

Now that KB has a second to think, what the hell is she about to tackle? Those incredible disguises—some kind of new technology? Does the Artisan have a weapon to match? If so, why didn't they use it?

Alarm cools her heat of the hunt, and a knot of fear forms in her belly. Still, she's going in. Has never backed away from danger, never will. KB unslings her camera and heads for the parking attendant's booth and raps on the glass.

The man inside, a few days away from his last shave, opens a window to peer at her, his gaze heavy-lidded and dull. "Yeah?" Warm air from a space heater rushes out, and she catches the aroma of alcohol on top of serious body odor.

"You see a kid run in here?"

The guy shrugs. "I'm here for cars coming to park, not people goin' in."

"So you didn't see where she went?"

He shrugs again.

"Didn't you hear shots?"

"I heard a couple backfires."

The man is useless. KB trots down the ramp to the first level. She grins with anticipation, lifts her camera, and aims at the rows of cars. There must be hundreds of them, but there'll be no hiding from her. She studies her viewfinder. "Shit!" A dozen spots flare as bright as the Artisan's glow. "What, we got a herd?"

Schultz's voice comes. "What're you seeing?"

"A bunch of hot spots, but none of 'em are tall like the Artisan. They're about as bright, but lower to the ground, and blocky." She focuses on the closest glow, then takes the camera away. She sees a red Explorer. She walks to it and hears the tick-tick of metal contracting in the cold. She lays her hand on the hood. Warm. KB sighs and reports. "I'm seeing heat blooms from motors in cars that recently came in. I'm gonna have to check each one."

She eyes the stairs to the lower levels. "I'm thinking it would have kept running down."

A snort in her earpiece, then Schultz says, "Somebody shooting at me like that, I sure would have."

Yeah, yeah, yeah. "So I'm starting with the bottom level and working my way up. Stay ready." KB grips her thermal camera in one hand and her Walther in her other. Heading for the stairs, she says, "Use your cameras. If I flush it out, order it to surrender. It speaks English. If it won't give up, shoot to wound. We want a live one."

4

Gabe sings the songs, dances the dances, and cracks the jokes. He wraps up his presentation by saying to Phil Esterhaus, the Allied Hardware client, "We recommend the Straight Talk campaign." Gabe takes his seat, a bad taste in his mind, nausea curdling his gut for the lie and anger simmering in his veins for being such an asswipe.

Lawrence smarms, "We all think we've got a winner here, Phil, just like last year." The two account executives nod like bobble-head dolls.

A winner? More like a wiener. Gabe wishes he could push a button and eliminate all stupid people. It would be fun to watch good old Lare melt into a noxious puddle. Maybe he should include liars, too. Whoa, can't do that; he's one of them now. He'd like to blame Lawrence, but it's yours truly that's turned himself into a prevaricator.

Phil smooths the sparse patch of hair left on top of his head and studies the storyboards lined up across the wall. He leans back and scratches his paunch, a gesture that means Phil sees something he likes. "Well, thanks, Gabe and Larry. I can sure see your reasons for recommending it."

Gabe spots glimmers of yellow-green around Phil's head. This is too much. The guy's always been honest before. Gabe's anger roils.

Whore.

The flickers of Phil's lie thicken to streams when he says, "Yessir, it's simple and straightforward. It really does the job."

Damn, it hurts to do this shameful thing. So he won't. He stands and says to Lawrence, "I can't do this." To Phil he says, "Please excuse me, Phil, but I've got to duck out. I'll see you later." He heads for the door.

He hears the smirk in Lawrence's voice behind his back. "Sure you can do this, Gabe." As if he is pulling on a leash, Lawrence says, "Sit."

There has never been a leash that worked on Gabe. He turns to face the room. Phil looks puzzled and Lawrence slouches in his chair, somehow managing to look down his nose at Gabe even though he is sitting. Gabe returns to the foot of the table and keeps his voice low when he says, "Maybe there is something I can contribute before I leave."

Lawrence's expression shifts from lord-of-the-manor to concerned. Gabe points to the Straight Talk storyboards and says to Phil, "There is *no* reason to recommend that crap."

Phil looks like he's just run into an invisible wall. He says, "But you said ... I ... ah ... pardon?"

Lawrence's tan cheeks redden. "Gabe."

Gabe likes Phil and feels bad about disconcerting him, but he isn't going to back off now. He'd feel worse about living the lie. "I'm sorry, Phil, but I just can't do it."

Phil says, "Do what?" He looks to Lawrence. "What can't he do?"

Lawrence pastes on a smile. "Gabe's having a little fun with me, Phil. We had a small disagreement earlier regarding the recommendation."

Gabe says, "We didn't *really* disagree, did we?" Knuckles on the table, he leans toward Lawrence. Lawrence shies back. "We both know Straight Talk is straight shit."

Lawrence says, "I think you're through, Gabe."

Gabe says, "Good. See you around, Lare." Lawrence hates being called "Lare."

Turning to Phil, Gabe says, "Good luck, Phil. If I were you, I'd do either one of the other two campaigns. That's the only way you're going to get a winner out of this meeting." He leaves Phil looking like he'd taken a sip of coffee and found motor oil instead.

Gabe is twenty feet down the hallway before Lawrence's voice attacks from behind. "You hold on there!"

Gabe stops and turns. Lawrence advances on him, his face flushed, his hands clenched into fists.

Lawrence comes to a halt close enough for Gabe to smell the cigarette smoke on his breath. "What the fuck do you think you're doing?"

Shackles lift from Gabe's mind. "How about the right thing?"

Lawrence sucks in air as if Gabe had thrown a jab to his belly. His face reddens even more. "You're one more word from being out of a job."

Out of a job. But this job, with Lawrence fouling his work and yanking on a leash, will be hell. Gabe has been here before, suffering the daily insult of working for a lesser man. Last time it had cost him lots of sleep and the beginnings of an ulcer. He'd vowed to never suffer fools again.

"One more word? I can do a lot better than just one, Lare." He smiles. "How about ass-kissing? Don't you have some to do? Phil's going to need a long, deep pucker if you want to keep him happy."

Like a fish, complete with round, glassy eyes, Lawrence opens and shuts his mouth a couple of times. Then he spins and hurries back to the conference room. Gabe heads for his office, a flush of triumph humming through him.

He stuffs personal things into his briefcase—a picture of Bonnie holding Berry when she was a baby and another one of his little girl in the saddle on Gabe's horse, Rusty, when Berry was five. He rounds up the small herd of wind-up toys that visitors love to play with, then looks around. That's all his personal stuff. He feels good, warmed by the glow of righteous anger.

He stops by Lily's office on the way out and sticks his head in. "It's all yours now, Lil." He heads for the elevator, not wanting any more talk.

Her voice comes from behind. "You didn't do anything stupid, did you?"

Yeah, stupid would be a good word for it.

Lily calls out, "What did you do?

He cuts through the lobby, summons the elevator, and turns. She stands at the lobby entrance. He shrugs. "Told the truth."

"About Lare's campaign?"

He nods.

Her eyes widen. "You didn't!"

The elevator door opens and he steps in. He punches the 1 harder than he needs to. It hurts his knuckle.

He's just been fired. Once again, he is a misfit. An outsider. Alien. Alone.

Screw 'em. He'd spoken truth to power. Fought the good fight.

He just wishes he felt like he had won.

Gabe trots along Michigan Avenue to the underground parking, trying to cheat the Hawk out of a share of his flesh. When he hits the ramp down to the first level, he isn't sure the tips of his ears made it. But earmuffs look so dumb.

By the entrance, a skinny guy in a black overcoat points a video camera his way. Gabe turns on him and vents a little. "You taking my picture?"

The guy lowers the camera and shakes his head. "Uh, just checking the white balance."

Gabe sees the color of lies spurt around his head. What is he up to? The guy turns away and Gabe decides to go on.

Some kind of wacky tourist. He looks back, but the guy now aims the camera at a mom leading a snotty-faced little boy into the garage.

Gabe hopes his stuff will still be in the back of his truck. He doesn't think anyone would steal a bale of hay and a hundred-pound sack of oats, but you never knew about Chicago, and this has not exactly been his day so far. His daughter will be pissed if they don't have anything to feed Rusty tomorrow at the farm.

On the other hand, Berry getting pissed would be great. It would be a breakthrough.

When Gabe nears his pickup, the hay and the oats are still there. Something is going right. No sense in letting wind tear at the hay any more than necessary, so he shoves the bale to snug it up to the side of the bed—but it doesn't budge.

He tries more force, but the bale seems blocked. Weird. He reaches into the deep shadow between the bale and the wall of the bed and his fingers jam on something firm. He grips it— kinda round, both hard and soft, and part of it gives ... a leg? Startled, he steps back and peers into the truck bed.

As if looking through veils made of shadow, he sees a girl huddled in the corner beside the sack of oats, her legs stretched alongside the hay. She looks Hispanic, is small and scrawny, just a kid. All Mister Quick-Wit can think of to say is, "Uh, hello."

The girl's eyes widen, then the shadows blink away and she's easy to see. He glances behind him to see if car head-lights had been turned on, but there's no one there. He turns back. The girl is plainly visible. He shakes his head. This thing with Lawrence and the lie color have him seeing things. The girl shivers and wraps her arms around herself. Her leopard jacket looks way too light for a Chicago winter. He says, "Are ... are you all right?"

She nods. Then shakes her head.

Something about the girl feels ... *familiar.* How can that be? "Are you hurt?"

Her voice barely makes it to his ears. "No."

"Well, I'm leaving. You'll have to find someplace else to ..." To what? What is she doing in the truck? Doesn't seem like a choice place to stay warm, not with all kinds of buildings nearby to choose from, including the Art Institute. "Well, I've gotta go." He extends a hand to help her out of the truck.

She shrinks from him. "I am scare."

"Scared?" Gabe looks around. Nobody in sight. He turns back. "Of what?"

"Some people chase me. They shoot gun."

Holy shit. "What people?"

"I don' know."

Is she trying to hustle him? Gabe squints at her and doesn't see the green of a lie. Okay, she's telling the truth and seems truly frightened. He wishes he could help her, but what can he do?

She solves it for him. "Can I just stay here when you drive away? I get out when you say." She looks up at him, her eyes huge, begging for help.

Hell, why not? "Okay. I'm going to the near-north side. That work for you?"

Her smile is quick and white. *"Gracias."*

But she'll freeze. "You ought to ride inside, though."

She shakes her head. "Here, I can hide. There, they can look and see."

He isn't going to push it. This time of afternoon it's no more than twenty minutes to his apartment. Still, the wind chill will be brutal ... he unlocks, pulls a green wool blanket from behind the seat and offers it to her. "It'll be awful cold when we're moving."

"Gracias." She takes the blanket and pulls it over her, then sinks down behind the oats. Shadows deepen and seem to envelop her. Barely able to make her out, he glances up at the burned-out bulb overhead. They need to do something about the lighting down here.

He starts up and pulls out, turns the heater on high and hopes it kicks in soon. When he stops to open the exit gate with his monthly permit card, the skinny guy with the camera is back, peering into the cab. The girl was right about that.

Then the man checks the front of the truck and writes on a pad. What the hell?

Gabe rolls down his window to ask what he's doing, but then thinks he'd better not attract attention; the guy'll spot the girl for sure. He readies to pop the clutch and burn out when the gate lifts. No, that isn't good either, might send the bale of hay sliding and reveal the girl. He gives the thin man another look—can he be the one who shot at her? Why is he hanging around a parking garage?

The gate lifts and Gabe pulls onto Michigan Avenue. Is he getting himself into a gang war? It's a little late to worry about that, isn't it? The perfect end to a perfect Friday: lose your job and acquire a bullet hole. Checking his rearview mirror for pursuit, he punches it through a yellow light and heads for Lake Shore Drive.

~

When the pickup surges forward, I rise up just enough to see over the truck-bed walls—and instantly duck back down. The slender man from the front of the Art Institute is there with his little video camera in his hand. But he seems not to have noticed me.

I relax when the truck picks up speed, but I have to stay alert. Even though the bearded man helps me now, and I have not *seen* any hint of deceit in him, he could be a danger. I'd had to stifle a scream when he said hello—a *lessi* could not have perceived me. So what is he? I recall no glow of *lledri* in use, not even to warm himself, something that's second nature to clansmen. And, although he pierced my shadow illusion, he did not seem to see my *truself* through my Rosa *glamère*.

Is he *elessi?* When I think back without the haze of fear clouding my mind, I remember him as he peered down at me. Yes, he had *read* me for truth. And it was residual *lledri* from him that drew me to his truck. Perhaps when he stops and gets out I can probe further, but now the glass and metal of the truck block my *sight*, and I cannot *see* if he is using *lledri*.

The strange events at the Art Institute have made this life even more hostile. How could that woman have tracked me? Perhaps she used her camera to see my *truface*. Even so, how is that cause for shooting at me? At least now the secret of my people is safe. I hate the guard for making me afraid. I have not felt such dread for more years than I can recall.

We move faster and the wind slashes me. I huddle under the blanket the bearded man gave me, a gesture I am increasingly thankful for. There is no use suffering, so I wrap *lledri* close to my body, and it warms me. Just now, surrendering to the cold seems an uncomfortable choice. I have heard that freezing to death is like going to sleep, but my body tells me differently. The cold hurts. Still, when this wild ride is over, that is what I will do.

An image of the fear in Graeme's eyes when he realized he was dying invades, and its cruel grip crushes me. Tears well, and one runs down my cheek.

I imagine it freezing there.

The sooner the better.

5

The percussive whup-whup-whup of a helicopter draws Drago to a porthole in his galleon's quarterdeck cabin. In the forest clearing where his ship and two others of his clan rest, a half-dozen clan children, teens to toddlers, build a snowman. The tall curved hulls of the sixteenth-century Spanish vessels, all grace when they sail on the sea and through the air, now seem awkward, supports angling out like spider legs to hold them upright as they rest on their keels. The daylight is depressingly dim under the gray January sky, but that doesn't seem to matter to the children.

The helicopter nears and the noise smothers the children's giggles. The galleons vanish behind *glamères* of snow-clad forest, the illusions broadcast by alert sentries.

All save one of the children disappear as well, disguised as young trees. Little Alexandra, her *lledri* skills not yet awakened at age four, bursts into tears.

Drago swings the porthole open to help her with a concealing *glamère,* but then a sapling scoops up the child. In the flicker of a thought, a fat squirrel appears in her place. Satisfied that the children are safe, he closes the port against the chill.

The helicopter sound fades, the ships and children blink back into view, and a snowball fight develops. Intrusions by *lessi*—and the danger they bring—are normal to clan children these days, but for Drago they are a long-endured infestation that he will soon eliminate.

He'd rather be basking in Louisiana warmth with the rest of his clan than skulking in a forest preserve on the outskirts of Chicago. But his research into recombinant DNA demands top university libraries close to a good hiding place, and it has been worth it. He is near to ending the murder and destruction ordinary humankind visits upon the world. The *lessi* killed his son, but no more. Drago's on the cusp of a final solution for the *lessi* blight. He feels it. Perhaps *this* day, yes!

And then he will have avenged Graeme's death, his son gone forever, cut down in the prime of manhood by a *lessi*. And killed by Rhianna, the best of Clan healers, who did nothing to save Graeme.

Drago shivers, gathers *lledri,* and controls the flow of the life force to create a blanket of energy that hugs his skin and repels the cold. Warm light from kerosene lamps gives the impression of comfort, but the cabin is unpleasantly chilly despite oaken wall panels and woolen Oriental rugs that insulate the hardwood floor.

The pot-bellied wood stove in the corner tempts him, but a column of smoke can't be disguised, and the danger of discovery is too great so close to a *lessi* city acrawl with people like maggots in a carcass.

He tests the chill of a wall panel with a fingertip and then traces the carving there, a scene of his ancestor Merlin, deep in conversation with King Arthur. The artist portrayed Merlin as tall and lean, with a handsome beard that reaches his chest. Drago wishes he looked like the carving instead of the balding, plump appearance he associates with a ruddy-cheeked butcher in a small-town grocery store. He suspects that the real Merlin looked much like he does, and the majesty portrayed on the panel is no more than an artist's imagination at work.

Drago smiles at Merlin's reputation as a wizard, created by using *lledri* to do tricks that looked like "magic" to medieval people. The *lessi* are so easily fooled.

He shakes his head at Merlin's brave but hopeless attempts to guide the *lessi* King Arthur to form a rational civilization. The wizard's blood runs true, though; Drago is close to creating his own remedy for a sick world. If he can just breach the last barrier, the *lessi's* constant attack on all he holds dear will vanish as if it had never been. The children of his clan—of all the clans—will prosper, free of peril. The natural balance of the world will return, and the danger of global warming will recede into history.

He strokes his moustache, the one thing he has in common with Merlin's carved image. Despite his centuries, Drago's moustache is still brown, as is what remains of his hair. If only he had found his *key* to rejuvenation before he reached his thirties and his scalp had become a bleak pink dome rising above a low hedge of hair. No matter how much *lledri* he pumps into his scalp, nary a hair grows there. That he is stuck with his looks for the rest of his days is one of life's minor irritants.

On the far wall, the painting of Lake Hallstatt and the surrounding hills of the Celtic homeland hangs crooked. Drago guides *lledri* to straighten it with *touch*. The picture flies from the wall and, luckily, lands on a cushioned easy chair. For the millionth time in his life, he curses the clumsiness of his *touch*. He can lift a galleon with it, but the most inept of his clan can best him with small objects.

He lifts the picture with his hands, re-hangs it, and then scowls at the grandfather clock, its pendulum patiently marking time: eight-fifteen. Vixen is late. They have work to do. He takes the iron spiral staircase that descends to below-decks, his footsteps clanging.

In the middle hold, at one time the mess hall for sailors and later a recreation room when Drago had a family, scattered sofas and chairs now host meetings in his role as clanmaster. Along the wall that separates the room from his quarters in the forward hold, wide wooden stairs rise to the above-decks door. A clatter comes from the galley at the rear. "Emmaline?"

"Doin' dishes."

He goes to the galley doorway. Her back to him, his house matron washes breakfast dishes, her broad shape and orange floor-length skirt swaying in time with the tune she hums. A big bow secures a yellow apron to her waist. He finds Emmaline pleasingly proficient but annoyingly cheerful.

Her competence matches that of the galley, a decidedly one-rump kitchen crafted with the efficiency needed for a sailing vessel. Even though his ship no longer bears masts and canvas, it sails the air, does it not? And, during the long voyage from the old world to the new centuries before, they had rested on the ocean's surface to replenish supplies with fish lured from the sea.

"Emmaline, I'll be working in the lab."

She pauses to glance back. "Aye, Drago. Will Vixen be comin' along, then?"

The door at the top of the stairs to the deck bursts open and admits an exasperating gust of freezing air. Vixen breezes down, her curly bush of long russet hair the color of a red fox flaring over her shoulders and rippling down her back like a cloak of curls.

Low-riding jeans and a halter top expose entirely too much flat belly that has a disgusting gold pin piercing her navel. Her fair cheeks fetchingly reddened by the cold, she looks no older than a teenager. She discovered her *key* at nineteen and holds herself there. He envies her having such youthful beauty that ages only one day a year.

When he searched his clan for someone who could wield *touch* finely enough for his needs, he hadn't expected the tiny dancer and musician to be the most talented, other than Rhianna, her *touch* exceeding even that of his clan healer.

He's never cared for Vixen's wild ways, and he finds little to like about her other than her small size; hardly five feet tall, she is one of the few adults in the clan shorter than he. But so far even she has not produced the delicate control needed to manipulate genetic structure the way his project requires.

He wonders if anyone can ... if only his own *touch* weren't so clumsy ... if only he and Rhianna weren't at such odds. He would never reach out to her, she would never answer if he did. Graeme's ghost haunts them both.

He'd like to lambaste Vixen about being late—she'd probably been up until the wee hours carousing in bars on Chicago's near-north side—but he plies her with a smile instead. "Are ye well rested, Vixen?"

She glares at him. "Eat shit and die, Drago."

Yes, he had pressed her hard the day before, but surely that was no cause for crudity. Young people have no etiquette, and the most recent generation might as well be Martians for all that he understands them. "I should think that after ninety years ye would have better manners."

"Yeah, well, I make an exception for a guy who thinks he's still the same old slave owner he was when Columbus was a pup."

"They were only *lessi.*"

Her eyes flare, the irises a morning sky blue rimmed with black. "Well, *I* am not *lessi!* And I will *not* be your slave!"

Emmaline bustles in from the galley, carrying a cup and saucer, steam rising from the cup. Drago winces; his finest antique English china, which he's had since the 1800s, is as fragile as the bones of a baby bird. He loves the Staffordshire blue-and-white rose pattern, beautifully detailed and botanically accurate, right down to the thorns on the stems.

Emmaline says, "Good day to you, Vixen. Care for a cuppa cinnamon tea?"

Vixen beams at Emmaline. "Oh, yes." She takes the cup and inhales the aroma.

For reasons he can't fathom, Emmaline likes Vixen. Drago would like to put a stop to the use of his best china, but then Emmaline might decide she no longer wants to work for him. She has no real need to, empowered as all Magians are by mastery of *lledri* to be as independent as she wishes, welcome anywhere in the worldwide community of clans.

Drago says, "Bring it with ye, then, we've work to do." He launches a scowl at Emmaline, who knows full well how he feels about giving Vixen the fine china. He gets a pleasant, galling smile in return. To Vixen, he adds, "And take care."

She widens her eyes. "Oh, yassuh, Master, I be doin' what you say."

Insolent little bitch. If they succeed today, perhaps she will be the first test of his final solution's lethality.

He smiles.

Upstairs, inside the forecastle structure that houses Drago's laboratory, a half-dozen animal cages line the outer walls of the otherwise bare first room. They hold rats, nests of white mice, and a trio of rhesus monkeys. He resents the smell of feces and urine that assaults him, but it's necessary. For now. The monkeys leap at their bars and screech at him; the rodents blessedly hold their tongues. He looks forward to the day his task will be done and he can cleanse his ship of machines and vermin.

Drago precedes Vixen into the laboratory. One of his wives, he doesn't recall which, had installed large windows and a skylight during its previous tour of duty as her art studio. Her delicate watercolors of flowers and wild birds still decorate the walls. The woman—what was her name?—had talent, and her paintings offer relief from the lifeless plastic and metal of the computers, steel dissection table, chemistry beakers, burners, and other lab equipment that clutter the room. A monkey, the next test subject, squats in a cage on a table. When Drago nears it, the beast screeches and slams against the bars of its cage that frustrate its attack.

From its place of honor on the bow wall of the room, the woman's portrait of Graeme gazes at him. Drago pushes down the volatile blend of love and fury that has filled him for many months and focuses on the task at hand.

Drago goes to the wall switch that starts the gasoline-fueled generator on the forecastle roof and, wishing he didn't have to, flips it on. The generator chugs into life with an irritating mechanical rhythm. Fluorescent lights hanging from the ceiling flicker and come on. Soon the stench of burned fuel will invade the lab, and he'll hate that, too. But solar panels and batteries don't provide enough power to sustain use of the scanning electron microscope, computer, and lights, so the generator is a necessary evil.

One day it will go, along with most of the other "modern" technology spawned by the *lessi* that he tolerates only for their current usefulness. Had he his way, there would be no technology in his clan that dated much past the nineteenth century.

Vixen sets her tea on the marble-topped lab table that holds the electron microscope and goes to the monkey. It calms as she approaches. Drago *sees* the stream of soothing *lledri* Vixen sends into the creature's brain to stimulate its pleasure center, a trick she no doubt uses on her lovers. Why is such deft skill squandered on a wastrel such as her?

She pokes a finger through the cage wire and strokes the animal's head. "Hi, little guy."

"Can we begin, please?"

Vixen leaves the monkey and, with a saucy swing of her hips, crosses to the lab table and settles on a stool in front of the microscope. Light from the skylight above her glistens on droplets formed by melted snowflakes in her hair, crowning her with a scattering of jewels. She says, "You still haven't told me why we're doing this."

"Why do you care?"

She raises an eyebrow. "Something to tell my grandchildren?"

Drago is sure that Vixen, despite her sexual appetites, has no desire to bear children. The discomfort and obligations would be too much for her frivolous life. It's only through her loyalty to the clan that he has been able to prevail upon her to help him. He strokes his moustache as he searches for exactly the right words. "By then they will know it as a cure for what ails the world."

She eyes him, and he suspects she's looking for the color of a lie. Like all clansmen, he never lies—what would be the use? But he is adept at thin-slicing the truth. Apparently satisfied, she glances at the microscope. "A bunch of bacteria are going to do all that?"

"Trust me, they will make a better life for the Clans." He takes a sample from a petri dish and prepares a slide, then inserts it into the microscope stage. The electron "gun" bombards the specimen and an image forms on the computer screen of the DNA of the bacteria he has created. It has taken him years of using restriction enzymes to select, cut, and transfer DNA molecules to assemble a completely new bacterium.

Vixen's voice breaks into his thoughts. "It's dark, like disease."

Yes, the microscopic bursts of *lledri* emitted by his new bacteria as they die in the vacuum of the microscope chamber are near-black, the color of disease. "True, but they are a medicine. Sometimes, with the right dose, a poison can be a cure."

Vixen shrugs. "You should know."

"Let's get to work. Focus."

She hesitates. "I'm not really good enough for this, Drago. It takes someone like Rhianna."

He scowls. "I've told ye not to mention her name."

She flicks a glance at him. "Are you never going to let that go?"

He turns on her and raises a hand to slap the impudence from her.

She lifts her chin and says, "Go ahead."

Damn the wench, he needs her. He turns the gesture into a wave of his hand and tries for a smile. "Your *touch* is almost as fine as hers, ye can do it. Please, let's get started."

She holds his gaze for a long moment, then nods. She closes her eyes, and a frown creases her fair brow while she narrows her *sight* to the level of the molecules on the slide.

On the slide are unique bacteria formed by his combination of *Bordetella pertussis,* the cause of whooping cough, with the anaerobic bacteria named *Clostridia,* the producer of botulism toxin. His tests on monkeys have shown that the combination brought on the symptoms of whooping cough in eight hours instead of the seven days normally required. Even better, the immunization vaccine that *lessi* children routinely get has no effect on his manufactured illness.

But his aim is not to simply create a fast-moving, highly infectious disease. He values *Clostridia* for a gene that creates a toxic protein. With Vixen's help, he will modify that gene to create the protein that is the basis of his "cure"—prions, the wrongly folded PrP proteins that cause mad cow disease. It will destroy the brains and spinal cords in infected humans. They will lose the ability to walk, to talk, to see, to think. And then die.

Also on the slide are cells taken from an infected Canadian cow that manufactured the infectious prions. Drago's research has been unable to find any restriction enzymes that act upon the propagons, the amino acid strings that produce the crippled PrP proteins, but he believes that a skilled clansman can use *touch* to achieve the cutting and splicing needed to complete his remedy, a fast-acting bacterium that manufactures prions that lead inevitably to death. He hopes his belief is true and not just the product of desire.

"Push upon each of the samples in the center of the slide until I tell ye to stop."

It takes long minutes, but at last a string of DNA centered in his screen jostles. Next to it is a cell that produced corrupted PrP proteins. "That one! Go into the membrane of the nerve cell immediately to the right of that bacterium and clip the protein structure that I showed ye."

Vixen's voice is tight. "I don't think I can."

Spare him the incompetent. "Ye can, ye can, just do it." He shuts his eyes and concentrates, joining his *sight* to hers. He *sees* the twisted spirals of proteins inside the membrane. "Go ahead. Sever the strand as I showed ye." If she succeeds, there will be a piece with a "sticky end" that will fasten onto the DNA in his bacterium. And then the fun will begin.

The propagon in the nerve cell begins to part ... but it's at the wrong place, too far up its molecular chain. He says, "No, no, ye must move dow—"

The electronic jangle of a cell phone cuts into his words. The cells in the viewfinder scatter.

Vixen takes a tiny phone from her pocket.

Rage takes him. "Damn ye!" He snatches the phone from her hand, hurls it onto the floor, and smashes it with his heel. "Ye know I banned these foul things!"

Her face clouds with equal fury. "You have no right—"

"I have every right! I am Clanmaster!" He slaps her.

His blow sends her staggering from the stool. She catches herself against the monkey cage. The monkey screeches and leaps from wall to wall. Vixen turns on Drago, a redheaded storm. "You bastard!"

Her gaze shifts. He follows it and understands too late. She lunges and sweeps the china cup and saucer from the table.

Drago stabs out with his *touch* to stop them. Instead, his effort shatters them on a wall.

He turns on her, gathering *lledri* to reach inside and crush her heart.

But Vixen knows of his temper, and she is quicker than he. Pressure wraps around his heart ... it tightens ... his knees weaken ... black spots appear in his vision ... She has him.

Her lips curl. "We're not going to hurt each other, are we?"

He forces his anger back into its cage. "Now, Vixen, it is against clan rules to use *lledri* against one another."

"Oh, you're such a follower of rules now, are you?" Her purple-red aura of anger diminishes, though.

Can he salvage this? "I apologize, Vixen. I was hasty. But ye know that cell phones are against the rules."

Her grip on his heart fades away. "Against *your* rules, not mine. You can't keep all of us in the Stone Age." She heads for the door.

"Don't go. We just need to complete one simple action—"

"No, *we* don't. Find someone else." She pauses at the door. "Besides, I really can't do what you want. I doubt anyone can." As she leaves, she tosses back, "Except maybe Rhianna, and you'll never get her to help you."

6

KB stomps out of the Michigan Avenue parking lot exit, empty-handed and pissed. Schultz lounges against a wall, smoking a cigarette. When he sees her, he drops it and crushes it with a foot. She says into her microphone, "I'm out. No luck."

Bailey's voice whines in her earbud, "I'm cold."

"Ain't that a cryin' shame." Even though Bailey is out of sight, KB can almost see her lips form the words, "Fuck you." Well, fuck her. "Schultz, what've you got?"

He flips through his pad. "Thirty-four vehicles pulled out since we got here. I looked, but I didn't see anybody suspicious." He holds up his camera. "Checked out everybody I saw with this, no luck."

"Bailey?"

"'Bout twenty. No glows."

Martinez says, "Same story, a couple dozen here."

"Shit." KB had checked out every hot spot in the garage, so the Artisan must have somehow escaped in one of those vehicles while she searched. KB exhales disappointment with a long sigh. But she can't show it in front of the troops. "All right. We have a few more hours of stakeout. Maybe there'll be another one." She forces energy into her voice. "Schultz, you take the inside and call license numbers in. Tomorrow we'll start with the ones that left first and work our way down."

He heads for the Institute, stretching his long legs, no doubt eager to get in out of the cold. Bailey says, "I'm really freezin'."

Even though she'd like to lean on Bailey for being such a wuss, KB knows a good leader has to be fair to her crew—or at least appear to be. "Okay, you take the inside for a while. Martinez and I'll cover outside." The wind blows up her skirt and she regrets her decision, but she has to stick to it. Her agents head for the Art Institute.

She goes into the parking lot opening until none of her team can see her. A cramp in her gut doubles her over and tears fall from her eyes. She's failed! The ghost of her father lashing her with his belt for bringing home a D on her report card strikes her again. That changes to an image of her brother and his glorious smile, and then it crumbles, wiped out on 9/11. She lets it out with a scream that echoes. "AIEEEEEE!"

KB leans on a concrete wall and forces herself upright. She draws in a deep breath and wills the cramp to go away. It does, the pain recedes.

Dammit, she's not a failure. She's one up on everybody else. She's the first to really see an Artisan. And now she knows what they can do. Talk about your masters of disguise.

The whole department will read her report. Then they'll give her the resources she needs to track down the one who escaped. KB takes out her phone and emails a heads-up to the RAC to set up a meeting for the morning. She can't help but anticipate the glow she'll feel when she walks in to the sound of the Resident Agent in Charge's applause. Even though it'll be Saturday, she'll order her team to come in, too.

She straightens and strides to the Institute's Michigan Avenue entrance, her shoulders back. If another Artisan comes, she's gonna nail it.

~

Gabe drives through the shadow under the El tracks. Ahead, Wrigley Field looks forlorn and friendless under the ashen sky. He wishes it were baseball season, if only for the warmth. An El train thunders overhead, and he tells himself he ought to ride it more instead of paying for parking. If he still has a need to go downtown, that is, after having pissed away his one and only job. But it wasn't all his doing. Lawrence had an agenda, and Gabe was pretty sure his life at the agency would have only gotten more miserable. He's been here before, attacked by superiors who feel threatened by his talent. His anger still smolders; shitheads shouldn't be allowed to win.

He checks his rearview mirror for the eleventy-leventh time. Still nobody following. The whole way he's felt like somebody was staring at the back of his neck. So this is what paranoia feels like. Or maybe it's reality—the girl said people were shooting at her. So what the hell is he doing carrying her around in his truck?

He pulls into the alley just past Magnolia Street and drives the half-block to his home, a 1940s three-story house modified into apartments. It isn't a great place, but it'll do until he and Bonnie figure out the marriage.

Parking in one of the spaces beside the Dumpster is never a problem because he's the only tenant with wheels. When he gets out, the girl in the bed of his truck is hard to see, even in the gray daylight. Then the shadows over her clear; he looks up to see if the cloud cover has thinned, but it's the same sullen gray.

The way this day is going, he figures this is a sure sign of a brain tumor and he'll probably be blind in a couple of hours.

The girl is pretty and small, with all the defenses of a butterfly. He tells her, "This is it."

Her gaze rests on him with an implacable inertia. *"Gracias, Señor."*

"Sure."

She doesn't stir.

"Ah, you'll need to get out."

He leans in and shoves the hay bale out of the way. When she gets to her feet it's like watching a bird with a broken wing. The thought sparks a flash of his daughter's solemn face. Is it the girl's frailty that gives him a sense of where-do-I-know-you-from?

Words pop out of him. "You want to come in and warm up?" Then he thinks that could be dumb move of the day number two—invite a complete stranger inside, a teenage girl, a minor? Not to mention the alleged shots being fired.

She shakes her head. "No. I am okay."

Relieved yet doubtful, he offers her a hand, but she clambers over the far side of the truck. So maybe she's scared of him, too. He locks the truck. "Well, take care of yourself." She just watches him. He says, "Listen, you need a ride someplace? I'd be glad to take you."

She looks around. "This is *bueno.*"

He shifts from foot to foot, lifts a hand, drops it. Seems like he ought to do more. "Ah, my name's Gabe River." She gazes at him with a heavy stare. Those aren't the eyes of a teenager; there's some serious history behind her windows.

Just when he thinks she's not going to respond, she says, "Rhianna."

Gabe points up at his apartment. "I'm there, the middle place, if you, ah ..."

"I will not." It feels as if she looks *into* him. She nods. *"Gracias.* You have been kind. I am grateful."

It strikes him that he has never seen deeper sadness in anyone's eyes. He offers a smile and a little rusty high-school Spanish to say you're welcome. *"De nada."* Having no more to give, and it being no business of his anyway, he leaves her there.

He trots up the back stairs to his little kitchen porch, glad to get out of the cold. Inside, he looks out the window. He can see his truck, but the girl is gone. Oh, well.

~

I watch the bearded man leave. He strides with strength and confidence—where has mine gone? When he closes the door behind him, I walk behind the Dumpster to a spot against a fence where it conceals me from the houses around me. I sit in the snow, my back to the cold metal. I'm well hidden. I stop using *lledri* to warm myself; it's time for winter's chill to do its work. I wish my *glamère* could continue after I die so no one will see the true Rhianna.

As if it were possible to feel shame in death.

I'm relieved to escape those who pursued me. Why had they? Why with such fervor? There was no cause.

Enough. I won't gnaw that bone any longer. I settle back and sink into the snow. The Dumpster is hard, the snow achingly cold. I resent the discomfort. Ha! What kind of suicide worries about discomfort?

I am a coward, seeking the hand of cold to do the deed for me. I have no need for pills or bullets or a leap from a building ledge; I could evoke the Final Fire and consume my body with *lledri*. But that's reserved for an honorable surcease. Punishment is what I deserve, not an easy ride into Valhalla.

I think of the bearded man ... Gabe. Giving him my true name broke a host of clan rules, but he was so vivid in his wish to help. And he felt like kin, his aura radiating the colors of strong *lledri* talents, although they were muted, like the strength of a sleeping tiger. He can't bend *lledri* to do his bidding. But he might if he learns how to turn his will to it. He *read* me for falsehood, and it's a short step from perceiving to wielding.

He is *elessi*, and I think a powerful one, but he'll never know all that he is. I have helped people like him into my clan, welcoming them into my tribe.

I shiver. No, this one will have to live as an ordinary man. Without Graeme, I have no help to give, no more life to live.

He was so full of life that day we strolled through Central Park ... if only I hadn't said that I thought the Met's new sculpture exhibit was excellent.

Graeme shrugged. "Perhaps." He gestured at the people plodding through the park. "But there's little else of excellence from that sorry race."

My contrary side reared its head at the unfairness of the bias against the *lessi* that Graeme inherited from his father. "There's plenty of good in them, and you know it."

"I do not." He surveyed the people around us. Dozens wandered, for it was a sunny day. "Observe their colors, Rhianna. Is there kindness or good will anywhere?"

I looked, and the *lledri* auras around their heads writhed with the nasty burgundy of hostility, the bilious color of lies, the ash-violet of depression, and the bruised red of violence. That, of course, only served to rally my resistance. "Perhaps not here, not now, but there are many good-hearted *lessi.*"

He made an exaggerated moue and said, "A wager?"

I picked up the gauntlet. "Yes." I pointed down a curving walk. "We'll go that way, and we'll find a worthy *lessi.*"

"The stakes?"

I ran my hands over my breasts and down my belly, pushing my pelvis at him. And then added a wiggle of my hips.

Oh, that lusty smile of his. He said, "It's a bet."

Only minutes later, I congratulated myself on my good luck when we came upon a woman pulling a two-wheeled shopping cart; her aura radiated a rosy gold, the rich hue of caring. Perhaps sixty years old, the woman was stout, solid, anchored to the earth like an oak tree. She stopped before a trio of homeless men who sprawled on ragged blankets.

When she opened a brown paper bag from her cart, I caught the aroma of bologna. The woman took a sandwich out and handed it to one of the men. He sat up and attacked the food.

Graeme spread his arms in surrender, lifted his gaze to the heavens and said, as if to a higher power, "Why have You once again given Rhianna victory over Your poor servant Graeme?"

I poked him in his ribs. "I believe you owe me."

He pulled me into his arms and pressed me to him. "I'm ready."

His body let me know that he was indeed ready. My pulse quickened, and I wanted to take him by the hand, find a cluster of bushes, cast a shadow *glamère* for concealment, and make love. But I pushed away and said, "If we're so advanced, we should help."

Oh, if only I hadn't ...

He laughed and then put on a thick French accent. "But of course, *ma cherie.*" Stepping to the woman's side, he bowed and then gestured to the sack of sandwiches. He said, "May I assist you?"

She smiled and nodded, and Graeme took a sandwich from the bag and thrust it at a whiskery man whose bristles made him look like a wild boar.

The boar man scrambled to his feet, digging into a pocket. Too late I *saw* in his aura the acrid tornado of colors that mean madness. He pulled a knife from a pocket, flicked it open and thrust it into Graeme's chest. Graeme collapsed as if he were a puppet whose strings had been cut.

I dropped to my knees beside him and plunged *lledri* into his chest to heal the wound—but his heart had been sliced almost in two. There was no way I could mend him in time. I looked into his eyes and saw terrible fear ... and then an even more terrible absence.

If only I hadn't ... if only ...

Here and now, the cold attacks and my body wants to fight it. I need to turn my thoughts away from the temptation to warm myself.

I picture the golden necklace I wore in the portrait at the Art Institute. In my imagination, it adorns a lady in a flowing gown. She sits by a roaring hearth, entertaining the men of her household with a story. I try to see her face.

Into my mind comes instead the beetling brows of the woman museum guard who chased me. Damn the woman. Will she pursue me even unto death?

7

Gabe's apartment is quiet. During evenings and weekends, he's sandwiched between a murmur of big band music from the garden apartment below and the stutter of hip-hop from the young couple on the top floor. He goes to the stereo and fills the emptiness with a classic-rock station.

Three months of living alone since the separation and he still hasn't gotten used to the silence of no kid activity, not that Berry is anywhere near noisy, but she's always busy. He slips off his shoes. The apartment is cold, so he opens valves on the radiators in the kitchen and living room and they ping as steam flows in.

Tension from the parting scene with Lawrence still churns through him, so he paces past the rented couch and chair. The furniture isn't all that comfortable, though he likes the clean contemporary lines and pastels. Bonnie would hate it; early American is the only thing she goes for.

Is their split going to be permanent? Should he go ahead and get a few rugs for the hardwood floors? So far the sessions with the marriage counselor haven't made much of a dent, mostly because of Gabe. He just can't come up with a yes to the question he keeps asking himself, "Can I spend the next forty years of my life with this person?"

But he can't come up with a no, either.

He steps into his daughter's room and a warm sense of Berry comes like a deep breath filled with her essence. Bright red curtains are closed against the drafty window. The soccer poster Gabe tacked to the wall in hopes of stirring interest in Berry curls at a bottom corner; a pushpin has fallen out. He finds the pin and puts it back. The room is fairly tidy, the sheets are clean.

He pictures a shy smile from his daughter when he picks her up in the morning. And the deep pleasure that glimmers in her eyes when she rides Rusty. Oh, if they could only break through to that secret place Berry seems to occupy, living inside herself, sometimes peeking out at the world that swirls around her as if she is a stranger in a very strange land, and then ducking back into her protective shell like an alarmed turtle.

For the thousandth time, Gabe wonders if he's in some way responsible for Berry's troubles. Always an outsider after the day he learned he was different from other kids, since then he hasn't felt a deep connection with another person, not even his mother. You don't want your mom thinking you are crazy. And he'd never had a father who might have been there for him.

Gabe's lifelong isolation opens the pit of his aloneness, and he falls. His job has provided professional friends, people he could connect with on some level. Gone now. His marriage means at least one human being who shares his concerns about daily life. Going. His daughter, the one person he'd die to truly connect with, unreachable.

He could call Lawrence and apologize. For doing the right thing? Gabe realizes that he's slumping, his shoulders sagging.

He straightens, chin up. Screw 'em. He's never given in to self-pity, and he isn't going to start now.

Berry's little soccer ball on the floor catches his eye and he puts his anger into a kick. The ball hits the wall with a satisfying thwack and caroms off the dresser.

He isn't due to pick up Berry from Bonnie until the morning, and she never lets her go early.

Call his headhunter? No, he's mentally fried and couldn't put the energy it would take to get her fired up for a job search. And maybe it's time to think about doing something else with his life besides inventing clever come-ons for bubble-gum and toilet paper.

Work on the novel? Naw, says the fried brain. Is it too early to drink? He checks his watch—almost four o'clock. They're bending elbows in New York. Close enough. He walks to the kitchen, pours a glass of Cabernet, and then digs his stash out of the freezer to see if there's enough weed left for a pipe or two.

After an hour of surfing the internet, Gabe gazes at a screen shot of new writing software on the monitor at his living-room computer station—two TV trays pushed together. He lifts his wine glass ... but nothing rolls onto his tongue. That's the last of it. He checks the clock on his screen: six-fifteen. The dope has nicely cottoned his mind and put the unpleasant scene in the conference room far enough away to ignore. It has also brought on a major case of munchies. He craves peanuts, more wine, and anything with the name Hershey on it.

In the kitchen, the only thing he can find to nosh is sal-tine crackers and peanut butter. And he knows that sooner or later he will lust for chocolate. Okay, so an outing to the store is in order. But first, another toke to gain a little altitude for the journey.

Outside, darkness has come, and the porch light reveals drifting snowflakes. Downstairs, there's enough of the city's pale, reflected luminescence to let him see a covering of new snow on the backyard. Good. It'll hide the nasty gray topping on last week's brief accumulation. He swipes snow off his windshield, starts up, and backs out.

His headlights swing across the Dumpster; the Latina girl's face is a brown spot in a field of white. She slumps against the Dumpster, legs stretched in front of her, arms limp at her sides, her chin on her chest.

He hits his brakes, then pulls back into his spot, shuts down, and rushes to her. There isn't enough light to see if she's breathing. He gets his flashlight from the glove compartment. A faint cloud of vapor streams from her nostrils. Relief rushes through him.

But what is the matter with her? Nobody just decides to take a nap and freeze to death. Drugs? Had she been shot by whoever was after her? She seemed weak when she got out of the truck. Dammit, he should have insisted on doing more—she *FLICKERS*.

For an instant, instead of a brown girl's face, he looks at a pale-skinned woman about his age, longish brunette hair, a deep frown crease between her eyebrows, eyes clamped shut—she *FLICKERS*—he sees the girl again.

He draws back and sits on his heels. Is his dope laced with acid? But nothing has happened with this batch before. He gazes at her. No more flickering. She looks dead. And might be soon, if he doesn't do something.

He pulls her away from the Dumpster, squats and slips an arm behind her back and the other under her knees—that is, he tries to. Where he expects her knees to be is solid lengths of thigh. Okay, maybe there is something in the dope. But he still has to get her inside.

He staggers when he lifts—she's far heavier than she looks. He almost dumps her on the ground, then steadies, lifts her high and carries her inside and into Berry's room. He lays her on the bed, wondering again how such a little person could be so heavy. Now what? Call 911.

He takes out his phone, but his thoughts spiral into scary scenarios. Paramedics are trained observers—what if they see that he's been smoking dope? What if she overdosed on a really nasty drug? What if she's been shot? They'll call the cops. It's hard to look for a job while you're in prison. Maybe she'll warm up by herself.

He pockets his phone, goes back to the girl, and takes her hand—it's like meat just out of the refrigerator. Why doesn't she shiver? The fog in his brain clears enough to let a memory through—shivering stops when hypothermia becomes severe.

He has to do *something.* Wait a minute—don't you take the clothes off a freezing person so the air's heat can warm them? He leans toward her—

FLICKER: he sees the stark white face again, a grimace of pain—*FLICKER:* he sees the Latina.

He lurches back a step, then runs his gaze over the room. All familiar, all steady, all the same. He feels fine, sober even, and he's never had trouble operating when high.

Back to the girl. Do something. He reaches for a button on her leopard coat, but his fingers find only cloth. He moves his hand down and finds a button where he sees fake fur. Oh, man, he's really tripping. But the cold he feels through whatever she's wearing tells him he has to keep going. He closes his eyes and lets his fingertips do the seeing. By feel, he unbuttons and peels off a cloth coat.

When he opens his eyes, he holds a long black wool coat and still sees the leopard coat and turquoise pants on the girl. But what he holds looks like a coat, feels like a coat. Good. He decides to believe that this is really happening. Tossing the coat onto a chair, he explores with his fingertips—eyes open this time—and discovers a long dress, buttoned down the front. He also encounters full breasts where he sees a flat chest. Wishing he'd taken acid in his wilder days so he'd know what to expect, he decides to worry about it later because she feels too cold to be alive much longer. Guided by touch, he removes the dress, which turns out to be white and silky with little purple flowers.

The girl still "wears" her fake fur coat. He reaches, and his fingers appear to encounter the coat, but his touch finds nothing but frigid skin. He should now be looking at a girl who is naked except for underwear—actually, thinking of those phantom breasts, a woman—but he still sees fake fur and blue pants. Talk about fucked up.

He would search for a wound, but that's useless with his eyes not working right. Better take care of the Popsicle part of her problem. Her limbs flop and she's hard to handle, but he manages to get her under the covers. He grabs Berry's daisy comforter from the closet and lays it over her. He sits in a chair beside the bed and watches. She just lies there, so ... low. Life is just about out of her.

Another factoid pops into his mind. Skin-to-skin is a great way to warm someone. Body heat. Yeah, but this is a mostly naked girl. But it isn't a girl. He looks at a teenager, but the face he saw when she flickered was a woman's. He shakes his head. Girl, woman, whatever she is, he can't just let her die. He strips to his briefs and slides into the bed.

He rolls her onto her side, facing away from him. Her skin is so cold he winces, but he spoons himself against her and wraps his arm around her. It takes concentration to detect her breathing, so shallow, hardly there.

Time passes. Her skin seems less cold, at least where he presses against her—either that or he's colder. The wine and marijuana dim his lights, and the strains of the day—goddam Lawrence—drain him. He closes his eyes.

8

Braaaaack.

Gabe comes awake just enough to hate his apartment buzzer. Why can't it ding-dong instead?

Braaaaack.

Go away.

Braaaaack.

He opens his eyes. Sunshine backlights Berry's red curtains. Gabe lies on his side, teetering on the edge of his daughter's single bed. Berry's bed? How messed up had he gotten last night? He tries to roll onto his back, but a warm body stops him. Reaching behind, his hand finds the curve of a woman's hip. He tenses. Who?

Oh, yeah, the girl was freezing and ... ohshit! He rolls out of the bed and scrambles to his feet. She faces away from him, all but the top of her brown hair covered by Berry's daisy comforter. Despite his briefs, Gabe feels naked. All night? He had slept with her all night?

Hold everything. *Brown* hair? But the girl had black—

Braaaaack.

It's Saturday morning, for Christ's sake! Who the hell—the meaning of the sunshine hits him and he checks his watch. Nine o'clock. He said he'd pick Berry up at eight! Gabe runs out, skids through a turn toward the front door, and then another brain cell kicks in. He detours into his bedroom for a robe.

Robe mostly on, he flings open his door and looks down the half-flight of stairs to the foyer. Through the glass in the foyer door he sees Bonnie; his wife wears an expression that could get her busted for assault with a deadly weapon.

Peeking out from behind her is Berry Sarah River, the most precious six-year-old on the planet, adorable in her puffy pink parka and cowboy boots, a pink knit hat on her head. Berry makes brief eye contact with Gabe, then drops her gaze to the floor, where it's usually aimed. She's so cut off—Gabe would give anything to find a cure for his daughter, to help her connect with the world and with people instead of being so isolated.

Bonnie glares up at Gabe, punches the buzzer again and holds it. *Braaaaaaaaaaaaaaaaaaaack!*

He thumbs the release button and Bonnie storms through the door, her curly brown hair bouncing as she runs up the steps. She wears a navy-blue suit she couldn't fit into six months back, but she looks good in it now. One hand clutches an orange backpack emblazoned with the Looney Tunes Tasmanian Devil.

Trying to head off the squall about to hit his shore, Gabe rattles, "I'm sorry, I don't know what happened, didn't set the alarm, fell asleep, hard day yester—"

"Dammit!" She stops on the landing and fumes. "Can't I count on you for anything?"

Actually, she can, and she does, and she knows that. But he doesn't think reminding her just now will be particularly soothing. Where is Berry? Gabe leans out. His daughter stands in the foyer doorway, her gaze still cast downward. "Come on up, honey." Berry starts up the stairs, watching her feet—one step and a pause, another step and a pause ...

Bonnie says, "Is it too much to ask for you to pick her up on time?"

"No, of course not, I'm sorry, but why didn't you call—"

"I told you I had a nine o'clock appointment. I'm trying to get a real estate business going, and I can't afford to piss off customers." She pokes him in the chest, one of those little things he hates, and she knows that, too. "I couldn't wait for you to drive out once you got around to getting up."

She has a point. It's forty minutes to Palatine. "It won't happen again." A draft invades his open robe and goose-bumps his skin. He shivers and closes the robe.

She tightens her eyes, pokes her head in the doorway, and sniffs the air. "You have a woman in there?"

An image of the woman in Berry's bed flashes into Gabe's mind. Mental clench of panic. He stays cool. "No, I—"

Hard and low, she says, "Not in front of Berry!"

"I don't. I haven't. I wouldn't. I mean, I—"

Face as sour as her tone, she says, "Yeah, Mister Playboy, living the life while I take care of Berry and the house—"

"Berry's hearing all this."

That shuts her up. She's a good mom, no matter what. Bonnie turns to find Berry behind her. Placing a hand on the back of her head, she guides her to stand beside Gabe. "You do want her for the weekend, right?"

"You bet I do." He tousles Berry's hair and teases out a quick glance up. Gabe adds, "We've got some riding to do." That earns him a small smile.

Bonnie goes for one more twist of the knife, her expression pretty close to a sneer when she says, "Are you bringing her home tomorrow, or do I have to come back?"

She's starting to piss Gabe off, and he lets her know with silence and a steady gaze.

She meets it for a moment, then backs off and shifts her attention to Berry. "All right. Make it early. She has day care Monday morning." She squats. "C'mere, honey." She wraps her in a hug, buries a kiss in her cheek, then stands.

Berry slips into the apartment. Bonnie hands Gabe the backpack. "Change of clothes. And her new favorite book, *Where the Wild Things Are*. You'll probably have to read it at least twice."

"Whatever she wants."

She lingers and says, "I don't think she should play in the snow. She sniffled a couple times this morning."

"I'll be careful."

She looks at her watch, says, "Damn!" and hurries down the stairs.

Gabe shuts the door. What a great way to start a day. He turns. Where's Berry?

Oh, shit ...

~

I awaken to a small girl's intense blue eyes. She holds a blanket up from my face and peers in at me. On a wall behind her is a soccer poster. I wonder where I am, then recall sitting in the snow, my body numb and useless, a great lassitude settling over me. I should be dead. Why am I not?

A man's voice says "Berry" and the girl drops the blanket. I brush it back from my face, then pause—my dress is gone. My Rosa *glamère* is gone and I'm *truself*. I'm not naked, still have my underwear ... but how?

The bearded man who rescued me steps behind the girl and puts his hands on the child's shoulders. The girl is black-haired like the man, who must be her father. The man's eyes widen when he sees my face, then he looks hard at me. His gaze has impact, and I sense a strong mind behind it.

The girl observes me.

No, she drinks me in.

The man says, "Who are you? Where's the girl? Rhianna."

"I am Rhianna."

He scowls at me. "Don't screw around with me, she was sick. Where'd she go?"

The man's determination to know is almost palpable—it will not go away. I decide to squelch it with a shock: I shift to my Rosa *glamère*.

He flinches as if I had struck him. "Holy shhhh ..."

The girl blinks, but that's all. Inside me, a ghost of a smile comes in appreciation of her steadiness. It has been a long time since any part of me smiled.

The man says, "How ... ?" He shakes his head. The bitter yellow of fear streaks his aura, but then the sturdy red-brown of courage overwhelms it. He steps in front of the girl, shielding her, although the child peeks out at me from behind him. The man—he told me his name ... Gabe—studies me. He says, "Which is the real you?"

I'm tempted to say that what he sees is, but I'm tired of playing games. I shift back to my *truface*.

He says, "I saw that face ..." He points at me. " ...last night."

I don't believe it. My control is too long practiced to have let my illusion slip, even when unconscious. But I can *read* that he thinks what he says is true. "Like this? As you see me now?"

"It was a … a flicker. A couple of times. An instant of—" He points. "*You,* then it was the other, the girl." He raises his hands. "Her clothes weren't real. I tried to take them off to warm her up, but found that—" he points to my dress and coat draped over a chair. "—instead"

I must have been very near death. So close. And he stopped me. By what right?! My cheeks warm with anger and my voice takes on an edge. "You had no business bringing me here. You had no right to undress me. To interfere with my life. *My* life."

"But you were dying!"

Wrath colors my response. "Yes."

He starts to protest, then peers at me, then shakes his head. "You're nuts."

I'm nuts? An image of a giant squirrel stuffing me into its cheek darts into my mind, and the absurdity pops a laugh out of me. By the look on Gabe's face, I have just confirmed his opinion. I think he could be right.

The girl grins. The effect is angelic, all innocence and heart. Reflex takes over, and I send a mini-burst of *lledri* to the pleasure center in her brain, sort of like an ephemeral pat on the head. Her grin widens and then falls.

Then a shock of recognition shoots through me. I see Graeme's little-boy-lost look there—although Berry's expression of bewilderment is shadowed with sadness. My heart tightens.

Gabe picks up the girl and holds her close. "Hey, Berry, how about some hot chocolate?"

A sense of loss rises in me when the girl turns her gaze to his father. She answers with a nod. I say, "I need to get dressed."

Gabe glances at the clothes tossed at a chair, the dress about to slide off the seat. "I was in a hurry." He scowls again, and his voice turns acid. "I thought I was saving a life." He carries the girl away.

The sound of a microwave oven at work hums into the room.

Sunshine brightens a patch of bed. I slide my hand into it. My traitorous flesh relishes the warmth.

The sweet brown aroma of hot cocoa drifts in.

In this safe comfort, I feel no urge to pursue my goal of yesterday. I don't know if I have the courage to go right back out and bare my neck to death's cold hands. Curse the man. He brought me back to life, and I don't know if I can easily give it up again.

I hear the girl—Berry—giggle under the rumble of her father's voice. That's another thing. First the man brings me back to life against my desire, and now he inflicts the infectious charm of a child on me. A child who echoes my lost Graeme. Oh, how her sad eyes call to me.

I rise and put on my dress. It's my current favorite, white silk flowing to my ankles, sprinkled with hints of lilac flowers. I would have been a tribute to post-mortem vanity.

Following the scent of hot chocolate, I enter a kitchen. Gabe and Berry sit at a small round table, done in the style of an old-time ice cream parlor. The white kitchen cabinets wear many years of paint. Big, old-fashioned black and white tiles checkerboard the floor to complete the image of an ice cream shoppe. Gabe has traded his robe for jeans and a green flannel shirt. Hiking boots suggest an outdoor expedition on their agenda.

They look at me. A line of cocoa gives little Berry a mustache. It strikes me that I have heard laughter but no words from her.

Gabe's face sours into a frown. He says, "You're not wearing your coat."

His irritation is contagious. "The Samaritan goes only so far, does he?"

"I'll get it for you." He stands, but Berry grabs his sleeve and stops him. Then Berry looks to me and points to the jar of Ovaltine on the table. Gold spurts of hope light her aura, and her wide eyes beseech me. A desire to see her smile displaces my anger at the father.

Gabe's expression shifts to surprise, and then wonder.

I say to Berry, "I would love some." She rewards me with a quick little grin, and I am ... glad?

I add a smile and say, "My name is Rhianna."

Berry looks to her father. Gabe says, "This is Berry." He tousles her hair, and the rosy gold of affection glows in his aura. "My daughter."

"That's an old Celtic name. I love it."

Berry grins. Gabe's eyebrows go up. More colors interweave into his aura—the green/gray of suspicion, a tinge of the acid yellow of fear. And slender gold threads of hope.

~

Gabe can't remove his gaze from Berry. Throat-choking love threatens to swamp him. Amazement and questions jostle in his mind. Gabe has never seen social behavior like this from Berry, not even when she's with children. Her level of Asperger Syndrome means that she simply does not engage with others. Yet here she is, a hint of a smile turning up the corners of her mouth, wanting to share her hot chocolate with a stranger. An adult stranger that she's seen for, what, five minutes?

But, God, what a moment this is. Can Berry's shell be cracking, the armor that constant love and attention from two parents and thousands of dollars of therapy have not pierced?

Gabe appraises the slender woman standing in the doorway. She's tall, he guesses close to six feet. Being a man, he can't help but appreciate the figure revealed by the cling of her dress, and his body remembers her shape, narrow-waisted and full-hipped. She stands ramrod-straight, poised like a dancer about to begin a pirouette.

Her eyes, the sea-blue of clear ocean water over white sand, train on Berry. The sadness he had seen in the woman has melted into something that looks a lot like affection. She's riveting, the contrast of her eyes with her milky skin like jewels on snow. He guesses her age at around thirty, pretty close to him.

What is there about this woman that makes Berry open like a shy flower that senses sunshine? A shadow cools Gabe's joy. Berry is opening herself to hurt, too. Gabe studies the woman as if he can see evil intent. Then he shakes his head. With a person who can change her appearance quicker than he can think about it, how the hell can he know *what* he's seeing?

Gabe stands. Might as well enjoy what comes 'cause, God knows, something nasty is just as likely to appear around the corner. He says, "Have a seat and I'll whip up a cup."

The woman's gaze chills when she glances at him, and he isn't surprised—he hasn't exactly been welcoming. She takes a seat next to Berry and Gabe heads for the refrigerator, glad she's here and wishing he'd never seen her.

When Rhianna finishes her hot chocolate, Gabe stands. As beneficial as she seems for Berry, he doesn't feel secure about the woman. It's time to end this strange interlude. She lifts her gaze to him, and the warmth Berry brought to her face fades. He collects the mugs, takes them to the sink, and runs water in them. Plenty of time to wash up later.

He turns to see Rhianna lean close to Berry. Her voice is soft. "Thank you, Berry."

Berry keeps her gaze on Rhianna when she stands. Gabe scoops Berry out of her chair. "Well, cowgirl, Rusty needs his breakfast. We better go."

Berry smiles and nods. Gabe chuckles, says "Hi ho!" and bustles about, dressing Berry in mittens and a bright pink parka, a knit hat over her dark hair.

Rhianna leaves the kitchen and returns wearing her coat, and she still looks like herself ... at least he thinks that's herself. Good. Things can get back to normal. He glances down at Berry, who seems ... softer, more relaxed than Gabe can remember.

He takes Berry's hand and leads her to the back door, the woman follows. When he opens the door, the woman gazes down at Berry, warmth returning to her expression.

She says, "I'm happy I met you." She brushes a hand across the top of Berry's head. "Be well." She steps toward the door, but stops when Berry reaches up and takes her hand. Her eyes widen with an expression of surprise.

Berry gazes up at her and then shifts her big eyes to look up at Gabe. She wants her to go with them? That's crazy. Gabe isn't about to take a suicidal magician along with them.

He says, "No, honey, she can't go with us. She has …" He uses his voice to lash the woman for what she tried to do to herself. "… other things to do."

She lifts her gaze to his and her eyes narrow. He senses emotion rising. She says, "No, I haven't."

Gabe kneels before Berry. "You really want her to come?"

Berry nods.

Gabe looks up at Rhianna, indecision flip-flopping his mind. "I need to talk to you." He heads for his bedroom and gestures her in.

The woman says to Berry, "I'll be right back," and slips her hand from Berry's grip.

In his room, Gabe regrets the soiled clothes piled on a chair and the rumpled bed linens, and then scolds himself for being an idiot. This is serious. He turns to the woman. "Listen, I don't know who or what you are, but the way Berry is responding to you is … well, amazing."

Rhianna says, "She is sweet."

"No. I mean, yes, she is, but it's not that. She has a … condition."

"Tell me."

He eyes her. Why should he trust her?

She says, "I am a healer."

He thinks that over. Maybe Berry senses that in her. Gabe says, "The doctor says it's Asperger Syndrome. It's on the autism spectrum. Berry does not ever respond to strangers the way she has to you. Ever."

She waits, her face a still pool of calm.

"We've tried everything. Doctors. Play groups with kids. Nothing has worked. But with you ..." He says, "What are you?" He focuses on her, watching for the color of a lie.

She shrugs. "A woman. A mother."

That isn't much of an answer, but it seems to be true. "How do you do that ... trick with your appearance?"

"I cannot say."

"Will not."

She raises her eyebrows, and a hint of amusement lifts her lips and crinkles the corners of her eyes.

Gabe says, "Berry wants you to go with us ..."

She nods.

"But ..." How does he ask this? "Are you dangerous?"

A small smile. "Not to you, nor Berry."

Gabe sees no hint of the lie color. Oh, hell, what now? Then he visualizes Berry's happy face as she looked up at Rhianna. "Listen, I can't pass up a chance to maybe crack that shell of hers. And you owe me—"

"I owe you nothing." Her eyes flare. "You brought me inside against my wishes!"

Anger bubbles up, but he stops it. Still, it flavors his words when he fires back, "I suppose it was all a lie, people shooting at you."

She blinks, and the heat leaves her face. She shakes her head. "That was no lie. And I am grateful for your help in the parking garage." She drops her gaze, and then lifts it. "I was very afraid."

No green color shows up. He says, "I know you have other ... plans, but if you'd spend a couple of hours with Berry and me, you'd be helping her ..." He gazes at her, hoping. For what he isn't sure, but hoping.

~

The bearded man trails off, a man unaccustomed to asking for favors, I think. Because he rescued me from that pit bull without question or hesitation, I say, "I'm glad to."

The openness of Gabe's smile lets me see the depth of his warmth. He claps his hands, which sparks a chuckle in me.

He gestures at my bare hands. "Ah, real cold out there, you have gloves?"

"I'll be fine."

He studies my face. "Another trick?"

"No, *lledri*. An old Welsh word for magic, though that's not what it is." What am I doing? What is there about this man that invites trust?

"Oh, sure, you whip up a warm-and-toasty spell for your tootsies."

I smile. "You're thinking of witches. We don't do spells."

He *reads* that I don't lie and does a double take a comedian would envy. Have I lost my mind? We do not speak of *lledri*. The cold must have frozen part of my brain.

His focus turns inward, likely filing this information to bring out for later examination. He claps his hands again. "Come on." He strides out. "Berry! Rhianna's going with us."

I tag along. The man feels as open and honest as a clansman, and we never lie. Gabe grabs a small paper sack from the refrigerator and opens the back door. "Let's hit the road!"

Berry waits for me there. She takes my hand and doesn't let go until we get into the truck. It has bucket seats, and she snuggles against me in the passenger seat, trusting me to be one of the good guys. *Lledri* radiates from her, a youthful fever of living energy.

She warms the deep part of me. Oh, why is life trying so hard to lure me back? What cruel trick waits?

Let it not harm this child.

8

KB slams her shoulder into the cockpit door. It bursts open. The pilot turns and smiles up at her. His face is Mohammed Atta's, the man who flew American Airlines Flight 11 into the north tower of the World Trade Center. Laughter sounds behind her, and KB looks back.

Her brother, charming devil that he is, smiles up at a flight attendant. He shares KB's brown hair and heavy brows, but Jeremy is lean, with looks that make her think of a movie hero. He's flying to New York for his first visit to the Big Apple to meet his new publisher for his debut novel, Flying. *It's a happy time for Jeremy. KB wants to shout a warning to him, but her open mouth makes no sound.*

She turns back, and the pilot's face morphs into the Artisan woman's— first the snooty woman, then the farmer, and then the Latina kid. The pilot faces front, and the glass wall of a skyscraper rushes at them. White-hot light blazes, she shrieks—

KB bolts upright in her bed, her chest heaving. Then a fist-sized ache of grief slams her and she doubles over, biting back a moan. Despite the chill in her bedroom, sweat beads her face.

The clock next to the picture of Jeremy on her nightstand says it's three in the morning. She collapses back on her pillow and works to control her breathing. She closes her eyes, and the Artisan pops into her mind. Her eyes spring open; sleep is not going to happen.

She swings her legs out of bed and turns on the lamp. The TV is tempting, but there is such shit on in the middle of the night. She runs a finger across the tattoo of Jeremy's book cover on her forearm. Jeremy. She wants to smile at the memory of him, and then she wants to cry.

There's only one thing to do. She gets up and slips sweatpants on, changes her T-shirt, and then heads to the kitchen for a glass of milk.

Goosebumps prickle on her arms, and she hugs herself to ward off the chill. The drawback of a charming old apartment in Evanston is that the windows can't say no to the cold. By morning they'll be decorated with crystalline art painted by thick coats of frost.

In the kitchen, she opens the refrigerator and uses the light to track down her last clean glass and pour milk. She chugs it as she makes her way to the living room, dimly illuminated by the street lamp outside. She mounts her exercycle—sometimes mindless exercise clears her thoughts enough to let her go back to sleep after the Jeremy nightmare. But she doesn't think it will work this time; the dream has changed. Now it's a warning of things to come.

Of an act of terror unleashed by the Artisan she failed to catch at the Museum.

Five hours and no sleep later, KB's Chevy sputters as she turns from Michigan Avenue onto Huron Street and heads for her office a half block away. If only the damn car will last until she saves up a little of the pay bump from her promotion. Hey, maybe they'll pop another nickel into the pot when she captures the Artisan.

She nears the Homeland Security building; KB likes the anonymity of the old, nondescript brick structure that houses the Chicago headquarters—although she could do without the musty smell of age that fills the fifteen-story building. But they have everything they need, including detention cells on the top floor. She parks in the lot behind the building and welcomes the rare sunshine on her walk inside. She shrugs off her weariness. It's gonna be a great day.

In her tiny office—not much more than a closet with a steel desk in it, and so new to her she hasn't hung her diploma on the wall—she checks her email. The RAC got her report and wants to see her ASAP; he's as much a workaholic as she is, the one thing she respects about him. All right! Maybe this will be the breakthrough that gets her the respect she's earned. The way she sees it, he dragged his feet on putting her promotion through. In putting a *woman's* promotion through.

On the way out of her office, she pauses at the photo on her desk of her and Jeremy, the two of them getting ready to sail his little catamaran on Lake Michigan. They beam at the camera, having just said "cheese," and Jeremy has his hand behind her head, holding up two fingers like little horns. What a goof her little brother was. She touches the frame and whispers, "Wish me luck."

She makes a quick stop in the restroom to be sure her shirt is tucked into her slacks and to give her shoes a buff with a paper towel. She leans into the mirror and peers at her eyes—yeah, bloodshot and puffy from lack of sleep, but that's the norm around the agency.

She splashes cold water on her face, blots dry and then takes the stairs two at a time to the floor above. She hates the elevator; it's so slow and creaky she suspects the original Otis installed it.

RAC Berman's door is open, as usual. His white-haired head is bent over a stack of paperwork, as usual. Adrenaline pumps her up, and she taps on the doorframe and goes in. The office is too warm, as usual; the radiator must be cranked all the way open.

He looks up and nods. "Take a seat, Agent." Where's the smile she's been looking forward to? The old fart is old-fashioned and formal, so maybe he's not gonna come right out with her attaboy. Sitting, she tells herself to be patient, something that never comes easy for her.

He signs a piece of paper, places it in an out box, leans back, laces his fingers over his belly, and gazes at her. "So, you think you found a subject of interest."

She smiles. "Yessir!"

"Did you see it with the thermal imaging device?"

Inside, she smirks at his fussy way of talking. "I did, sir."

"Did you record it?"

Oh, shit. She'd been too excited. "Ah, no, sir."

"I see." He leans forward and studies a printout of her email. "You say it changed appearance on three occasions?"

"From a youngish woman to an older woman, then to a hick, then to a girl. Yessir."

"Did any of your team see these apparitions?"

Can't the old idiot read? "Schultz saw it come in as a red-headed woman. Martinez saw it on the stairs as a farmer, and Bailey saw it come out as a teenage girl."

"After receiving your email, I asked your team for their input." He picks up a printout. "Schultz didn't see a face."

"No, ah, he didn't get a good look." Why does she feel like she's on trial? "But he saw the glow in the camera."

"I see." He reads more. "No one else saw the older woman?"

"Not before she, uh, changed into a farmer."

"Martinez saw the farmer."

"Yessir."

RAC Berman studies another piece of paper. "He did not report using his thermal imaging camera. Nor did he report seeing a subject of interest."

"Well, he talked to him. It."

"Or he talked to a farmer that you *suspected* was the subject of interest."

This is not going anything like she had imagined. "Sir, it was, I'm certain."

"Hmmm." He examines another piece of paper. "Then you say it changed into a teenager as it fled. Did you see this transformation?"

"Not directly, sir, but it's the only explana—"

"Agent Bailey confirms your report of a girl fleeing the Institute. And that she apparently had high infrared output."

KB nods. "That was the Artisan, sir."

He studies her. "Perhaps Bailey's camera did show a subject of interest. Or perhaps it malfunctioned; these infrared cameras are new to us." He looks into KB's eyes. "You fired shots at this suspect."

"Warning shots. It was escaping."

"Or was *she* simply running because she was frightened?"

This can't be happening. KB shakes her head. "Oh, no, sir. There was highly suspicious behavior all the way, starting with her—it—shoving me in the exhibit room."

"Ah, yes. You do have that going for you." He scans a printout. "I don't see the witness's name."

"Sir, I was in pursuit. There was no time!"

"Don't ruffle your feathers, Agent." He gazes at her with those old eyes she can't read and then says, "The Department doesn't know enough about these, ah, curious individuals or their terrorist intentions. Our mission is surveillance and acquisition for questioning." He frowns. "Were you not aware of this?"

Of course she was. "I was aware."

"Yet you discharged your weapon. In public."

Anger simmers behind her eyes. She hopes it doesn't show on her face. Then a stab of fear punctures her irritation—he could come down on her hard for this. Maybe suspend her. She takes a breath. "I was using initiative, sir."

He raises his eyebrows. "I've never thought highly of initiative. Causes too much trouble."

The old goat means it causes too much paper to push. "But, sir, I'm the first one who's gotten a look at a Artisan with infrared. I saw what it really looks like!"

"And what did you see?"

She concentrates on recalling that brief image, wishing she'd taken time to study it. And to push the damn record button. "A woman's face, sir. Attractive. Twenties or thirties, I couldn't tell much more with the infrared image."

"How do you know that wasn't just another disguise?"

"I ..." She doesn't know. "I believe it was the individual."

"Is this a hunch?"

She has a hunch he doesn't like hunches any better than he likes initiative, so she keeps her yap shut.

One corner of his mouth tips up the tiniest bit, and the smug bastard nods. "Unfortunate that you didn't record it."

The RAC inserts the reports into a folder. "So what we have is a suspicion that one or more of the individuals called 'Artisans' visited the Art Institute."

Godammit, it's a *fact!* "Sir, I—"

"There is no physical evidence or witnesses of the changes in appearance you report."

Holding on to her temper with both hands, she says, "I *saw* them. The different disguises."

"Indeed." He leans back in his chair and does the finger-lacing thing on his belly again. "Your email requested surveillance for approximately seventy-five vehicles that left the parking garage after the alleged subject of interest entered."

He isn't gonna go for it, is he? "Yes, sir."

"And you want authority to search the homes of individuals owning those vehicles."

Her lack of sleep yawns inside her, sucking out her energy in a rush. Not trusting herself to speak, she nods. Christ, that can't be tears she feels building up in her eyes.

RAC Berman shakes his head. "I'm afraid we don't have the resources or authority for all that."

"But this is our chance!"

"You can have Schultz and Bailey."

She needs twenty and he gives her two. "Can we search?"

"Only with proper authority. My men do things by the book."

My *men?*

He leans forward and scowls at her. "I want evidence when you apply for a warrant. I want evidence before you detain someone. And you are not to use force unless endangered. I trust this is clear."

Tears are about to spurt out of her stupid eyes. She doesn't let her expression change. "Yes, Sir."

"Good luck, then."

She stands and leaves. Races down to her floor and into her office. She locks the door and muffles sobs with her hands.

When the storm passes, she dries her eyes. The heat of anger takes over, anger at the RAC and his male pig attitudes, anger at the Artisan for getting away. She flashes on her nightmare and shivers. The Artisan is up to something nasty, KB knows it. If not, why such a desperate effort to hide, to escape? Why can't the RAC see that it's a terrible danger?

9

Gabe settles into the fast lane on the Kennedy Expressway and heads west for his "farm" in Cary. It's nice that, at this time on a Saturday morning, there really is such a thing as a fast lane. They'll be there in less than an hour.

Twenty-five minutes out of the city, they pass through the forest preserve. He glances at the gray-brown of the hibernating forest and grins. "Hey, Berry-girl, remember those geese?"

On an October hike deep into the preserve, they'd come upon a pond, its shores inhabited by migrating Canada geese. Berry had delighted in dashing through them, flapping her "wings" to make them scatter. Until, that is, the boss gander decided enough was enough. It stood taller than Berry, flared its wings, lowered its head and charged with a screech that had started even Gabe's adrenaline to pumping. Berry had run for the safety of fatherly arms.

Berry smiles into Gabe's eyes. That has to be at the memory of chasing the geese.

Then Berry frowns. Ah, the specter of the gander.

Gabe smiles. "Wonder where Old Man Gander is now? Maybe his goose got cooked."

Berry's frown turns upside down. It's such a blessing to reach her. Is the woman making a difference? Gabe casts a quick look at Rhianna.

Her eyes train on him as if she studies him. He snaps his attention to the front, partly because he got caught looking, partly to do the driving thing. Last night's snow has been cleared from the lanes, but slushy spots make his speed problematic. Yeah, he drives a little fast, but he doesn't have accidents.

Is this the real her? What does he *actually* see? He snatches a quick look. Still the same, except now she gazes at the road ahead. Her arm is around Berry—almost a necessity, buckled into a single seat as they are. But the way her fingers stroke his daughter's hair isn't at all necessary. Berry smiles up at her, and she answers with a tiny one of her own. What magic is she working on his child?

Gabe says, "Is this the real you?" He catches her frown, and then has to attend to his driving.

After a pause, she says, "Yes. I'm *truself.*"

Okay, she says she's the real thing, and a glance discovers none of a lie's yellow-green sparks glowing around her head. But he doesn't know if his color-in-the-air lie detector works with someone like her. Maybe she can hide that, too.

They cross the Fox River, the road to Cary comes up, and he exits the expressway. The two-lane road is still afflicted with snow, so he slows.

Ten minutes later, he spots his little house with the horse barn behind, both painted "barn red." The sight brings on the usual rush of pleasure. And longing; maybe if he sells a novel or two he can just hole up here forever, safe from the Lawrences of the world. It hits him—no job, no way to pay the mortgage. He could lose everything.

Set a couple of hundred yards from the road, the house sits in eleven acres of pasture and woods. With snow a foot deep on its cedar-shake roof, the place has a storybook look to it. Gabe sometimes feels as if he's arriving at his own small kingdom.

The barn behind the house is a miniature classic dairy barn, just large enough for a two-horse stall and a tack-and-feed room. The Fox River, choked with thick slabs of ice this time of year, borders the back of the property and adds to the illusion of a country apart. The nearest neighbor, Mitch, is up the road and out of sight beyond a low hill.

Gabe turns onto the driveway and shifts into four-wheel drive. Snowmobile tracks go to the barn—Mitch looking after Rusty during the week. As Gabe pulls up and parks behind the house, Rusty appears from the barn and trots to the corral fence. White mist steams from his nostrils in the frosty air; his bay coat is long and shaggy.

The second Rhianna unbuckles and opens her door, Berry scrambles over her lap to plow through the snow toward Rusty. Gabe calls out, "You forgot something!"

Berry turns, and Gabe hands Rhianna the paper sack he'd brought from the refrigerator. Carrots peek out. "Toss it to her?"

She underhands the sack toward Berry, misses wide, and Berry makes a diving catch and lands on her belly in the snow. Not bad; just like her dad back in college, laying out for a disk in Ultimate Frisbee. Berry gallops toward the horse, waving a carrot in the air like a sword.

A low laugh comes from Rhianna. She says, "Such joy." She turns to Gabe. "Are you sure she's autistic?"

He corrects her. "Asperger Syndrome. That's what the doctors say."

She gazes at Berry, now at the corral fence and feeding a carrot into Rusty's eager mouth. "I wonder."

She has his attention. "You see something?"

Turning her gaze on him, she says, "Perhaps. I also think that *she* sees something."

"What?"

"Me."

She slides out of the car and follows Berry's tracks to the corral.

Okay, she has to mean more than Berry gets the standard image of her on her retinas. But what?

~

I plow through the snow and join Berry, using *lledri* to keep the cold from my body. The air, so frosty and crisp I feel like I could snap my breath like an icicle, refreshes me after the stuffy heat of the truck. Leaning on the corral fence, I relish the air's clean taste. Beside me, Berry stands on the middle fence rail and leans over the top, patting Rusty's neck. The horse munches a carrot, and the pale orange of contentment fills his aura. Berry gives me a shy smile, and the buttery color of happiness shimmers around her head.

Berry's emotion reminds me of my son when he was a little boy. Cael, too, had loved a horse. But he hadn't been trapped inside a shell of isolation like Berry. At least, not when he was a child. He was with our clan, with people who understood what he was. Just like them.

Gabe unloads the oats and hay from his truck into a room partitioned off from the stall in the barn. Then he emerges carrying a saddle with one hand and a bridle and saddle blanket with the other. Rusty spots the gear and frisks away from Berry's stroking hand to trot to the far side of the corral.

Gabe chuckles. "Oh, boy, here we go." He looks at me. "I don't think Rusty actually minds being saddled, but he gets a kick out of making me work for it."

I turn my gaze on the horse. Yes, I see a pink ghost of amusement like a mist above Rusty's head. I smile, gather a slender stream of *lledri,* and ease it through the latticework of the horse's skin and skull and into its brain. I find his pleasure center and stimulate it with a micro-surge of *lledri* as I stretch a hand out to him and say, "Here, Rusty."

He associates my voice with his sudden pleasant feeling; I strengthen the stimulation and say again, "Rusty. Come here, boy." He walks to me. I keep the stimulus going until he steps close enough for me to reach the bump atop his head, between his ears. Scratching that bump works as well as *lledri* with a horse, and Rusty stands before me, docile and happy. Berry offers Rusty the last carrot, and Rusty takes it in with his lips and then crunches, pleasure in his big brown eyes.

Berry stretches to scratch the same spot on the horse's head. I steady the girl with an arm around her waist, and the vigor of her young life spills over me, into me. It prods my despair into grudging retreat.

Gabe hasn't moved, his gaze like a drill trying to punch a hole into my skull. I say, "It isn't polite to stare."

He shakes his head. "I'm not sure it's polite to bewitch my livestock, either. What did you do?"

As always, I tell the truth. "I called to him."

"Yeah, but ..." He sees that he will get no more from me, so he saddles Rusty and then bridles him.

Gabe lifts Berry over the fence and swings her onto the horse. She pulls on the reins and kicks Rusty's ribs to start him moving. We watch Berry trot her mount in circles inside the corral. The only sounds are the muffled thud of hooves on snow and rhythmic creaks of saddle leather. Back when there was no more to Chicago than the trading post of the black man from Haiti who founded it, Jean Baptiste Point du Sable, I raced across these plains on a long-legged black mare, riding bareback, my sweat mixing with that of my horse. But I was a teenager then, and there is wisdom in using a saddle for such a small child as Berry.

Gabe's aura fairly glows with the rosy gold of affection. I can't recall seeing a more vivid bond between a father and his child. And whenever Berry glances at her father, the same colors spike in her aura. More than that, Berry also radiates the hues of *lledri* ability as rich as her father's, but hers are active, lively rather than muted as his are. It's as if he suppresses his nature. Why? But then, he likely does not know of it.

I take in the lean beauty of snow-swept fields and barren trees. I should have come to the countryside yesterday instead of the Institute.

Would I be alive now if I had?

Standing here, my body is pleased to be living. It doesn't care a fig for my mind's tortured rationales for cessation. No, my body is perfectly happy to keep on breathing, unconcerned by my grief and guilt for the loss of my Graeme, my One.

I watch Berry bounce in the saddle, wearing a smile that would make the Cheshire cat proud. My reason to die pales beside the girl's joyfulness. And she has that happiness even though she is troubled in a deeper way than I can imagine, trouble that I am coming to think is needless.

Gabe turns to look at me. If I could read minds, the flood of questions I see in his eyes would drown me. I should leave before—

A rabbit bursts from a bush beyond the barn, a fox at its heels. The rabbit dashes through the corral, straight into the horse's path. Rusty rears, his back hooves slip in the snow. He topples and lands with a great thud, legs windmilling in the air. Berry flies into a snowdrift. The fox veers, and the rabbit escapes.

Gabe dashes for his daughter; a quick glance at Berry shows the bitter yellow of fright in her aura, but no sign of pain. The horse screams, a call I cannot resist. I scramble over the fence and run to the horse's side. It writhes and struggles to get to its feet.

I kneel and lay hands to its neck, and then stream *lledri* into its brain to stimulate its pleasure center and counter the pain. The horse quiets, and I can focus on *seeing* what harm has been done.

I deepen my *sight* to include the streams of *lledri* that emerge from the cells in the horse's body. Each tiny burst of the living energy is a unique signal shaped by the cell that emanates it. I search for threads distorted by damage.

The combined patterns of *lledri* from the horse tell me that one of his ribs is broken, and a hamstring is torn in a hind leg, though not severed. If the horse lies there much longer, his weight will force the rib to pierce a lung. But his leg injury keeps him from getting up.

Gabe lifts his daughter to her feet and brushes snow from her. "Are you hurt?"

Berry's wide-eyed gaze is fastened on the horse. She shakes her head.

I cry, "Gabe!"

Gabe looks to me. "What?"

"I need your help to get Rusty to his feet."

Gabe says to Berry, "You sure you're not hurt?"

Berry nods and then points to the horse and me. "Help."

Gabe's eyes widen at Berry's communication. I see his reluctance to leave Berry, but he rushes to me. "What do you need?"

I stand. "He has a broken rib and an injured leg, and we need to get him to his feet before there's further damage. Lend him your strength when I say. You can use the saddle girth to lift."

Gabe doesn't hesitate or question. He positions himself by the horse's side, crouching until his hands are almost under the horse's belly, gripping the broad strap that holds the saddle on.

I stroke the horse's head and speak soft words. "Easy, Rusty, easy." I know he can't understand, but a calming human voice affects many animals. "Rusty, you're going to stand up now, and we will help you."

I take the reins, stand in front of the horse, and pull them taut. "Rusty, I want you to come to me." I put my weight into pulling on the reins. At the same time, I stop my soothing *lledri* and let the pain exert its full strength. Rusty's struggles begin again.

There is little free *lledri* in this isolated place to draw upon—trees are in the near-death of winter and there are few animals about, other than the horse and we humans. I gather what I can.

The horse gets its front hooves on the ground. I shout, "Now!" I focus the *lledri* and *push* up against the horse's torso from underneath.

Gabe heaves ... the horse gets its good hind leg under it and lunges to its feet.

We all breathe hard. I resume the flow of *lledri* to Rusty's pleasure center and he calms, but he shivers. I say, "The saddle."

While Gabe unbuckles the girth and takes the saddle and saddle blanket off, I worry about the horse going into shock. "Do you have a horse blanket for him?"

Berry comes close and Gabe says, "Stand back, honey. Rusty is hurt."

But I see empathy streaming from Berry, and know that it will reach the horse. "Come around by me, Berry, and lay your hand on Rusty's neck."

Gabe shoots a sharp look at me.

"It's safe, and she can help." The horse's shivering increases. "A blanket?"

"In the barn." He runs through the snow.

Berry has to tiptoe, but when she presses her hand against Rusty's neck, a powerful wash of love enters the horse. Human love is a unique and dynamic emotion, and it often has a potent effect on animals. The horse calms even more, though it stands with a rear hoof off the ground. I can set my mind to carrying out what I have spent most of my life doing.

I move to the horse's side, where the broken rib is. Easing my *sight* inside, I find the break, its ruptured cells hemorrhaging the energy of life.

I draw *lledri* from my body and use *touch* to move the broken ends of the rib together, and then flood the join with *lledri*. My added energy stimulates the cells to begin knitting together. The bone is on its way to healing, and there is no more danger to his lung. And no more pain from his rib.

My strength sapped for the moment, I back my focus out. The horse turns its head to me and nickers softly. There is always a bond when my *lledri* mixes with that of another creature, sometimes minimal, sometimes significant, a resonance between us that will remain.

Gabe returns and places a horse blanket over Rusty's back. Gabe gazes at me. "What did you just do?"

"I ... helped the healing. The rib will be all right."

"Are you an X-ray machine too? How ... ?"

"Another time. There's more to be done." I move to the horse's injured rear leg. Berry appears beside me. Placing a hand on the horse's hip, I take a breath and ease my *sight* into his flesh.

Berry slips her little hand into my free hand and closes her fingers. A a rush of *lledri* from her flows to me! Stronger now, I leave my surprise for later and finish my job, finding the tear in the tendon and accelerating the healing process.

Soon the horse straightens its leg and eases weight onto it, and I can relax. I withdraw my *sight* and stretch, drawing a deep breath. Berry releases my hand and grins up at me. Gabe stares at me as if he has seen a miracle. Perhaps he has, but for me a mundane one. This child is the miracle.

Her pink hat must have fallen off, and I run my fingers through Berry's hair and smile. "Well done. Thank you. Rusty will be all right now."

The girl beams back at me, then moves to the horse's shoulder to stroke and nourish him with love. Berry can show affection for the animal, but so much of the girl is trapped in a prison of her own making. She needs my help as much as the horse did.

How can I abandon her now?

10

Recovered from her meeting with the RAC and ready to kick butt again, KB hits the break room. She fills her mug with the last of the coffee-flavored sludge in the pot. A note taped to the wall above the coffee machine says, "You empty it, you fill it," but she's not in the mood to be a good guy. She turns her back on it and goes to Schultz's cubicle, where she finds him sorting printouts into stacks.

He glances at her and bitches, "I don't see what's so hot about this we gotta come in on Saturday."

She decides to pimp him, just a little. "There are no days off when it comes to the security of our nation."

It bounces off his calloused ex-cop brain. "It ain't the end of the friggin' world."

Terrorists were the end of the friggin' world for her brother. She took a moment to steady her voice. "Could be for somebody." She sits in his side chair and pokes at the papers. "Those the people from the parking garage?"

"Yeah." He taps a stack with a cigarette-stained finger. "DMV reports, sorted by parking garage exit and when they left."

"What about the ones you saw?"

He thumbs through the top pages and shrugs. "No red flags." He pulls one out. "This guy gave me a look when I pointed my camera at him. Some kinda farmer."

KB's instincts prickle. "Farmer?"

"Well, maybe. He didn't look like a farmer, but he left in a black pickup truck with hay and a sack of feed in the back."

She takes the paper and skims through a name, address, date of birth, and details on the truck. "One of the disguises the Artisan used was a farmer."

"You said a big blond guy. This one was lean and dark-haired, with a beard. Looked like an A-rab. Besides, the thermal thing showed nothin' weird."

Disappointed, she sinks back and sips coffee. What more could they have done? They checked every person ... Wait a minute. "There was hay in the truck?"

"Yeah." He stretches his arms wide. "Big bale."

She straightens, excitement growing. "You use the thermal camera on it?"

He snorts a laugh. "On a bale of hay?"

"For all we know, this whatever-it-is can look like anything, including my Aunt Sally's refrigerator." She scans the information on the printout. Gabriel River. Couple of speeding tickets. Likes to break the law, does he? "I'll take this one."

Schultz shrugs. "Whatever."

"Anybody in particular interest you?"

He thinks a second, then paws through the papers and pulls one out. "This one. Good-looking blonde."

If men didn't have dicks, they wouldn't be able to think at all. "Sure, you take her. Stick with her for twenty-four hours, then move on to the next one."

"Tomorrow's Sunday."

"So?"

"Never mind."

KB says, "Gimmie some of those and I'll start Bailey working too." Bailey will understand that the women need to get this done.

Bailey has managed to make her cubicle look homey with a couple of pastel landscapes on the walls and a vase of fake daisies on top of a file cabinet. She looks up from a file folder when KB enters, closes it, and smiles. "Well, what'd the RAC say?"

What to tell her? KB plops into Bailey's side chair and tosses the DMV reports on the desk.

Bailey's smile fades away. "He didn't believe you, did he?" She shakes her head. "'Cause you're a chick."

So Bailey sees the RAC the same way KB does. "I don't know that for sure, but, well ..."

"Men ain't got the sense God gave a goose." Bailey places her brown hand over KB's. It's warm and soft. Bailey says, "I want you to know I think you done great." She laughs. "Hell, I'd'a never taken a shot at that thing."

Her touch feels good. KB gazes down at the hand covering hers, and Bailey eases it away. KB sees warmth in her eyes. She hasn't really paid attention, but Bailey is kinda pretty even if she is older—lean, with big eyes and a friendly smile.

KB shakes off her thoughts and divides the stack of reports into halves. "I'm going to cover these, starting with a place out in Palatine." She slides papers toward Bailey. "You check out this bunch."

Bailey's smile is big and white. "You got it. You and me, we'll catch it, you'll see."

KB leaves for her office. She's stoked.

The hunt is on.

~

I can't help but smile at Berry.

With the intense expression of a little woman doing a grown-up job, Berry fetches Rusty a helping of oats in a bucket from the feed room next to the stall while Gabe picks up the saddle and leads the horse to the barn. I follow with the saddle blanket and I'm glad to see that the horse hardly limps.

When I enter the barn, I am pleased to find that it is chilly but not freezing, and at a temperature that the horse's winter coat can easily handle. These *lessi* care well for their beast. Though *"lessi"* is not correct; they are clearly *elessi*, and potent ones at that.

Must I do something about that?

Gabe pats the horse on the neck, a frown furrowing his brow. He turns his gaze on me. "Think he'll be all right?"

Now there's an interesting turn; he appreciates my healing skill even though still puzzled by what has happened. "He's a happy horse. With rest, he will soon be ready to take Berry for rides again." I glance at Berry. I had *seen* in Rusty's aura a horsey affection for the child. "I happen to know that Rusty really likes to do that."

Berry tosses me a wide-eyed glance when she hears that, and then empties her pail of oats into a wooden box fastened to a hayrack at the rear of the stall. Gabe slips off the horse's bridle and Rusty nickers, steps forward and plunges his nose into the oats. A misty hue of pleasure rises from his head as he nibbles. Berry stands by, stroking the horse's shoulder. The girl almost gleams with love.

Gabe smiles down at the scene, then flicks a tight glance at me. Oh, the conflict in his eyes ... and his colors. Swirls and spikes of suspicion, love, curiosity, and fear surge and tangle above his head.

He puts the saddle and gear at the front of the stall. Rusty no longer shivers, so I check his aura for discomfort—finding none, I remove the horse blanket.

After fetching Berry's hat and putting it back on her, Gabe takes a currycomb from a hook on the wall and grooms Rusty, taking special care with the injured leg. Probing the leg with his fingers and getting no reaction, he looks up at me, his colors gaining the airy sky-blue of wonder.

I glance at Berry and catch her shifting her attention back and forth between her father and me. In her colors I *see* curiosity and puzzlement. Since we are doing nothing out of the ordinary, I believe that she's examining our colors. Kneeling beside Berry, I circle my hand over my head and then whisper into her ear. "Do you *see?*"

She gazes into my eyes. She understands what I mean. I see fear ... weariness ... and hope. At last, she nods. Poor child, so alone in her secret knowledge. I smile and say, "That's good." Her eyes widen and I *see* a white flash of amazement. "Very good."

Gabe takes the saddle, blankets, and bridle to the feed room. When he returns, he says, "Anybody here interested in toasting marshmallows?"

Berry raises her hand with the eagerness of a student who knows the right answer. I add my vote. "I, for one, am weary, and something warm would restore me." It occurs to me that I have eaten nothing since the day before. It wouldn't matter if my death wish had not been forestalled. Hunger. A curse. A blessing.

Gabe scoops Berry up, lifts her over his head and settles the girl onto his shoulders, her legs around his neck. "Let's go, then ..." He eyes me. "Miracle worker."

I do not rise to his bait, but follow them to the back door of the little red house. A dormer room juts out of the roof on this side, and I see a teddy bear propped in the window, looking out.

A sense of lightness comes over me, as if a weight has lifted. I look inwardly for the swamp of guilt that I've been drowning in. It's smaller—I'm not up to my neck but knee-deep, near the shore.

Perhaps Berry is *my* healer ...

Inside the house, a large room serves as living space and kitchen. Two bedrooms and a bath are visible through doors, and stairs lead up to the dormer room. It surprises me to feel at ease; the overstuffed furniture, clean but well-worn into comfortableness by many human lives, offers welcome.

Gabe lays kindling in the firebox of an honest-to-goodness Ajax pot-bellied wood stove. Now an antique, I remember when my parents bought one of the first ones made in the early 1800s. Berry fetches a piece of firewood from a tidy stack beside the back door and stands ready with it at Gabe's side. I sit in a chair at a gray kitchen table rich with character from countless scars in its painted surface.

Gabe takes the firewood from Berry and says, "Thank you. One more like this would be great." He smiles as she hurries to the wood supply.

When the fire is going well, Gabe fetches a sack of marshmallows from a cabinet. The mother in me cringes at the sugar in those fluffy candy pills. "You're really going to give her that?"

"I know, I know. But just a couple, and we'll have a good lunch later." He watches Berry, who stares with fascination at the fire. "She likes to do it, and, frankly, there aren't many things she likes to do. Besides, a glass of milk is part of the deal."

He opens a round-shouldered old refrigerator, takes out a jug of milk and sets it on the table. He adds three jelly-jar glasses from a cabinet.

Gabe goes to a closet and takes out three wire hangers. Two have been straightened and have gummy residue on the tips. Gabe sits at the table, unmakes the third hanger and straightens it. "You'll need a toaster."

I shake my head. "Maybe just the milk."

"Your loss." He shrugs and sets the straightened hanger on the table. "Hey, Berry."

Berry comes to him, pleasure curving her lips. She takes a marshmallow, skewers it, and goes to the open door of the stove. Gabe does the same and joins her to hold his marshmallow over the flames.

Berry holds her hanger with both hands. The tip of her tongue poking between her lips, she eases the marshmallow into the stove and rotates it as it browns. Just as it begins to sag, she pulls it out.

She comes to me, holding the marshmallow out to me.

Gabe watches us. His colors show hope. And fear.

Inside, a part of me goes as soft as the toasted marshmallow. I blow on the treat to cool it, and then slide it from the hanger's tip. "Thank you, Berry. This looks delicious." I take a bite and, of course, the warm taste of caramelized sugar *is* delicious.

Gabe and Berry smile identically.

Gabe's marshmallow flames. "Whoa!" He jerks it from the fire, blowing out his mini-inferno. Even though his marshmallow is blackened, he cools it and pops it into his mouth. I remember that, even scorched, they taste good.

I pick up the roaster Gabe made for me. "My turn." I take a marshmallow from the sack and spit it with my hanger. After countless clan campfires, I am an expert, and I soon have a reciprocal treat in Berry's fingers. I usher her to a chair at the table and pour a glass of milk for her. She knows just what to do with both. I sit next to her and enjoy her enjoyment.

Gabe closes the stove door and comes to stand behind Berry. He rests his hands on Berry's small shoulders and pins me with a stare. His voice and manner are forceful, though not threatening, when he says to me, "Enough games, Rhianna. What did you mean when you said that Berry sees you?"

His aura flares. I *see* the burnt orange of combat; he's ready to fight for his daughter. For the girl's sake, I will not deny him.

I say, "You see a greenish color around people's heads when they lie to you."

Gabe's eyes widen. Berry looks up at her father. After a thoughtful pause, Gabe nods. Berry returns her attention to me.

I look into Berry's eyes even though I address Gabe. "So do I." Berry's eyes grow wider ... and then her expression relaxes.

Buttery lights of happiness glimmer around her. "So does Berry." Now her colors include the blue of wonder. I return to Gabe. "Have you seen that green from me?"

"No."

"You won't. All my people see lies and, because it's useless to try, we just don't think of doing it."

"Your people?"

"I am one of a Celtic race that ... acquired certain abilities in ancient times. Over the centuries, our blood has mixed with ordinary humanity, what we call *lessi*, and produced people like you and Berry. *Elessi*." I *see* that he's *reading* me, searching for an untruth. "Do you see other colors?"

He shakes his head.

I shape a sphere around Berry's head with my hands. "Our cells emit tiny bursts of living energy. We call it *lledri*."

He lifts his brows. "The *'lledri'* for warming your hands?"

I nod. "Each energy pulse from a living cell is unique, shaped by what the cell is or does. My people see these pulses as streaming motes of light. When the part of the brain used for lying is active, it produces the color of bile."

He nods again. "A nasty yellow-green." He looks at Berry, and then me. "There are more colors?"

"Many more." I shift to Berry. Her eyebrows lift as if she senses what I am about to say. "And Berry *sees* them."

Berry nods. I turn my attention back to Gabe. "I think you understand the effect that possessing this ability can have on a child, don't you?"

~

Oh, yeah, Gabe knows how seeing a weird color in the air can affect a kid. In second grade, he'd watched Marty Simmons swipe an oatmeal cookie from Heather's lunch sack. It was scorched on the bottom like all the cookies Heather's mom made. When Heather saw Marty eating it, she accused him of taking her cookie.

He told her his mom had baked cookies yesterday and that Heather was crazy—and a nasty greenish color had flickered around his head. Gabe studied the other kids at the table as they watched Marty tell his lie. Their eyes never shifted and they didn't react to the color swirling around Marty's head, not even when Heather started to cry.

That wasn't right. He said, "It is too her cookie."

Marty said, "You're crazy. It's mine." The strands of green color thickened. Marty's cheeks reddened, and Gabe knew he was mad.

Gabe decided he wasn't crazy because he knew what he saw was true, but he felt ... *outside,* as though he was across the room from everybody else. His friendship with Marty ended that day, and soon he'd had no friends.

He had wanted to ask his mother about it, but he'd been afraid she would look at him in that scared-angry way that said he was nuts ... strange ... weird. Crazy. It wasn't until his mother moved and he changed schools that he was able to make himself pretend he was like everybody else and be friendly again.

Gabe strokes Berry's hair. Berry sees lots of colors? And Rhianna does too?

"So what are you saying? Does seeing these colors have something to do with Berry's—" The warble of Gabe's cell phone intrudes. He glances at the screen and mutters, "Shit." Then he pushes a button. "Hello, Bonnie."

"I'm glad I caught you."

He isn't. Whenever she interrupts a day with Berry it never works out in Gabe's favor.

Bonnie says, as she always does, "I'm sorry to call, Gabe, but something has come up. Are you at the apartment?"

"No. The farm." Does she plan these things just to foul up his time with Berry? Was she that pissed off about this morning? He lets a little of his frustration sharpen his tone. "Having a great time, I might add."

"Oh, I'm sorry ..."

Damn, she sounds sincere, which makes it harder to be irritated. "What is it?"

"A birthday party invitation just came in the mail. It must have been delayed, because the party is today. In an hour."

A birthday party? He glances at Berry—his daughter and Rhianna have moved to the kitchen sink. They're letting the water run, and Rhianna pokes a finger into the stream. Checking the temperature, he guesses, waiting for warm. Berry watches her, licking marshmallow from her fingers, her blue eyes bright and focused instead of lost. Rhianna brushes a lock from Berry's forehead and gives her a soft smile.

He turns his attention back to Bonnie. "Well, that's unfortunate."

Now her voice pleads and demands at the same time, a mother moving full tilt to get something her offspring needs. "Gabe, this is the first party she's ever been invited to. This could be a breakthrough for her."

She's right, it could be important. He glances at Berry. She's a lot looser today, and this chance to connect with other kids might be too good to miss.

Bonnie says, "Please bring her home. I'll run get a present, and we can still make it. She'll have so much fun! And make friends."

Rhianna checks the water with a finger again, then tugs Berry's hands to it. She wets them, then she takes the Lava soap bar and lathers them. Berry giggles—even her hands can be ticklish. What was happening here could be just as important.

"I don't know, Bonnie. You know she doesn't like to have her routine messed with."

He hears the old, familiar anger smolder under her words. "She needs friends, Gabe. We can't deny her this chance."

Rhianna turns off the faucet and wraps Berry's hands in a dish towel. Smiling, she rubs them with vigor. Is that a trace of yellow shimmering around Berry's head, like melting margarine on toast?

Bonnie's voice cuts in. "Are you listening? This could mean a friend for her! You know how important the doctor says it is for her to connect with other kids."

She's right. The doc made a big point of that ... although nothing else the doctor does seems to make a difference. Even though Berry has clearly bonded with this strange woman, friends her own age would be huge.

It's a half hour to the house. "All right. We're having a treat. I'll bring her as soon as we're finished."

Now Bonnie's voice smiles. "Great! That'll give me time to dash out for a present. See ya."

Gabe kills the connection and gazes at Rhianna and Berry. He has to find a way not to let this go. But how can he hold onto a suicidal woman who can change appearance at will, doesn't feel the cold, and can remote-control a horse?

~

I have no need of *sight* to see Gabe's consternation when he ends his conversation. His brows draw down as he gazes at Berry and then me. He puts his phone away and tells Berry, "That was Mommy."

I rehang the dish towel on its hook by the sink and Berry turns to her father. What has made Gabe turn sour? Yet I also *see* twinkling gold threads of hope in his aura.

He kneels before Berry. I like the way Gabe is careful to be at eye level with the child instead of speaking down at her.

"Mommy says you've been invited to a birthday party."

Berry's aura shifts from the warm yellow of happiness to the acid, yellowish hue of fear. It's always struck me as odd that the colors are so near and the emotions so far apart. Berry takes a step back and presses against me. I want to wrap her in my arms, but that is not my place here. I do, though, rest my hand on her shoulder.

Gabe offers a smile. "C'mon, it'll be fun. And you could make a friend. There'll be cake and ice cream!"

Berry's colors warm a little at that, and she nods. Gabe stands and says to me, "Please come with me while I take her home. You need to tell me more about ..." He waves a hand above Berry's head, through the colors I can *see* but he can't.

"I know you have something you want to do, but an hour or two won't make a difference."

Now I'm the one who feels a thrill of fear. Expose myself further? Expose my race? But I have done this before with *elessi*, even those who had far less potential than this man. I discover that he is wrong about one thing; my desperate need to end my pain has withered under the warmth of Berry's … love. Yes, she radiates a puppy's innocent love when she looks my way. And she needs what I have to offer far more than Gabe does. Leaving for later the question of what to do with my life, I say, "Yes. I want to help. And, as for what I want to do … that seems to have changed." It was true. The wall of grief that had cut me off from feeling has crumbled.

I squeeze Berry's shoulders. "Well, where's your coat?"

11

Slumped low in the seat of her car, KB sits just high enough to peer over the dashboard and watch Gabriel River's house three doors down, a middle-class ranch-style house amid a neighborhood full of them. A shiver starts between her shoulder blades and spreads until even her legs tremble. She hates to start the engine to warm herself and broadcast her presence with vapor from her exhaust pipe, but she's so cold she can hardly think. At least she's parked in front of a home with a For Sale sign in front; maybe she'll appear to be someone waiting to see the house.

She turns the key and the engine catches. It's been an hour with no sign of a black pickup. Should she move on to the next possibility? A brunette woman had dashed from River's house earlier and raced down the street in a gray SUV, but she hadn't looked like any of the disguises the Artisan had used. A quick shot with KB's thermal camera had caught no suspicious infrared from her.

The woman had left the two-car garage door open and KB had done a quick drive-by. No black pickup inside. She'd circled the block and returned to her vantage point to watch. Shit, the guy could be gone all day.

She glances in her rear-view mirror—a truck turns onto the street. It's her target. She lunges to turn off her engine and duck low. He pulls into his driveway but not into the garage.

From KB's vantage she can see a dark-haired woman on the passenger side.

KB rolls down her window. Cursing the cold air that spills in, she aims her thermal camera at the truck. Its engine heat shows, and a low-level glow from the cab. Probably just from the truck's heater. Nothing special.

She pulls her camera back in, then remembers the RAC's hard-on for evidence. Everything looks normal now, but what if it changes? Easing the camera back out, she records the scene for a few seconds.

That done, she rolls her window up and settles in for a wait. Her intuition is yelling "This is it!" Even though she thinks it's right, she tells it to shut up and pay attention. She's not making a move without proof.

~

Gabe wishes Bonnie wouldn't leave the garage door open. The side he'd parked his truck on is accumulating the detritus of living.

Anybody could walk into the house. He glances at Rhianna. Man, there's gonna be an explosion when Bonnie sees her. A fight with Bonnie in front of Berry could kill all the good things that have happened this day.

Maybe she could slide down in the seat ... no, way too easy for Bonnie to see inside the truck. Half joking, half hoping, he says, "I don't suppose you can make yourself invisible?"

She turns those sea-blue eyes on him. Even though he doesn't see colors the way she says she and Berry do, her comprehension and wisdom are impossible to miss. She says, "Your woman?"

"Yeah. She'll go straight to thinking that I'm ... well, I don't know, exactly, but it won't be pleasant."

"I can't make myself invisible. I could adopt the *glamère* of a man ... but then you'd have to explain that. And you don't like to lie."

"No." Down the street, Bonnie's car turns the corner and splashes through slush. What can he tell her? "Hey, Berry, here comes Mommy." He gets out, reaches in and lifts Berry to him.

Rhianna says, "Perhaps a shadow *glamère* would do the job, especially with you out of the truck. Her attention will be on you and Berry."

With that, she slumps down in her seat and seems to fade until she's no more than a suggestion with shadows flickering over it. So that's what he had seen in the underground garage. Berry glances at her, and then her eyes widen. The shadows ripple away. Rhianna places a kiss on the tip of her forefinger, and then leans across and touches it to Berry's forehead. She says, "Bye, Berry. Maybe I can show you how to do this one day." Again shadows ripple and she might as well not have been there.

Bonnie pulls into the garage and Gabe shuts the truck door. Berry stares at the area where Rhianna sits, then lifts her hand and says, "Bye."

Damn, what will Berry say to Bonnie about this strange woman? "Berry, honey, I think Rhianna needs to be our secret for a little while. Just you and me. We won't talk about her to anyone, not even Mommy. Okay?"

Berry shifts her gaze to Gabe, her expression serious. Gabe warms at the intelligence and understanding he sees there, so opposite the avoidance she usually displays. Berry nods.

"Atta girl." He carries Berry around to the open garage—he glances at his truck and can't see Rhianna even though he knows she's there.

Bonnie hustles out with a broad smile of love and hope aimed at their daughter. She holds up a shopping bag. "Got her the sweetest little doll."

He sets Berry down, and she takes her daughter's hand.

Bonnie gazes at Gabe. "I know you hate it when I do things like this, and I understand."

Of course she would know. Bonnie has always cared about how other people feel—except, of course, when she comes down on him. He nods. "Maybe this will be good for Berry, and that's what comes first." The one thing they always agree on.

She glances at her watch. "We'd better hurry." She lifts the bag. "Gotta get this wrapped."

"Her backpack's at the apartment. I'll run it out later ... maybe I could take her out for a burger tonight?"

"Sure."

He squats low and pulls Berry close for a hug. "I'll call you, okay?"

Berry wraps her arms around Gabe's neck and returns the hug. "Bye, Daddy."

Gabe hears an intake of breath from Bonnie. He stands and enjoys the surprise on her face. The "opening" that Rhianna seems to have started in Berry is still happening. Maybe this is a terrific day after all.

~

Watching the family scene in River's driveway, something strikes KB as different. She studies the truck. She can't see the woman who arrived with River. Did she scrunch down, trying to hide? But that would be foolish—the brunette woman from the house can see into the cab from where she stands.

Excitement flutters in KB's gut. She rolls her window down and edges the lens of her thermal camera out. The family is clear in the viewfinder as people-shaped hot spots. The glow from the truck's cooling engine has dimmed ... and the truck's passenger window shines like there's a floodlight inside! KB can make out no detail, just a rectangular glow. Maybe the window glass diffuses whatever it is. She centers on the truck window and presses Record. She pans to the family, still producing normal infrared signatures.

She presses Stop when the guy squats down and hugs his kid. Holy shit. River's infrared flickers and then flares bright like the Artisan's had. She fingers the Record button, but too late—the suspect has stood and his infrared output is back to normal. Still, she saw it. He's one of them.

She shuts off the camera and rolls up her window. Now what?

Backup. Her fingers clumsy with cold, she keys on her radio. "KB calling. You guys out there?"

After a moment, Bailey says, "Yeah. Parked in front of a condo. If I had balls, they'd be freezing off."

Schultz's voice joins in. "I do have balls, and they are freezing off."

KB grins. "So your babe is giving you the cold shoulder, hunh?"

"You're a hard woman, KB."

"Listen, I've found our suspect. In that black pickup you saw at the garage, Schultz. It looks like there are two of them now, a man and a woman."

Bailey catches on. "You needin' backup?"

"Yeah. Here's the address—" She glances at the truck. "Hold on." River gets into his truck as the woman and girl enter the garage. The garage door closes. Exhaust plumes from the truck's tailpipe, and the quarry backs out of the driveway.

KB slides down in her seat and listens to it pass. "Suspects moving. I'll follow and call when they settle. Be ready to move." KB starts her car, and after the truck turns the corner, she does a quick U-turn and follows. Woo-hoo! Gonna get her a couple of terrorists. No, that isn't right. Yet. Technically they are only suspects. But not for long, she's certain of that. Woo-hoo!

~

I'm a little nervous as I lead Gabe from a parking garage to the plaza beside the Tribune Tower above the Chicago River. There are Saturday strollers, although not the throngs of *lessi* who fill the plaza on weekdays. One less aggravation to deal with.

It's time to expose his true nature to him, and that is an act of consequence. Some people can't handle it, though I have little doubt about this man.

Gabe has been patient, respecting my wish to wait to talk until we arrived. Underneath the pavement, just east of the Michigan Avenue bridge, lies land that is special to me. I'm not sure why I wanted to come here. Perhaps because it's where I became an adult, and, in a sense, that's what could happen to Gabe today.

We pass the Equitable Building as we cross the plaza, its barren concrete so alien to the prairie I knew as a young woman when I rode to the lone trading post that was here. But it is within the embrace of those memories that I want to tell Gabe of the Clans. And, perhaps, to begin the recovery of my own life.

We take the steps down to the walkway along the river. There are no people there, and I feel that our conversation will be private. The cold is bitter, and I use *lledri* to warm myself. Gabe has his hands jammed in his pockets and hunches his shoulders.

He turns to me. "You don't think Berry has Asperger Syndrome, do you?"

Clever man, he's been putting the pieces together. "Do you remember how you felt when you discovered that others don't see the color of lies as you do?"

"Yeah. Like an outsider. Alien, as if I had to pretend to be human."

He looks away, and I see pain draw the corners of his mouth down. He says, "I still do."

"Imagine, then, what it must have done to Berry when, from her earliest days, she has seen a rainbow of colors that no one refers to or teaches her about."

"It must have been bewildering. Incomprehensible."

"To protect herself she withdrew, like a turtle retreating into its shell. I've seen it before in highly talented *elessi*. It's her Magian blood." I see the question rise in his eyes.

"Magian?"

"What we call ourselves, our race. It's an old word for magician."

Gabe's eyebrows make a move for his hairline. "But ... Berry? How? I mean ... how?"

"Because of the ways Magians can use *lledri,* we are, let's say, gifted at seduction. Even though, as a people, we withdrew from ordinary humanity centuries ago, our men and women have philandered merrily across the world, leaving behind their offspring. By now I suspect there are millions with Magian blood. Although they are kin, they are distant, their blood so diluted they will never wield *lledri.* But you ... you are at least half Magian. And Berry favors you."

"But I see only one color." He pauses. "Although, come to think of it, I did see a yellowish something around Berry's head when you were helping her wash her hands."

"Like butter?"

He nods.

I'm warmed and somewhat pleased. "That's the color of happiness. It may be that exposure to me is breaking down whatever holds your perceptions at bay."

"Like I've repressed it?" He gazes at the river, a thoughtful expression softening his features. "Are you telling me that— besides seeing colors—Berry is normal?"

"I can't be certain yet, but it explains her behavior. And the way she responded to me." How lonely the girl must be, a feeling the Clans well know. "As for 'normal,' seeing the colors of auras *is* normal for me and my kin."

Gabe turns to me, shaking his head but grinning at the same time. "This is crazy. You must be crazy." He runs a hand through his hair. "Hell, *I* must be crazy."

Alongside excitement, I *see* a flood of indigo blue emerge from him, the dark hue of a deep, aching longing. An urge to take his hand and comfort him forms, but I shy from it. Other than Berry, I have not touched another human being for months. Perhaps that's one of the things wrong with me. I brace for the avalanche of questions he's sure to rain on me.

~

KB pushes the Record button on her thermal camera and takes in the scene on the walkway below. In her viewfinder, Gabriel River looks normal, but he stands next to a tall, slender glow. The guy hasn't shown any more of the weird infrared radiation the female Artisan puts out, but that could be just because he hasn't needed to. For sure he's an accomplice.

Turning down the gain, the Artisan's glow dims until it shows a tall, slender woman. Gotcha. The RAC can't deny this.

KB zooms in and captures the woman's profile. It's the same face she saw through the camera at the Art Institute, a youngish woman with regular—hell, pretty—features. What's confusing this time is that the Artisan looks the same with infrared and normal vision—no weird disguise, no nothing. KB presses Stop. She's recorded enough evidence of the Artisan glowing like an electric person to satisfy the need for evidence. It's time to move.

Triggering her collar microphone, she says, "Bailey. Schultz. You here?" She'd called them in as soon as she saw the Artisan and her accomplice go into a parking garage.

Schultz is the first voice in her earpiece. "Yeah, I'm behind you, by the south side of the Tribune Tower."

Bailey says, "Across Michigan Avenue, at the Wrigley Building."

"Okay, guys, it's party time."

Schultz says, "I hope you got something worth spending my Saturday on."

His attitude pisses off KB; this is serious business. But she keeps her irritation out of her voice when she says, "There are two of them. One is the guy you saw in the pickup at the garage, Schultz, and the other one is the woman from the Art Institute. Bailey, you approach on the river walk from the west. Schultz, you circle around and come at them from the east. I'll stay here and cover the stairs down to the river. When we've got them boxed, we'll move in—but not until you hear from me."

Bailey says, "You got it. Uh, which way is west?"

KB hears Schultz snort. The woman isn't exactly helping with the female rep for helplessness. "From where you are, the lake is east, you're west."

She slings the camera strap onto a shoulder and surveys the plaza. Schultz moves toward another approach to the river walk. KB turns back to the river. Without the camera, she sees only an innocent scene of a couple standing by the water and chatting. She bounces on her toes, eager to move. Don't attract attention, you goof. She stills, then slips off a glove and reaches inside her parka to the butt of her gun. It's warm and ready.

~

The intensity of emotion that Rhianna's revelations bring chokes Gabe's throat. He turns away from her and scans the buildings across the river. She has kin! And he's one of them?

What whirs in mad circles in his mind is not joy at her idea that Berry is normal, though that's there. No, it's a fluorescent hope that the crushing loneliness he's felt all his life could end. He can be part of something, not an outsider. He isn't weird, there are others like him. Kin!

He takes a breath to settle himself, but excitement still hums through him. He turns back and re-examines her.

Rhianna seems as human as he feels. He sees a beautiful woman, but none of the colors she talks about ... although he believes they exist. They have to, for his sake and for Berry's.

He'd like to reach for her, just to make contact with someone who is like him. Oh, the questions.

At last the lump in his throat eases enough to allow him to speak. "Is this real? Are you real?"

She smiles. It feels good to have that warmth turned his way. She says, "Yes. Very real."

"Can Berry learn ... can I?" God, she has to say yes. She's a healer, and they are both so damn broken.

Now she's the one to send her gaze roving over skyscrapers, but at last it returns to him. "I think so. It will take time—clan children learn the meanings of colors over the years of childhood. Berry should find it easier because of her youth. And there are no guarantees that either of you will be able to control *lledri.*"

"So you'll, what, teach us?"

She nods. "I will try to bring you into my clan, as well. They will help."

"But will you be ..." He fishes for a word. "... around to do that? I mean, you did try to turn yourself into an icicle."

Rhianna's expression sobers. "I ... you and your daughter have forced open a door in a prison wall for me."

"What do we do? When? How? Where?" He has more questions. Who was his father? Can he find him? It strikes him that his mother's stories about the "angel" she met and loved are maybe not the fantasies he always thought they were. He visualizes her rocking in her room at the nursing home, a bemused smile on her face. Since the stroke, she always smiles. Next weekend he's going to go see her. Can he tell her about this?

Rhianna glances behind him and stiffens, then she takes a step back. He swivels and catches sight of a skinny man in a black overcoat on the walkway. There's something familiar—

A woman's shout comes from the plaza above. "Now!"

He turns, Rhianna spins and looks up. She cries, "How can this be?"

A woman in the plaza points a gun at them. He glances toward the skinny man. The man advances, a pistol in two hands, the weapon aimed dead at Gabe's chest. It's the wacky video guy from the parking lot. Gabe wheels. A Black woman approaches along the river walkway on the other side, aiming a pistol their way. They don't look like gangbangers. They act like cops.

Rhianna turns to him. He doesn't need to see colors to perceive her terror. He says, "The people who were after you yesterday?"

"I don't know what's happening!"

The woman above calls out, "Department of Homeland Security. Hands up!"

Gabe raises his hands. Rhianna becomes shadows. The female agent above raises a small camcorder to her eye and then fires her pistol into the air. The pistol lowers to aim at Rhianna. "I can see what you do. Stop your tricks!"

Rhianna's shadows disappear and she backs against the railing. "Oh, what have I done?" She wraps her arms around her abdomen and bends as if bearing a crushing weight.

Gabe steps close and puts his arm around her shoulders, careful to keep his other hand raised. He draws her close.

The agents advance, their weapons scary, the grim hostility on their faces even scarier.

12

After a morning of fuming at Vixen for her intransigence and at the bacteria on a slide for the same damnable characteristic, Drago powers off the electron microscope. Maybe he can get her to work on it one more time—no, she isn't going to forgive him for smashing her cursed phone.

Drago shakes his head. Why are people so bloody hard to get along with? The one thing he can threaten Vixen with is banishment from the clan. She has enough kin in Clan Bleddyn she would lose that it might work. But then the whole family might revolt and leave. Controlling clansmen is like trying to herd cats, creatures he's never liked very much, too damned independent. Better to save the banishment option until he's had a chance to explore alternatives.

He gazes at the portrait of Graeme on the laboratory wall. Will there be no vengeance? Is his work a waste? Not yet. Maybe Lewinna, the Clan Bleddyn healer, can do this if she tries hard enough.

Drago goes to a cabinet for the cell phone Lewinna insists he keep for medical emergencies that she can't handle. He speed-dials her number.

Lewinna's voice, as always, evokes honey pouring over a hot biscuit. Her voice is almost as healing as her *touch*. "Well, Drago. You about ready to head south?"

"Work yet to do. And I need your help."

"That micro stuff? I thought Vixen was helping you."

"Well, not anymore. When can ye be here?"

"Not going to happen. I've got two cases of chickenpox and a broken leg to care for, and the chickenpox will likely spread."

Anger swells in him. "Lewinna, I—"

"Don't even think of trying to pull clanmaster rank on me, Drago. Besides, I don't like the way you won't look at me when you talk about your 'cure.'"

Damn all uppity women! Keeping his voice civil, he says, "Ye will thank me for it one day."

At her end a child's voice wails. Lewinna says, "Oh, damn, here comes another snakebite. I wish we didn't have to hide out in this swamp. Gotta go."

Drago ends the call. Yes, she *will* thank him when they no longer have to hide. He puts the phone away and then studies the image from the electron microscope. The bacterium lives and it can sicken the *lessi*, but as it is it can do nothing to further his cause.

Vixen is right about Rhianna. She has always been the best with deep *touch*. Though he despises the truth of it, Rhianna is the most likely of the clansmen in this hemisphere to be able to splice the genes.

He straightens. Putting his hatred aside—temporarily—is a sacrifice he must make. The stench of burning hydrocarbons reaches him, and he turns off the generator. The fluorescent lights go dark, and the lab is lit by the skylight.

Will Rhianna speak to him? Does she still feel the sting of his blame for the loss of his son? No matter, she has to do her duty. She has always had an outsized sense of integrity; maybe he can use it to force her to do his bidding. Surely she will do all she can to help her race. He will persuade her.

He strides onto the deck. Vixen plays with the children in the clearing, helping little Alexandra in a snowball fight. Drago calls down, "Where is Rhianna?"

Hands on her hips, Vixen cocks her head and studies him. "You think she will talk to you?"

"She must."

Her bush of hair shakes. "I sure as hell wouldn't."

Damned woman. "Where?"

"I can call Mary Fay in Rhianna's clan and ask—she keeps track of everybody in Clan Deverell." She digs into a pocket and then stops. "Oh, gosh, my phone doesn't work." She beams a smile through an aura of red-black malice. "So sorry."

Thrice-damned, wretched, cheeky bitch! It will do him no good to call Rhianna's clan—he and the Deverell clanmaster share a grudge going back a century. Drago wheels away from the railing and storms down into the amidships hold. "Emmaline!"

Emmaline emerges from Drago's sleeping quarters off the main room, a feather duster in her hand. "No need to bellow."

"I need to find Rhianna."

She raises her brows. "And what would you be wantin' with her?"

She knows him too well to believe he wants to reconcile. "Clan business."

He *sees* doubt blossom in her aura, but he hasn't lied. He *is* the clan; his business is its business.

She shrugs. "I got a note from my cousin Betha in Clan Deverell and she asked if I'd seen Rhianna. Seems she went walkabout to Chicago some time back. Rhianna wasn't doin' so well, says Betha." She eyes Drago. "No surprise, considerin' what happened to her husband."

He ignores the wince of pain that stabs at his heart. Why can't these women keep their opinions to themselves? "Thank ye." He charges back up the stairs to the forecastle. Taking out the cell phone once more, he calls the number at the clan safe house in Chicago. He has used similar places owned and maintained by the clans in other cities, but not this one in a riverside high-rise. There's no answer, so he leaves a voice mail message for Rhianna and then returns to the deck. Well, he prefers traditional methods of communication anyway. If she's in the Chicago area, Merlin and Arthur might be able to find her.

He goes to the stern deck and seeks his blue jays. He finds one huddled in a nearby oak, homes in on it and focuses. The gray of hunger clouds the bird's aura, its empty belly no surprise in this winter land. Though not as easy for Drago as for most clansmen, he manages to project at the bird a *glamère* of seeds held in his hand.

The jay launches into a glide toward the galleon, and Drago searches for his other feathered friend. He finds its familiar aura among four other clan jays in a cedar tree and lures it to him with another seed *glamère*. As the two birds fly in, he takes birdseed from a ceramic container that rests on the deck rail and scatters a small serving on it. He wants to reward them, but not with so large a helping that they won't be motivated to do the task he has for them in return for more food.

The first to land is Merlin. Drago strokes his back as the jay pecks up seeds. "Wise old bird, will ye be the one to find her?"

The other jay lands on the railing. "Arthur, lad, ready for an adventure today?" Drago has spent many hours training his jays, and he thinks they are the best at the scouting he needs done. It isn't written which clan discovered blue jays' ability to perceive and recognize human auras, but he's grateful for it. Because each Magian's DNA is different, each of their auras has a unique, distinct "flavor" that the jays can recognize.

After Merlin and Arthur clean up the seed, Drago holds his hands near them and the birds roost on his outstretched fingers. "All right, boys, time to earn your supper."

Flooding their little minds with his memory of Rhianna's aura, he adds an image of birdseed in her outstretched hand. He commands the birds, "Seek and home. Seek and home." Search and return.

He tosses them upward and the birds, under the compulsion of powerful Pavlovian conditioning, spiral upward, seeking Rhianna's aura. He calls after them, "Seek and home!"

Far above the birds, a jet roars toward O'Hare Airport, trailing foul plumes of exhaust. Not for much longer, Drago vows, not for much longer. How ironic that Rhianna, a healer, will deliver the final solution into his hands.

13

The RAC stands beside KB in the tenth-floor conference room. As she plays the recordings from her thermal camera, she lets a little smirk curl the side of her mouth that he can't see. Behind her, Bailey and Schultz also stare at the scene on the monitor. After it shows a close-up of the female Artisan's real face on the river walk just before the arrest, KB stops the video.

She waits for the RAC to sing a praise or two.

Still gazing at the television screen, he says, "Well, it looks like you might have something, Agent."

She stifles a snort. Yeah, she *might*—just two of the Artisans the Department has been searching the country for.

He looks her way. "You say the man also showed signs of this exceptional infrared radiation?"

"Yessir. At his house. He's clearly an accomplice."

He indicates the TV. "I didn't see it here."

Yeah, but he has seen the other one. Why can't he take her word for it? "I wasn't recording when I saw it, but it was there. I tell you, it is no coincidence that she met up with him after she left the Art Institute. Besides, he aided and abetted her escape."

The RAC shrugs. "I wouldn't call it an escape. After all, these people have done nothing illegal."

"She ran for it outside the Institute."

He arches an eyebrow. *"If* the child you saw was this woman, perhaps she was running from the bullets coming at her. From *your* gun."

Christ, what did the Artisans have to do, knock on his office door with a bloody hatchet in one hand and the mayor's head in the other? "But you didn't see—" KB puts on the brakes. Words aren't gonna get her anywhere with this guy. But a confession from the Artisans will. They'll give it, now that she has them in cells on the top floor. "The woman has no ID, no money, no nothing. We ran her fingerprints. No hits. But we'll find something."

"The man?"

"His ID looks real, but we're checking. He could be a sleeper."

The RAC surveys KB and her crew. "We'll see what happens when our interrogators get here tomorrow."

Why wait? What the hell, she made an A in interrogation. She has the perps confused and shaken—*now* is the time to move, just like the textbooks teach. She gears up to say so, but the RAC has that flat, you're-getting-nowhere-with-me-today look. Doesn't he get it? Lives could be at stake.

He points at the camera. "You've logged that video in as evidence?"

Mister Procedure. Although she hasn't, she says, "Of course, sir."

The RAC nods and leaves. The old fart isn't going to give her diddly-squat, is he?

Bailey beams a big, fat grin and holds up her hand for a high-five. "Damn! You go, girl!"

KB laughs and gives her the five.

Schultz says, "Am I done now?"

KB is in too good a mood to care about his crummy attitude. "Yeah. I'm gonna do guard duty for a while." She needs two people, one stationed by the cells, the other at the elevator lobby. "I'll get Martinez to take the front."

Schultz grins. "Hey, good job." He adds a casual salute. "Sir."

Holy cow, a nice word from Schultz? Now she has icing on her cake.

Bailey says, "I can come in after supper and spell you."

Schultz says, "Tell you what, I'll take over for Martinez then."

Now that's good. She can trust her team to help her do the right thing. She checks her watch. Three o'clock. "Great. Seven?"

Schultz nods and Bailey says, "I'll be there."

KB removes the video and follows them out to log it in and round up Martinez.

What is it gonna take to break through with the RAC? She has the most incredible catch in the agency and he wants paperwork? Paperwork is what a file clerk does, not an agent. Agents take action. Maybe she can soften up the Artisans, get something before the interrogation guys rip into them. It'll have to be tonight.

The woman had looked scared, so she could be vulnerable. The guy is acting brave, but he has that little kid to worry about, could be a weak spot. Hot damn! This is gettin' good.

She meets Martinez in the fifteenth-floor lobby by the elevators. He's pulling on a sweater—it's always chilly up here this time of year. She's tempted to go downstairs and get her jacket, but decides to tough it out.

He says, "Temperature outside's dropped ten degrees since this morning—down to zero and heading south."

"I'd like to head south." She points to the desk in the lobby. "You stay here and I'll go back with the bad guys."

"You really caught one?"

"Caught two. It's just a matter of proving it."

Martinez settles in at the desk and opens a *People* magazine. Monitors show surveillance camera views of the lobby and hallways.

Down a forty-foot hall lined with doors that once opened upon offices, KB rounds a corner to find Rudy, the agent she drafted to watch the prisoners while she set things up. He sits at a desk, gazing at a bank of small video monitors that show the interiors of the five rooms converted to cells with bars on the windows.

Three cells are empty, and her prisoners pace in the other two, free to move but hands cuffed in front, a wooden chair is bolted to the floor. The power lights on the recorders are green; the cameras will catch anything the suspects do, especially glowing—she's added thermal cameras to the regular video surveillance equipment in the cells that hold River and the female Artisan. The RAC wants evidence, KB is damn well gonna get it.

"Anything happen? Any weird glows from the perps?"

Rudy, a Native American guy almost as wide as he is tall, pushes up from his chair. "Nope. They just walk. I think I've lost a couple pounds watching them."

She smiles. "Yeah, I thought you looked thinner."

He laughs and gestures at a bulging nine-by-twelve manila envelope. "Here's the guy's stuff—cell phone, keys, money. She had zip."

"How could anybody have nothing?"

He shrugs, then taps a large thermos. "Fresh coffee, you're all set."

"Thanks, Chief."

After he gives her a friendly middle finger and leaves, she sits, leans back, puts her feet on the desktop, and checks the monitors.

The guy is a puzzle. KB hates to think about it, but her case against him is pretty anemic. She needs hard evidence. Like catching him generating that extra infrared. KB reviews what she knows ... the female Artisan first caught Schultz's attention because she didn't act like she was cold in a sub-zero wind. So she must have been doing something to keep warm, and whatever it was showed up on Shultz's thermal camera. Can KB use cold to force something to happen?

She gets up and heads for the woman's cell, then stops and returns to the desk to switch off the recorders. Nobody will think anything of it—power outages happen all the time in the old building.

~

I wish I believed in God for I'm in sore need of someone to pray to for help. But in my centuries I have seen no evidence of a deity willing to lend a hand to mortals. No, as far as I can tell, all the good and evil in this world is created by human beings, the same people who dreamed up God and Satan and all the other divinity notions that are, the way I see it, reflections of human impulses.

But then, I haven't seen everything yet. There is room for doubt.

A shiver runs through me. Even though there is an old-fashioned steam radiator in the corner, the one window in the room is drafty. Stout iron bars block any thought of escape. Bare white walls seem to intensify the chill; it's as though I'm inside a refrigerator.

The handcuffs create circles of pain around my wrists as well as an ache in my shoulders from the unnatural position of my arms locked in front of my body. I long to ease *lledri* into the keyhole and manipulate the handcuff to release myself.

But I can't use *lledri* to free my hands or warm my body now that I know that dogged woman somehow sees it with her video camera. Such a camera perches high out of reach in a corner, next to a second video camera, waiting for me to betray myself. And my kind. No, the best thing to do is to wait this out. I have committed no crime, and they will have to let me go sooner or later.

My thoughts turn to Gabe and his embrace at the river flashes into my mind. It had been unexpected, although welcome. Far more unforeseen, though, had been a gentle *touch* from him. Along with the firm embrace of his arm had come a light but steady pressure of *lledri* where his arm wrapped my body. *Touching* with that delicacy of control is unprecedented in someone untrained and rare in any case, untrained or not.

He must be unaware of it; he would surely have mentioned it when we talked about Berry's ability to *see* the colors of emotion. I think perhaps Gabe's feeling of isolation has somehow led him to the spontaneous use of *touch* to try to bond with other human beings. His need must indeed be powerful ... perhaps as great as the desperate need that drove my ancestor when she first discovered *lledri* and how to control it during the Ice Age. If Gabe has similar talents, he could become very strong in his use of *lledri*.

Movement draws my attention to the window—two blue jays jostle for position on the window ledge. I know blue jays well, and they wouldn't naturally venture this deeply into the heart of the city. The only reason these birds would be here is that a clansman seeks me.

I go to the window—if I can open it, I can give the jays a command that will send them to bring the searcher to me. At the least, I must warn the Clans of this new danger of discovery. And perhaps I can get help for Gabe; he has no place in this, and no defenses.

Thinking of his helplessness, my son's image comes to mind, his body so frail and bent with age. I have been criminally neglectful of him these last few months, lost in the swamp of my depression. I want to make it up to him before I die. I examine the window.

It's bolted shut. Hope withers. Maybe I can break the glass ... I go to the single piece of furniture, a wooden chair, intent on using it to smash the window. But it's secured to the floor.

A key rattles in the door lock. The door swings open to reveal the woman who has become my nemesis. The burnt orange of combat dominates her aura. "Sit in the chair."

I oblige her, resisting an urge to reach out with *lledri* and bring her to her knees. But that cursed camera watches. And

I must not let them see me use *lledri* and lead them to the existence of the Clans.

Her hand is inside her coat where the pistol in a shoulder holster sits. Yet the woman smiles and says, "I don't think you'll be escaping me here." She enters and locks the door behind her.

Another of these ruffians could be poised outside the door, ready to rush in. I have to pretend to be one of them, a *lessi,* an innocent.

The woman says, "I'm Supervisory Special Agent KB Volmer. You are a guest of the Department of Homeland Security." She gestures at one of the cameras. "Thanks to our thermal cameras, we know when you do your little tricks. You want to tell me about it?"

"I've done nothing illegal. Why am I here?"

"Why don't you have any identification?"

"I left it at home."

"Where is home?"

"Why do you want to know?"

The agent circles the room. "Why were you at the Art Institute?"

"To see art."

"You don't need disguises to see art."

I have no rejoinder to that.

"You want to destroy the Institute, don't you? You were scouting for a bomb attack, weren't you?"

I'm so stunned by these bizarre accusations I can think of nothing to say. What could inspire paranoia such as this? At last I say, "I am innocent. You have no right to keep me here."

"Yeah? The Patriot Act says I do." She circles Rhianna, her colors vivid with combat and disgust. "You're gonna steal art to pay for your attacks, that it? Gonna get yourself a plane and fly it into the Willis Tower, right?"

It's clear that reason will have no influence on this woman. "What have you done with the man who was with me?"

She points to a wall. "Your accomplice is right next door. He tells me you're the one organizing the attack."

Could Gabe really be saying—I stop myself. The color of lies joins the woman's aura. A lie designed to extort the truth is standard procedure in *lessi* police dramas. "He only helped me when I was cold."

"Oh, sure, the innocent man fooled by the terrorist. I've seen that movie, and it's not gonna play here."

I open my mouth to protest, but realize the futility. I shudder from both my captor's madness and the chill.

"You cold?" The woman stops by the window and takes her pistol from its holster.

I brace myself, but then flinch when the woman shatters the lower window glass with the gun butt. The blue jays on the ledge flee, and arctic air rushes in. She smiles at me. "Aw, now why would you want to go and do that? A desperate attempt to escape? Trying to warn your accomplices?"

The air spilling in is like ice knives slashing at my flesh. I start to wrap my arms around myself, but my handcuffs bind me. What is this madwoman doing?

Pointing her weapon at me, she orders, "Come here."

I rise and go to her.

She says, "Hold out your arms."

I do as I'm told. One-handed, the woman digs a key out of a pocket, unlocks one handcuff, and then snaps it shut around a window bar.

The agent goes to the radiator in the corner and closes the valve. "Let's see what you remember after you chill out a little." She goes to the door. "And your partner, too."

Oh, no, Gabe has no way to fight this. "You can't do that. He's not one of—" The woman has almost tricked me.

"Not one of what?" A smile comes to her face, but the result is cruel. "Your terrorist cell? Funny, but I don't believe that."

She glances at the broken window. "But you help me out and I'll move you to a nice warm room." She points to the cameras. "I'll be seeing you."

She slips out the door and I hear the lock turn. The woman's brutality crushes my fledgling return to life created by Gabe and Berry. The insane face of the man who killed Graeme leers at me, and all the pain of my One's death returns.

What a fool I am. As long as the *lessi* swarm, there is no hope of peace and freedom for Magians. Shame for my brief, selfish lust for life adds to my guilt. I'm sorry for Gabe and Berry, but I just can't continue. In a final irony, the cold death I sought yesterday will find me in a cell today.

At last my suffering will stop. And they will learn nothing from me about the Clans.

I sit on the floor, back against the wall, and let the chill air flow over me. Long minutes pass, and then the two blue jays return to the window ledge. Their persistence confirms that they are not wild birds but clan-trained scouts sent to find me. I stare up at them, the representatives of my people. My family. My gaze shifts to the handcuff around my wrist. Will this be their fate too?

It could be. They have no idea of the new threat to the Clans. Agent Volmer's zealotry will not die with me. No, the woman is onto the scent of our secret. I have to warn them.

Why won't life leave me be?

I stand and turn my back to the cameras, and then say to the birds, low and intense, the words clan jays are taught to respond to when sent to find someone. "Home and back. Home and back." I chance a brief burst of *lledri* to project a *glamère* of a hand holding seed and once again say, "Home and back." Return home and then come back here.

They fly. I step aside from the window and put my back to the wall to avoid the cold as much as possible. What irony. Moments ago, I sought its release, and now I fear it will succeed before I can warn my people. But perhaps this is the end that is meant for me. At least the secrets of my race will die with me, and Agent Volmer will have to begin again. No, I can't hope for that ... more clansmen will come to the Art Institute, unsuspecting, and Volmer will be lying in wait.

I shiver, and my instinct is to counter the cold with *lledri*. I stare at the camera in the corner. No ... I will fight to reveal no more to that hound.

But someone had better come soon.

14

Gabe paces. What's happening? Guns aimed at his heart? Homeland Security? He looks at his wrists. Handcuffs? Why the hell do they have him in handcuffs ... to keep him from typing ad copy like "free" and "act now?"

He stops and stares out the window at the blank brick wall of a neighboring building. Out the *barred* window of a *cell*. Admit it, Gabe old buddy, you're scared shitless. He hasn't been offered a phone call. No lawyer. Nobody has spoken about his rights. When he asked, as nicely as he could, he was told to shut up. He's a worm, helpless in the grip of a fisherman's fingers, and he has a bad feeling that a hook is on the way.

Okay, it's time to calm down. This is America. He has rights. He's going to be okay.

A click sounds behind him. The woman who arrested them enters and then locks the dead bolt. She faces him, her stocky legs apart, hands at her sides—he thinks of John Wayne ready for a showdown in the old West. And he knows she has a gun under her jacket. Her eyes, brown under heavy black brows, appraise him like someone looking at a thing, not a person. A name tag identifies her as KB Volmer.

He puts on the smile that has been known to charm the sourest of his clients. "Agent Volmer, please tell me what's going on."

Her expression doesn't change. "Well, how about the United States of America working damn hard to protect itself from terrorists."

He'd like to zap back a retort, but he stifles himself. Not smart to rile people with guns. "And I support that a hundred percent. What does it have to do with me?"

The agent ambles to the other side of the window and gazes out. She scrapes a line through the frost on the glass with a fingernail. "Heard it's down to zero out there now."

He quashes a snappy "thanks for the weather report" and waits.

The agent glances at him, then shrugs. She keeps her tone conversational, which makes her words doubly scary. "What does my job have to do with you and ..." She tilts her head at a wall. " ...your terrorist buddy next door? How about stopping your asses before you bomb the Art Institute?"

This is seriously nuts. Panic churns in his gut. Pushing it aside, he says, "Listen, I don't even go to the Art Institute. I don't have a terrorist buddy next door or anywhere. You've made a terrible mistake."

Agent Volmer smiles at him the way a hungry man smiles at a piece of meat before he sticks a fork in it. "So you deny it."

"Of course! Because it's not true."

She aims a thumb at the wall between him and Rhianna. "Not what your comrade says. I wish I had a canary sang as good as her." The agent points at him. "You're the one behind all this."

The green of a lie appears above her head. Give me a break. "Come on, this isn't a *Law and Order* rerun." He wishes the agent could see lies the way he does, she'd know he was telling the truth.

"Don't say I didn't give you a chance." She jams her hand inside her coat and yanks out a very black pistol. A crazy thought of leaping at her charges into his mind. He tenses ...

She reverses the pistol and shatters the lower window glass with the butt. The air that rushes in feels every bit like zero degrees. He backs away.

Aiming the pistol at his face—God, all he can see is the black hole of the barrel—she says, "Come here and hold your hands out."

He does, and she jams the gun muzzle against his neck. "It would be okay with me if you make a wrong move."

He holds rock still. She unlocks one handcuff and then snaps it closed around a window bar. She slips the gun back into its holster, turns off the out-of-reach radiator, and then saunters to the door. "I'll make you the same deal I made your partner. You talk and I'll take you to a nice warm room like I did her after she talked. Or you can stay here and do one of your little tricks to stop freezing to death. Or just go ahead and freeze. Your choice."

His mind says this can't be real but his fear knows it is. Then he thinks of Berry, so helpless. "Listen, I have a little girl—"

"Saw her. Cute kid." She shakes her head. "What a shame, a little girl growing up without her daddy."

She closes the door behind her, and Gabe steps to the side of the window. He stretches his arm and flattens against the wall so that only his hand and forearm are hit by the cold flowing into the room. It'll help, but not for long.

He shouts up at the cameras, "I didn't do anything! I want a lawyer! I'm an American!"

He tugs at the handcuff hooked to the bars. That he's an American doesn't seem to mean much to these people.

~

Four hours and four cups of coffee later, KB figures it has to be below freezing in the cells, but the prisoners have shown no weird glows. The guy jogs in place once in a while. Doesn't want to give himself away. But he will. He will. The woman just shivers and glares up at the cameras now and then. Glare all you want, honey, you're mine now.

God, she hates terrorists. These two deserve a lot worse than what she's giving them.

Right on time, Bailey's voice comes down the hall. "Brr. Doesn't seem any warmer up here than outside. It's ten below out there now." She appears from around the corner, wearing a thick cable-knit sweater and carrying a thermos.

Glad to see her, KB stands and stretches. "You're savin' my life. I'm gettin' hungry, and coffee's not doing the job anymore." She steps aside and Bailey takes her place.

Bailey sweeps her gaze across the monitors, the recorders turned back on. The two prisoners, handcuffed to window bars, sit on the floor and huddle as best they can with an arm stretched in the air. Bailey leans forward and squints at the images. "Are those windows broken?"

"A little experiment to see if we can learn something." To Bailey's shocked expression she says, "Listen, I think we can, um, persuade them to do their infrared thing to keep warm.

I'm sure that's what the female did when Schultz spotted her outside the Art Institute. I think the guy's weakening, and we get him doing his thing on video I think he's ours."

"We can do this?"

"Well, you saw that busload of kids outside the Art Institute. Think about a bomb going off."

"Yeah." Bailey nods. "Okay."

"I'll grab a bite. You good for an hour or so?"

Bailey opens her thermos and pours a cup of coffee. "Got all the time you need."

"Maybe make it an hour and a half? I want to grab a bite and then visit my mother." As much as going to the Cook County cancer ward troubled her, she was overdue. Not that she could do anything more than hold her mother's hand. To comfort the only person she's ever felt close to other than her brother. And he's gone.

"No problem." Bailey glances at the monitors showing the prisoners. "They don't seem to be doing anything."

"Yeah." But they might. "Tell you what. If they do the glow thing and you get it recorded, move them to a warm cell. I told 'em that we would do that."

"Got it." Bailey turns back to the monitors.

In the elevator lobby, KB finds Martinez gone and Schultz settling in at the desk, looking through back issues of *True Detective* magazine. He says, "Any luck?"

She eyes him. The guy isn't as dumb as he looks; he knows what she wants to do. "Nope. But I think we're getting there."

She punches the down elevator button. When the door opens, she says, "Thanks for helping out."

He grins. "Hey, it never hurts to suck up to the boss."

She laughs and steps into the elevator. After she comes back, she'll work on River again. Maybe she can leverage his kid.

~

Drago stalks the deck of his galleon, wrapped by *lledri* for warmth and using *sight* to scan the night sky. Dark came at five o'clock, an hour has since passed, and still no sign of his blue jays. Has some *lessi* shot them? He wouldn't put it past them. Or is Rhianna simply not in the area?

A flutter sounds behind him. He turns around as Merlin settles onto a rail. The blue jay would have gone to his tree instead of the ship if he hadn't found Rhianna. Drago digs into a pocket for seed and then holds it in his hand for the bird. "Where's Arthur, brave bird, where's Arthur?" He peers into the dark. Curse the *lessi* if they've harmed him.

After a few seeds go down Merlin's gullet, Drago goes to the rear of the deck. The jay flaps briefly into the air and lands on the rail in front of him. Drago strokes its back and gives it a few more seeds. "Good bird."

He takes a parka from the rail and puts it on so he's prepared to pass for a *lessi*. Then he lifts a skimmer from the deck. Crafted from wood in a shape like the bowl of a spoon, it's big enough to hold two people lying side by side. The narrower, pointed front has a low wind screen, and the broader back end is squared off to give *lledri* a vertical surface to push against. He's ready to bring Rhianna back with him.

He brushes snow from the skimmer's floor and gathers *lledri*. Shaping it into a broad stream, he guides it to *push* up underneath the skimmer until it hovers waist-high above the deck. He grasps the steering lever and checks under the skimmer to see that the rudder works.

Clambering in and lying prone to avoid wind resistance, he lifts to the level of the deck rail. "Back," he says to the blue jay. He projects a *glamère* of birdseed at the bird and says, "Merlin, back."

The jay launches into the night and Drago follows, using his *lledri* to keep warm as well as to propel his skimmer by *pushing* against the flat end. He tracks the bird with his *sight,* its radiation of *lledri* clear to him and its speed easily accommodated.

It surprises Drago that the jay leads him into Chicago; Rhianna hates big cities almost as much as he does, especially after Graeme's death. At last, the jay lands on a window ledge at the top floor of an older building. The room is lighted, but Drago sees no one inside. When he gets closer, though, he discovers a slender arm handcuffed to a metal bar. The glass on the lower window is missing. He hovers close to the opening and decides to risk a call. After all, if it isn't Rhianna, he can disappear behind a shadow *glamère.* "Rhianna? Rhianna?"

The hand stirs and Rhianna appears, kneeling before the window and peering into the darkness. She shivers and wraps herself with one arm. She whispers, "Drago? It is you who seeks me? I thought you would only want to see me dead."

A tempting thought, but he brushes it aside. Why does she suffer the cold when she can warm herself? "What has happened?"

She gestures behind her with her free hand. "This is Homeland Security. The *lessi* have taken me prisoner. The one in charge talks about terrorists, but I think it's because they have found out about *lledri*."

The shock of that distracts him and his stream of *lledri* falters. The skimmer dips and he hurries to steady it. If the *lessi* know of *lledri*, he must waste no time. "I will help ye, but ye have to agree to help me in turn."

Massive shivering shakes her, and it's a moment before she can speak. "What do you want of me?"

Might as well be forthright. To an extent, that is. "I need your *touch* for a delicate scientific operation."

"That 'cure' you've been obsessed with?"

The woman is quick. "It has to do with that, yes."

"You've never said the actual nature of your 'cure.' Graeme would only tell me that you searched for a way to ease the pressure of the *lessi* on the Clans."

He must not forget that he deals with a healer. "It's a bio-logical tool that will change their ways." Terminally.

Though she shivers, she narrows her eyes and he *sees* the murky gray of suspicion join her aura. "I know you, Drago, and I know the depth of your hatred. I'm amazed that you are even speaking to me, so you must be desperate. Have you forsaken your lust for the death of the *lessi*?"

The woman is too acute. He *pushes* his skimmer upward until the unbroken upper pane of window glass is a barrier between her head and his. Her *sight* cannot penetrate the glass to *see* untruth in his aura. "Yes. Even I would not go that far."

She shakes her head. "I can't *see* you lie, Drago, but I know you too well. I will not help you kill."

Blast! "That's not my intention, Rhianna, but I need your unfettered commitment to help my cause."

"I can't give it, Drago, not as long as you conceal your colors from me."

"Well, then ..." He calls to the blue jay. "Home." It springs from the ledge and glides into the night, and he turns the skimmer.

She cries, "Wait!"

He turns back to her.

"You must warn the Clans." She glances at something inside the room. "Tell them these people have cameras that somehow detect the use of *lledri*."

His cure will take care of that if he can find the means to finish his work. "I will alert them." Again he turns away, again her voice stops him.

"If you won't help me, then help the *elessi* in the next room. He was captured with me, but knows nothing of the Clans. He is an innocent."

Drago notes the broken window to the right, and now sees a male hand cuffed to the bar. An *elessi?* "Ye know I don't care for half-breeds. Let him fend for himself."

"But he can't! He's untrained, even though I think he has immense potential. All by himself he has come to a masterful use of *touch*."

The information gives Drago pause. Now *that* is something. It had taken him a dozen years and the coaching of the best teachers in the clan to acquire his own clumsy skill. If the *elessi* is a natural adept then perhaps, in conjunction with Vixen's ability, he can ... "I will speak with him."

He starts for the other broken window. She calls, "His name is Gabe. He has a daughter with equal potential. Help them."

Drago drifts to the *elessi's* window. Edging close to the broken pane, he peers inside. A lanky, black-bearded man slumps sideways, his arm stretched taut by the weight of his body. The hand cuffed to the window bar is stark white. Drago can't tell if the man's eyes are open or not. "You there," he calls.

No response. He edges close enough to grasp the man's hand and shake it. "You! Answer me!"

There's no reaction, though the man's dim aura says he still lives. Well, there's nothing to do but go inside. Drago rises to the roof of the building and sets his skimmer down by a door. He gathers *lledri* and focuses it into a narrow beam, then propels it at the lock. The door bursts open and he enters a darkened stairwell.

15

I wonder if Drago has reached the point in his many years where he is no longer quite sane. Like any of the Magians who can turn their *key,* he has stayed physically healthy, but clansmen have never found a way to rejuvenate a mind. Sooner or later, for many their sanity crumbles.

Drago is at least five hundred years old and, while I know a number of clansmen who have lived beyond that age and remained relatively unwarped, I know of an equal number who, by his time of life, have become unhinged as memories and experiences pile up--some minds seem to ossify and then break up.

Will he warn the Clans of this new danger from the *lessi?* We could face a modern pogrom made more terrible by technology. I don't think I can trust the faltering mind of a man who seeks to deceive me, a man lost in a fury of vengeance and hatred for me. I can't surrender. Not yet.

My people must be warned, and it's mine to do.

I look at the cameras in the corner of the ceiling. These agents already know something about *lledri,* so what will it hurt to let them see a little more in order to save myself and break free?

After I warm myself with *lledri,* my thoughts come quick and sure. I divert a slender stream of *lledri* into the lock of the handcuff around my wrist. Nudging its elements, I ease the cuff open. But the cameras still watch, and I do not remove my hand. Not yet.

The woman who hunted me will see if I leave my place by the window. There's no doubt it would alarm her, and I believe she will not hesitate to use her weapon. There's nothing I can do to stop a bullet—if the agent rushes in with her gun ready, I'm not sure I'll be quick enough to stop her with *lledri*. My odds are better if the agent thinks I'm helpless.

I gaze at the cameras, wishing I could see what waits on the other side. Surely the agent is witnessing my use of *lledri* for warmth through her technology. What she sees now should bring her. Perhaps I can sweeten the pot with words. Once the agent is in sight, I hope I can render her unconscious in time to prevent an attack.

I weaken my voice and call to the cameras, "Please, help me. I will tell you what I know ... just help me. I'm so cold."

Soon Agent Volmer will be within *my* grasp.

~

Drago steps from the stairwell door on the top floor and finds a slender man at a desk in front of a pair of elevators, his attention on a magazine. The man shoots upright and then leans forward. "Who the hell?"

Drago reaches out with *touch* to close off the man's carotid artery and knock him out by denying his brain of oxygen.

The man says, "I said—" He looks at Drago and fear spikes in his aura. He collapses across the desk.

Drago steps close and observes. The reek of stale cigarette smoke rises from the man's clothing.

Bother, the man no longer breathes. Drago probes with *lledri* and *sees* that he has crushed the artery. Well, clearly it was weak to begin with—a normal vein would surely have stood up to his *touch*, clumsy as it is. It's the smoker's own fault. But the man is a *lessi*, so there's no loss.

He sees the man's pack of cigarettes on the desk next to a lighter and recalls the rush of nicotine and the fun of making smoke billow in the air. It's been a while, and this man has just kicked his habit. Drago takes a cigarette and lights it. A deep inhale, then a cloud of smoke. Ahhh.

Before heading down the hall to the *elessi's* cell, he studies the dead man, lifting and turning the head to get a good look at the features. Holding what he sees firmly in his mind, Drago conjures a *glamère* of the man.

Careful to tread lightly down the hallway, he comes to a corner. He peers around it and glimpses a Black woman at a desk, her back to him. She leans forward, watching a small monitor in a bank of similar monitors. He sees a body-shaped glow on one. On another, the *elessi* man slumps beneath the broken window.

The woman says, "God damn! She's doin' it! KB was right."

Drago takes a drag off his cigarette and rounds the corner.

The Black woman says, "Who that smokin' in here? Damn it, Schultz ..." She spins in her swivel chair to face him. " ...you know better. What you doin' back here, anyway?"

Hoping he can make his voice match the dead man's closely enough, he points at a monitor. "Came to get the guy."

The woman scowls, and Drago doesn't need to see the murky gray of suspicion rise from her to know what will come next. The woman says, "Where you taking him? And who's covering your station?"

Drago sends *lledri* through the skin of the woman's neck, wraps her carotid artery with it, and then compresses it with the lightest *touch* he can wield. As much as he hates the *lessi*, he's not an indiscriminate killer. Her eyes widen and she starts to stand.

Then she clutches at the left side of her chest. She folds forward and spills from the chair to the floor. Releasing the pressure of his *touch,* he stands over her and probes for a pulse. He finds one, though it's ragged and weak. The woman moans. He congratulates himself on his skill and picks up a ring of keys from the desktop.

He studies the surveillance apparatus on the desk, and then turns off the power—no sense in having his *truface* recorded by objective machines unaffected by his *glamère.* The monitors go dark. After scanning the corridor and listening, he decides he's alone and drops the appearance of the man he killed. He goes to the bearded man's cell and tries keys until one opens the door.

~

My cell door remains closed. All right, perhaps if I seem to escape I can draw Agent Volmer in. I slip my hand from the unlocked cuff and dart to the corner beneath the cameras, out of their view. When the agent can't see me and charges in, I will have an advantage, although a brief one.

~

Drago enters the elessi's cell. The cold is intense. *Pushing* up with lledri to aid his strength, he lifts the man to a standing position. My, he's a tall one. Drago slips his arms around the man's torso and pulls him close. The elessi's head falls onto Drago's shoulder. As distasteful as contact with an ordinary human is, it's the most effective way to revive him.

Joining his own *lledri* with the man's feeble emissions, Drago wraps both of them with it, holding in their heat. The energy seeps into the man's body. Within minutes, he lifts his head and stands on his own.

Drago releases him and backs a step. The bearded man's expression shifts from confusion to comprehension as he looks around. He tugs on the handcuff and then scowls at Drago. "Who are you, another torturer?"

The denseness of these people never fails to astonish. "It should be obvious that I've saved your life. Ye feel warm now, do ye not?"

The man—Rhianna said his name is Gabe—turns his attention inward. His eyes widen. He looks to Drago. "I ... I do. Who ... what ... ?"

Drago knows how to charm a bumpkin. He smiles big and sticks out his hand for a shake. When the *elessi* takes it, there's a gentle pressure of *touch* from the *elessi*. Good, Rhianna is right about his talent for *touch*. "Hello, Cousin Gabe. My name is Drago, and I've come to help ye."

~

KB pulls a chair close to her mom's bedside and takes her all-but-lifeless hand. It's so thin—no, scrawny—and cold. Her eyes are closed and likely to never open again. Thank God for Medicaid; she can end her days untroubled by pain and the old trauma of her life.

To KB's eyes, she actually looks pretty good, mostly thanks to the lack of bruises KB's father had caused over and over again. He'd done the same thing to KB until the day she kneed him in the balls and then kicked them again when he was down.

When hospice admissions asked for his contact information, KB was glad to be able to tell them that she had no idea. He's been gone for a couple of years now. If only breast cancer hadn't hit her mother, they could be having a good life together.

She strokes her mother's hand. "I'm sorry, Mom, so sorry I couldn't get rid of that bastard sooner."

There's nothing more to say, so she sits in silence, petting her mom's hand and wiping away tears. Finally, a glance at her watch tells her it's time to head back, so she leans over and kisses her mom's forehead. "I love you."

~

Gabe shakes the little man's hand. Plump, with ruddy cheeks and a bald head, the guy looks like he stepped out of a Norman Rockwell painting of a small-town butcher shop.

The man—Drago—had called him "cousin." "Are you one of Rhianna's people?"

Drago pumps his hand and lets go. "One of *your* people, to hear Rhianna tell it."

"You've talked to her? She's okay?" Wind gusts through the broken window, and Gabe shivers.

"She is well enough." Drago peels off the parka he wears and holds it out. "I don't need this."

Gabe accepts the coat, but then pauses and lifts his cuffed hand. "Maybe you can help me get it on one arm?"

"I can do better than that." Drago shifts his gaze to the handcuff attached to the window bars. His eyes narrow, and the cuff snaps against the bar as if pulled by a powerful magnet. Bit by bit it elongates, losing its circular shape. A metallic ping, and it breaks and jerks away from the bar. Its release unbalances Gabe, and he sprawls on the floor.

He gets up and puts the parka on. The sleeves are too short, but it's a help. He examines the broken handcuff. These people have amazing abilities. He rubs his wrist, the cuffs dangling from it.

Drago goes to the door. "Come on." He steps out.

Outside the cell, Gabe sees the Black woman who'd helped capture Rhianna and him sprawled on the floor. When he pulls up short, Drago catches his reaction and says, "She's just unconscious."

The monitors on the guard's desk are blank. Rhianna must be in one of the rooms. "What about Rhianna?"

The little man says, "She's already gone."

She got away but left Gabe behind? Then he notices the green of a lie about Drago's head. "That's not true."

The man's eyes widen. "I mean, she has chosen a different path."

As confusing as it is, Gabe sees that this is no lie. "I don't get it."

"Truly, I spoke with her and she refused my help. But she told me about ye."

Again, the truth. Gabe spots his cell phone protruding from a manila envelope on the desk. He dumps the contents out and pockets his money, wallet, keys, and the phone.

He follows Drago down the hall to find the skinny agent slumped over a desk. He seems too still. "Is he all right?"

Drago glances at the man, then opens a door to a stairwell. "Quickly, others may come."

Gabe follows him up toward the roof. What does Drago have up there, a helicopter? A magic broom? It doesn't matter to Gabe, anything to get away from people determined to torture and kill him. He wonders if he should call the police when he gets home.

Yeah, right, a guy on the run from Homeland Security is somebody the cops will for sure want to help.

~

I'm surprised that Agent Volmer has not barged into my cell. Perhaps she's no longer out there. I ease *touch* into the door lock and work the tumblers. A soft click soon rewards me and I open the door a crack.

No one sits at the desk in the hallway where I thought the agent would be. And then I spot the Black woman who helped arrest us sprawled on the floor behind the desk. All is quiet.

I burst out, ready to disable attackers, but no one else is in sight. The door to the room Gabe was taken into is open. The window is broken as mine is, but Gabe is gone. Good. Drago might not be one of my favorite people, but if he thinks he has a use for you, you'll be well taken care of. I can concentrate on warning the Clans.

The woman on the floor moans. Kneeling beside her, I sense pain. The woman's brown eyes open and fix on me. They widen, and then the woman struggles to sit, but she falls back, clutching her chest.

"Be at ease," I say. "I mean you no harm." I study the *lledri* coming from the woman; she's had a heart attack. I slip my *sight* into the woman's chest and discover a small blockage in the main artery to her heart's left ventricle.

Using the most delicate bursts of energy possible, I dissolve the obstruction bit by microscopic bit until the blood flows easily. A healing flood of *lledri* to her heart muscle reverses the damage there.

When I return my concentration to the outside, the expression of pain is gone from the woman's face, replaced by wonder. "What did you do?"

"Your heart was damaged. I ... helped it. What happened to you?"

The woman rubbed her neck. "I don't know. I was just sittin' here, then Schultz came back. He was smoking even though he knows he shouldn't. He wanted the other ..." She hesitates.

"Prisoner?"

"Yeah. I guess if you're going to save my life, there ain't no sense in being coy about this." She lifts herself onto her elbows and I help her sit up. "Anyway, here comes Schultz, then I feel pressure in my neck, and I got dizzy. It scared me. A lot. I started to stand up and then ... then a pain here ..." She touches her left chest. "And that's it. 'Till you came along."

I use *sight* to examine the woman's neck and find her carotid artery bruised. Clumsy Drago at work. Damn the man.

"I think you'll be all right. I have to go." I brush the bruise with *lledri* to encourage healing and then begin to rise, but the woman grips my arm. It does not escape me that she could pull out the pistol she wears on her hip. But I can stop her from using it if I have to.

The agent looks down at her body. "That was a heart attack, wasn't it? And you helped me." She looks up, her expression one of someone lost. "What ... what are you? I mean, you can do these things ..."

"I'm just a person who can, as you say, do things. A healer. I don't hurt people. And I don't understand why you people are doing this to me."

"We're afraid that you're dangerous."

"Well, now you know." I stand. Thinking of Drago and his rage, I add, "At least you know about me."

I leave the woman and hurry down the hall. I find the slender man who wielded a camera outside the Art Institute lying across a desk. I don't need to get close to see that he is dead—*lledri* no longer streams from his body. More of Drago's work. I go to the man and close his staring eyes—he wouldn't want to be seen that way. "I'm sorry."

The old-fashioned floor indicator above the elevator comes to life, the pointer like the hand of a clock moving from the number one and rising steadily, floor by floor. I dash to the doorway marked Exit and hurtle down the stairs.

~

KB hums *She'll Be Comin' 'Round the Mountain* as the elevator door opens on the fifteenth floor. Schultz sprawls on his desk, his eyes closed. "Schultz, you are the laziest man alive." She strides to him and shakes his shoulder. "C'mon, get your shit together."

His head wobbles, but he doesn't stir. She bends close and studies him. He's not breathing? Jesus Christ, is he dead? She puts a finger to his neck. His flesh is cool, and there's no pulse.

Breathing deeply, she draws her pistol and assesses the scene. No signs of violence. Nothing but empty hallways, no sounds. Maybe he had a heart attack or a stroke. He smoked like a chimney.

Then Bailey rounds the corner and walks down the hall toward KB, taking slow, careful steps instead of her usual loping gait. KB says, "Bailey, what's wrong?"

"I think I'm okay now, just a little shaky—" She reaches the lobby, stops and stares at Schultz. "What's the matter with Schultz?"

KB goes to her. "He's dead. Did something happen while I was away?"

Bailey slumps and leans against the wall. "They're gone."

"No!" KB runs to the cells, first to the woman's. Just a pair of handcuffs dangle from the window bars. Oh, God. She dashes to River's cell. No handcuffs, no prisoner. When she emerges, she finds Bailey settling into her chair, powering up the surveillance equipment. KB says, "Tell me."

Bailey shakes her head. "I was sittin' here, watching that woman. She started to glow just like you said, and then she yakked at the camera that she was cold and wanted to talk, and the guy was just slumped on the floor, and then I smelled a cigarette and Schultz was here ... I got dizzy ... and then I was lookin' up into that woman's face. Look at this ..."

She hits the rewind button and soon the image from the woman's cell shows her begin to glow, and then the glow leaves the window to duck out of sight. The handcuffs dangle empty from the bars. KB stares. How did she do that?

Bailey says, "I never saw her slip the cuffs. Musta been after Schultz showed up." She fast-forwards and the screens go dark. Bailey glances up the hallway, and then at KB, her eyes widening. "I thought it was Schultz, but something about his voice was funny." She gazes into the past. "He wanted to take the guy away."

"It was one of them!"

"I was talking to him when I felt dizzy all of a sudden, and then my chest hurt ..." She rubbed her chest. "It was my heart." She looked to KB. "That woman saved my life."

"And then she killed Schultz? Doesn't make sense. Maybe River did the killing." KB paces. She's well and truly screwed. What will the RAC do? What *can* she do? Her duty, that's what. "Call Security, lock down the building. Maybe they're still inside." She remembers the surveillance cameras for the hallways and hopes, just a little. She snaps, "Do it now!" As Bailey reaches for the phone, KB runs for the lobby desk. Please, oh, please let there be something on the videos.

Working around Schultz's body, rage at the Artisans building inside her, KB rewinds the videos. On the lobby camera a little guy who looks like he ought to be running a mom-and-pop grocery store walks out of the door to the stairwell. Schultz says something, then collapses across his desk. The little guy doesn't seem to do anything, but KB knows he did. She watches him take one of Schultz's cigarettes, light up, and head down the hall. What kind of ghouls are they dealing with?

She switches to the camera covering the cell area. The little guy enters and talks to Bailey. KB doesn't see him make a move, but Bailey falls from her chair and then the guy turns off the recorders and goes to River's cell. Bailey sure as hell hadn't been talking to Schultz. Soon the Artisan and River leave the cell and the two of them head for the lobby. The woman's cell door remains locked.

Back to the lobby camera; she watches River leave with the little guy out the stairwell door. Schultz is still unconscious, if not dead, and River hadn't gone near him. So it was definitely the little guy who was the killer. Bailey saw him as Schultz, but he was an Artisan. It's that disguise thing that they do.

They could have gone up to the roof or down. KB fast-forwards, then hits play when the Artisan woman hurries into the lobby. She closes Schultz's eyes. Grainy as the video is, KB sees anger on her face. The woman runs into the stairwell. KB stops the video.

Bailey joins her and stares down at Schultz. KB places a hand on his shoulder. A wave of affection followed by sorrow surprises her. "I'm sorry, Schultz." He was a good man. She looks to Bailey, who has a tear trail glistening on one cheek.

A piercing alarm rips into the silence and a voice shouts over the PA system. "Lockdown! Prisoners escaped. Begin search and use extreme caution."

The alarm breaks the spell. KB runs for the roof. She finds nothing there but bitter wind and bitter truth—her prisoners have escaped. Schultz's killer is free. Not for long, she vows, not for long. There will be justice for Schultz.

16

A teeth-clenched cry wrenches from Gabe and he bolts up-right. He sees himself frozen, white with frost, blind eyes open and staring, arms reaching for his daughter but doomed to never embrace her.

A quilt falls from him, cold air strikes his bare torso, and his nightmare blinks away. He's in a bunk that's fastened to a paneled wall. The room isn't much more than sleeping quarters, maybe five feet by eight. There's space enough in a corner for an antique-looking washstand and an old-fashioned pitcher in a large bowl. Next to it, the handcuffs gleam at him. Neatly folded, a small towel and washcloth sit ready for use. His shirt and jeans are draped over a single chair. Reddish sunlight glows through a porthole.

A porthole?

He swings his legs out and sits on the edge of the bunk, drawing the quilt around him. Memory rises of flying over a dark forest on a sled-like thing and landing on a shape that was a deeper blackness in the night. There had been trees all around, hardly visible. His rescuer, Drago, had taken him to this room.

His wrist hurts. He touches a red line of bruised flesh that circles it, and he remembers the handcuff being ripped from the window bar by the force of ... *lledri?* There had been a middle-aged woman frowning at the cuff left on his wrist and easing it open. Then his memories cut off as if he had passed out.

Yesterday he awakened in bed with a woman who changed appearance and healed with *lledri*. Yesterday Berry began to emerge from her isolation. Yesterday there were guns ... and being handcuffed to a window and freezing ... and guards lying unconscious and dead ... How could all that be real? He doesn't feel as if he's nuts.

He has to find out where he is, get back to his life, to his daughter.

Rhianna. Did she escape? Does this close the door to ending his lifelong loneliness and to the hope that she can help Berry?

He stands and sheds the quilt. Goosebumps prickle his skin. He dresses and wishes he had his parka. It must be at Homeland Security—will he ever see it again? Is he in trouble? He hasn't done anything ... except he broke out of jail, and that has to look guilty as hell. Does that mean he's a fugitive? He should find a lawyer.

Gabe looks out the porthole and discovers a snow-covered meadow surrounded by trees. Across the meadow is ... a pirate ship? Propped up on stilts? It's dawn or sunset, the sun just above the horizon. Does he face east or west?

He opens the door and enters a large room, maybe twenty by thirty feet, with a beamed ceiling. Most of the floor is covered with Oriental rugs, and the sofas, chairs and tables project a comfortable, lived-in look.

An eclectic array of oil paintings, from landscapes to portraits, brings the dark walls to life. Light comes from a half-dozen kerosene lamps on tables throughout the room and portholes along the opposite wall. As large as it is, the room seems intimate and warm, although it isn't warm at all.

Aromas of garlic and roasting meat hit him. His mouth waters, his stomach so empty it hurts. The metallic clatter of a pot being set on a stove comes from beyond a doorway at one end of the room. A woman's voice, humming a lively tune, joins the rattle of cookware.

He heads for the room and calls, "Hello?"

A ruddy-cheeked, heavy-set woman appears in the doorway, a floral apron over her long blue dress. She's the one who took off the handcuff. A wide smile stretches across her broad face, and it cheers him. There's an Irish lilt to her voice when she says, "Ah, you've rejoined the land of the living. Lordy, you've slept most of a day, and I'll wager you're starvin' right about now."

That's sunset out the window? He hasn't called Berry. How did the birthday party work out? Is Berry all right? Is she still opening up? Gabe pats his pants pocket and is glad his cell phone is still there.

The woman gestures toward a table with place settings for two. "Take a seat and I'll be bringin' you some vittles. Start with coffee?"

"Please." He heads for the table.

She calls out, "Drago! Your guest is up and supper's on."

At the other end of the room a door opens and his rescuer emerges. He smiles at Gabe. "I thought I heard voices. Welcome to my humble abode, Cousin Gabe."

"Mister Drago. I ... 'thank you' doesn't seem like enough to say to someone who saved your life, but thank you."

"Just 'Drago,' please. And ye are welcome. Have a seat."

As they sit, the woman returns carrying a round metal tray laden with a carved roasted chicken, a bowl of boiled new potatoes and another filled with Brussels sprouts—he's hungry enough to eat even those. The yeasty aroma of hot dinner rolls escapes from a basket covered with a cloth napkin. A tall mug sends out the rich aroma of strong coffee. She smiles. "Here you go."

She sets the tray on the table and places the mug before him. "This oughta get your heart started." She holds out her hand for a shake. "M'name's Emmaline."

He takes it, and her eyes widen just a bit. "Gabe. Gabriel River."

As she releases his hand, Emmaline glances at Drago. "As you say, he's got the *touch*. Coffee for you?"

Drago says, "No, I'd rather a glass of pinot noir. The '93."

"On the way." She bustles out.

Gabe sips his coffee—it has muscle, maybe it will clear his mind. "I've got to get back and straighten this mess out. I still don't understand what's happening."

"More *lessi* incompetence, I suspect." At Gabe's glance, Drago adds, "*Lessi* is what our people call ordinary humans."

Gabe files that away. And the phrase, "our people." *His* people. "Can you help me?"

"Of course. But I need your help with something first. It won't take long."

"Whatever you need, whenever you need it." He shivers. Remembering the cold in the cell, he says, "It was awful. I've never been so cold. I owe you my life."

Drago says, "I forget, ye haven't the ability yet."

A sensation of warmth eases around Gabe's body, close to his skin, and soon he's comfortable. "That's what you did in the cell. Is this more of the *'lledri'* Rhianna talked about?"

"Aye. Seeing the range of colors coming from your brain, I think ye will catch on quickly enough. After all, ye can already detect lies and have the *touch*."

Touch? "You've got the lies part right, but I don't know anything about touch."

"*Touch* is using *lledri* to physically touch or move things." Drago lifts his eyebrows. "So it's not intentional? I know just the person to fix that. Vixen will get ye started. Ye must have control if you're to help me."

"Vixen?"

He says, "That's what she likes to call herself. I can't remember what her real name is. She's a teacher of sorts."

Emmaline arrives with Drago's wine and chimes in. "Lovely girl, you'll like her."

Drago grimaces and then says, "A wonderful young woman." Gabe sees a spurt of yellow-green above the little man's head. Not quite a lie, but close. No love lost there.

Rhianna had been going to teach him and Berry. "What about Rhianna? Did she get away?"

Drago shakes his head. "I simply don't know. As I told ye, she declined my help. She was quite capable of freeing herself."

Emmaline touches Gabe's shoulder—it's a motherly gesture, a welcome one. "I wouldn't be worrying about Rhianna, a stronger woman I've never met. If you need anything more, just call." She returns to the kitchen and the clank of pots and the splashes of washing soon emerge.

Drago sips, sets his goblet down, and leans forward. "Vixen can help ye if that's what ye wish. If ye want to join us."

Want to join them? All the fears and weirdness of the last day vanish in a flare of joy. Drago smiles at him—does he see

Gabe's feelings? Gabe tries to maintain his cool. "Yeah. I'm interested." Hell, he's *dying* to be a part of this mysterious kinship. And Berry can be a part of it, too, and not spend her years isolated. Gabe vows to do whatever it takes to become a clansman.

Drago nods. "Well, then. Eat first, and then the next thing is to awaken your *touch*."

Gabe fills his plate and listens as Drago tells him of the loose alliance of the dozens of clans that wander through Europe and America in secret.

His belly full and his sense of well-being restored, Gabe follows Drago up stairs to the deck of the galleon. Three other ships are visible in the dusk, lights gleaming from portholes. What an amazing story they are, and he's just getting started.

He digs out his cell phone to call Berry— "Shit." The battery is flat dead.

Drago's voice comes from behind him. "Problem?"

"Phone's dead and I can't call my daughter. I promised."

"I can help ye with that later. But first, Vixen is conducting a calling-out. It's a ... ceremony, but more than that, it is instruction to help youngsters gain control of their *lledri*."

Gabe smiles. "And I'm one of the youngsters?" He gazes at the ships in front of them. "Listen, I mean no disrespect, but I'm having a hard enough time believing this is real ..." He waves at the nearest ship. "... and these pirate ships aren't helping."

Drago laughs. "They're so much a part of my life I don't even notice them." He rubs the railing, a half-smile on his face that looks like affection—no, love. "They are a tradition for my people. They were among the first vessels capable of voyaging across an ocean. While we could move them swiftly through the air on our migration from Europe, we could also set down on the sea to rest and to call fish from the water."

He points at the *Noah's Pride,* balanced on its stilts a hundred feet away. "And why change? The bows cleave the air as well as anything modern, they're quite roomy, and as watertight as ever."

Gabe shakes his head. It makes perfect sense ... if you're crazy.

The thin sound of a flute drifts through the air. Drago says, "Ah, it is begun. Ye need to attend."

Excitement kindles in Gabe, and he feels like a kid. Berry will be fine. He wonders how he and Berry will do without Rhianna, and then realizes that he has hooked up with a whole bunch of his new kin. Maybe she decided to continue with her suicide mission. That's a black thought. "Do you have any way of finding out what's happened to Rhianna?"

"Perhaps." Pointing at the nearest ship, Drago says, "Just beyond the *Pride.*" He indicates an opening in the deck rail. "The ladder's there. Ye can return here when you're done."

When Gabe starts down the ladder, the cloak of warmth leaves him and the winter air attacks. "Can I borrow that coat?"

Drago shoos him on. "Hurry along and you'll find ye won't need one."

17

Eager to see the ships of my clan afloat on our hidden lake, I peer ahead as I steer an airboat through saw-grass marsh deep within the three million acres of the Everglades. I need to pass on word of the *lessi* threat, and I yearn to see Cael. It shames me that it has been months since I have been with my son.

The warm air coddles me, such a relief from the energy drain of having to warm myself with *lledri* in Chicago. Sunset colors the sky with bands of pink and mauve. A silhouetted heron wings past, grace in motion. After spending all night and most of the day travelling, I relish the idea of coming to rest.

The contrast of Florida's green abundance to the dirty snow of Illinois is like that of little Berry's vivid spirit to my days of depression. I wonder how Berry fared at the birthday party. Not well, I suspect, and I hope that being surrounded by the crush of aura colors from sugar-crazed children did not overwhelm the fragile beginnings I had made with her. And where is Gabe now? What has Drago done with him? Or *to* him? Thinking of Drago's deadly removal of Gabe from captivity, I think it's no coincidence his clan name derives from the Welsh word for "wolf."

I remember Gabe's fledgling *touch*—I would like him to be here now. I would welcome him into my clan and teach him the things he needs to help Berry.

My thoughts fly ahead to my son.

I reach a familiar creek that winds through mangrove hummocks, small islands formed by clusters of the trees. A crocodile eyes my passage, its aura dominated by the thin gray of hunger. You'll have to wait a bit longer, my toothy friend, I am not meant for you.

At least I think not … currently I am at sea about what I am meant for.

At last I enter the small lake that forms Clan Deverell's winter quarters, warm and safe—thus far—from *lessi* intrusion, many miles from *lessi* activity, from the flight paths of air travel. It's an appropriate place for a clan with a name that means "from the riverbank." The fourteen vessels that ring the lake, ramps leading from their decks to the sandy shore, are home for the two hundred or so members of the clan, all of whom are family to me. Wildly eclectic in nature, our ships range from sleek sailing vessels to broad-beamed cargo ships, avoiding the lock-step sameness of Drago's Clan Bleddyn with their galleons-and-nothing-but-galleons.

I cut the engine and glide onto the sandy beach next to the rounded hull of my family's home, the *Wanderer,* a carrack like Christopher Columbus's *Santa Maria,* and roomier than Drago's sleeker galleons. Into the silence comes the screeches and hoots of the wetlands, the calls of myriad birds that bring color and motion to the swamps and broad sweeps of saw grass.

A young voice cries, "It's Rhianna!" and I look up to see my cousin Bryn leaning over the deck rail. He waves, all grin and energy, and I wave back, smiling my pleasure at his youthful vigor. At fourteen, he's the youngest of the family and has not yet found his *key*. Not that anyone would start their

renewal at such an early age—it's best to wait for young adult-
hood, though it takes some much longer to find their *key*.

And some never do.

I step onto shore and make my way to the ramp. "How are
you, Bryn? How is everyone?"

"I'm fine." His expression clouds. "But Cael ... he ..." The
forlorn ash color of sadness rises in his aura. "He wouldn't let
us send for you."

Spurred by fear, I race up the ramp and plunge into the
hold. Belowdecks, my brother Finnian and his current amore,
Nessa, look up from setting the supper table. They smile greetings as I hurry past, and I *see* sympathy in their auras.

The door to my son's cabin is open, and he lies in his
bunk, his eyes closed. I pause at the doorway, awash with
love and sorrow. My only child, one of the dearest human
beings in the universe, has never found his *key*. Constant care
and the deep healing of my *lledri* have kept him vigorous for
110 years. But now he appears wasted, his arms sticklike, his
cheeks sunken, deep creases in his tired flesh, unlike the vigorous man I left a few months back. I look deeper and *see* the
malevolent darkness of cancer spread through his body. I have
wandered for too long. Has my neglect killed him?

Kneeling beside him, I whisper, "Cael?"

Blue-veined eyelids flicker open, then the smile I love appears. "Mother." He lifts a bony hand and I take it. There's a
quiver in his thin, old voice. "I'm glad ..." He chokes off, and
a tear runs from his eye.

I wipe it with a fingertip. Now tears fill my eyes. I brush
them aside and run my fingers through his hair, still full
and thick even though white. I focus on his body, and learn

that the source of his cancer is his prostate. The disease has metastasized and invaded his bones. It will take many hours, perhaps days, but I can clean it out. "Don't worry, I can help you. You'll be all right."

He shakes his head. "No. No. I am weary, mother, so tired of being an ever-failing carcass in the midst of eternal youth."

"But you can have many good years—"

He raises his hand. "You don't understand. My years are no longer good, no matter what my health is." He gazes into my eyes. We know each other so well it feels as if he reads my soul. He says, "I would think you can sympathize."

He had watched my surrender to despair after the death of his father. Perhaps because Cael knows the slow death of aging, Graeme's passing did not strike him as severely as it did me. "But you still might find your *key*—"

"And then what? I live for centuries as a feeble old man? If my *key* could reverse aging, yes. But to just slow it and live surrounded by youth ..." He cringes, and I *see* the jagged spikes of reds and purples that signal pain. His gaze shifts to his dresser. "Morphine." On it sits disposable syringes and vials of the drug. "Four hundred milligrams."

I hurry to give him an injection. When his pain subsides, I use my "mother's voice" to say, "We will speak of this again."

He laughs. "Won't do you any good."

He's as stubborn as his father was. And me, for that matter. "I have to see Mary Fay." I don't want to argue now and waste his strength, so I rise and leave.

His voice follows me. "I'm glad, Mother, very glad that you're here."

So am I—I will care for him. And persuade him to live.

On the way to Mary Fay's vessel, I wave to children in a meadow enjoying a game of Red Rover in the fading light, two opposing lines of children, hands linked, calling out the challenge to try to break through. They know me, of course, and I them. Little Jonathon, a slight ten-year-old, hurtles at a line and bounces off the barrier of tightly held hands. He has not found his *key* ... but there's plenty of time for him.

I signal him to come over to me. He runs to my side and I whisper, "Next time, when you run, aim at one spot and then at the last second shift to the next one. You'll get through."

He smiles and shoots back to the line. That was the tactic I used as a child. The element of surprise always worked.

Mary Fay's ship, the *Wings of Freedom*, is a short walk around the shore. It has been hers since she was made clanmaster, though she shares it with two families.

I find Mary Fay standing on the deck. She hails me. "I hear that a ghost has come haunting."

I love Mary Fay's wry humor. For me, that alone made bringing her into the clan worthwhile, and it has been a marvelous bonus that an *elessi* could also grow into a strong leader despite lacking a lifetime of clan tradition. Besides her wisdom, one of her strengths is her powerful intuition –although an ordinary human trait, I have rarely seen it as deeply insightful and accurate as hers. When Mary Fay has a "feeling," it's wise to pay attention.

I love the color of Mary Fay's skin, too, so close to black that there are bluish highlights to it. The white of her smile is like a full moon in a midnight sky. She found her *key* at a comfortable forty and remains a youthful matron.

When I reach the deck, we embrace. Mary Fay says, "I've missed you."

I'm tempted to say, "And I you," but that would be a polite lie. Except for the brief distraction of Berry and Gabe, I have thought of no one but Graeme and my miserable self for many months. Too many.

Mary Fay studies me. "I see fear, and that's unlike you." She leads me to one of the benches clustered amidships, the clan equivalent of a patio at a *lessi* home. We sit quietly for a moment, letting the giggles of the nearby children flutter around us. Then she says, "Tell me."

I relate the pursuit in the Art Institute and my rescue by Gabe. Of little Berry and her trouble, and Mary Fay nods with empathy. Then I tell of my imprisonment and the *lessi* agent's revelation that her cameras detect *lledri* in use. And of Drago's furtive mission and "rescue" of Gabe.

Mary Fay scowls. "We've always known that cameras see through a *glamère,* but now they have one that sees *lledri?*"

"That's the only explanation."

She shakes her head. "This is trouble." It hasn't taken Mary Fay more than seconds to reach the same conclusion I have—the Clans could again become prey, sought, persecuted, and killed for their difference. The pogrom to end all pogroms, made possible by *lessi* technology.

She says, "This is the first I've heard of this. Is it widespread?"

"I don't know."

She stands and paces, the burnt orange of combat coming from her so strongly it seems it would be visible even to a *lessi.* Her scowl would have made her warrior ancestors proud. She stops and turns to me. "You have to lead a team there. Maybe we can infiltrate this organization and somehow divert them."

Now I stand. "I can't leave Cael."

Mary Fay's expression softens. "I know how you feel. He won't allow us to bring in another healer, but you can persuade him to. We can care for him."

"No. I've done my duty and told you of the threat. It's the Clans' to handle now. If you need me, well, it has to wait."

Mary Fay faces north. I ready myself to counter her arguments. Instead, Mary Fay says, "I have a sense that it can't wait." She turns her gaze full on me. Now it's my turn to *see* the acid yellow of fear stream from Mary Fay. "A strong sense."

18

Gabe follows a tune that spills from an unseen flute. Rhythm from a tom-tom joins it as he crosses the meadow. Rounding the galleon's hull, he finds a group of children sitting cross-legged in a twenty-foot circle on green grass. A young woman stands motionless in the center. About a dozen adults stand behind the children, and then the grass gives way to snow within a foot or so.

Of the children, two little girls and a boy are about Berry's age, perhaps five or six, then a half-dozen more look to range in age from eight to teen. A teenage boy taps the drum, held in his lap. A plump girl of about twelve plays the flute, her body swaying to the beat and the lilting melody of the song.

Murmurs of chatter and flickers of smiles ebb and surge among the adults, and the children fidget the way children do when waiting for something exciting to begin. Gabe thinks of Berry's open gaze when she was with Rhianna. If only his daughter can join these children. Somehow, Gabe will make it happen. Drago will make it happen.

The grown-ups glance at Gabe. The closest, a woman who looks to be in her twenties, nods in welcome. She wears a sundress, her shoulders bare in the middle of an Illinois winter. Gabe steps from snow to grass, and the air becomes comfortably warm.

He focuses on the still figure in the center. A red-brown bush of untamed curls frames a delicate face and falls past her shoulders. Barefooted, barelegged, she seems to be wearing nothing but wisps of color suspended by a collar around her neck. Veils, hardly more dense than air, hint at reds and blues and yellows and greens and drape over her body to her knees. She's no more than five feet tall, lithe and slender ... yet he sees curves that make him very much aware of a woman's body.

Her gaze comes to him. She gestures to an opening in the circle of children seated on the grass. He points to his chest, raising his eyebrows in question. At her nod, he sits on the grass, not quite as comfortably cross-legged as the children around him.

Conversation dies as she begins to move her feet in place to the rhythm of the music.

She arches her body, her shoulders back, her arms out, and the curve of her belly parts the veils; she wears a white leotard that fits so closely it could be her pale flesh. His gaze follows the bow of her back down to the taut arc of her buttocks.

She turns to face Gabe. Her eyes fix on him, and her lips curl up at the corners. They part, as if to take him in. Her gaze has weight, like Rhianna's, but there's heat, too. The sensation is so vivid that it seems real ... then he realizes that it *is* real, a warm pressure as light as a lover's breath against his neck. Is this the *touch* Drago talked about? It travels down his body, under his clothing, caressing his chest ... his belly ... and then it moves lower. It explores what it finds there, encircling, stroking, and his body responds.

God, she's copping a feel from ten feet away. Does anybody see what's going on? He scans the faces around the circle, but all are focused on the dancer. Then her *touch* withdraws, leaving a disappointing absence. And a feeling of flushed cheeks.

Lifting her arms above her head to place her palms together, she sways her hips from side to side, and the shape of her arouses thoughts of gliding his fingertips over her skin. With his marriage apparently in its death throes, it has been many, many months since he's made love to anything other than his right hand.

He scolds himself. She—Vixen, Drago said—can't be older than nineteen or twenty. What a dirty old man he is. But there's the way she eyes him, *touched* him—then she says to him, her voice soft, hardly more than a murmur, "This is the Song of Beginning." She spreads her arms as if to embrace them all and then dances to the drum's steady beat. She twirls with grace to the somber tune that rises and falls from the flute, and her voice joins it in song.

"Mother she was, mother of us all.
"She faced, one night, the last of her fire.
"Not far away rose the glacier's ice
"Looming bitter, cold, and tall."

As she dances, darkness eases into the circle, stealing the last of the light, yet Gabe has no trouble seeing. She drifts to the three smallest children, kneels and rings them with her arms.

"Mother pulled her children tight
"Three there were, there'd been more.
"They huddled by the ashes and she wept;
"Her man was lost to the night."

The flute takes on a breathy tone, and her voice softens until it could be a breeze. She releases the children to stand and turn in a slow spin in the center of the circle as her veils flare out and trail in the air. Voice and flute weave a spell, and Gabe sees the scene she sings about as if through a cold mist.

"Night wind fell from the ice face,
"It stole from Mother and her bairns,
"And it took into the black night
"The deep, bright warmth of their flesh."

One by one, veils detach from the dancer's collar and fly through the air toward the children. A waft of pink wraps the shoulders of the smallest child, a little girl with wide green eyes. A veil that hints at tangerine comes to Gabe. He reaches for it, and it nestles into his hand like a small animal. It's warm to the touch.

The dancer becomes still, yet her last veil, a shimmer of gold, streams out from her as if in a breeze. The dancer's body could not seem more naked, more vulnerable. Sorrow for the mother's loss wells in Gabe, along with anger at the cruelty of the cold.

The drum beats faster, the flute quickens, the dancer reaches for the night and cries,

"Her mind fired with fury and fight
"And suddenly she could see so clear
"The stuff of life stealing away
"To die in the black of night."

Gabe's vision somehow deepens to see gossamer threads of yellow-gold motes streaming through the air, flowing from the dancer, around her, around him. Threads also rise from the adults around the perimeter of the circle, joining to create a dome over them all, its circumference matching the border where snow meets grass.

The dancer's gaze touches his and she nods as if she knows what he sees. Handing the tip of the last veil to the small boy, she holds her arms out, begins a slow rotation, and sings,

"Her thoughts reached for what she'd found,

"And grasped those shining strands."

The gold scarf wraps, inch by inch, around her.

"Back, she cried, to me, to me!

"Curling back, golden warmth wrapped her round."

Her words lift with the melody.

"Swathed by her body's own heat

"She pulled her children to her

"But still they shivered, still they died.

"You have to see, she cried, you have to see!"

The green-eyed tot springs to her feet. She points into the air and cries, "I *see!* I *see!*"

The dancer drops to her knees in front of the child, grips her shoulders, and urges, "Now reach. Reach! I will help you."

The girl scowls at the glowing sparks of energy that stream away from her, and then Gabe *sees* them quiver, and then some curl back. The dancer smiles. "Well done, Alexandra, well done!" The ... *lledri,* it must be the *lledri,* swirls around the little girl's head. Then she giggles and the *lledri* shoots upward to join the dome created by the adults.

Gabe eyes the threads of sparks that leave his body. He tries to reach with his thoughts, to force something from his head to touch them. The dancer gazes at him. A feathery touch eases into his mind and then withdraws. As it does, his thought follows, riding along streams that join to make a tight glow that he knows is his *lledri*. He visualizes the glow going up, and it curves upward. He thinks it back, and it curves his way.

Gabe whispers, "I see."

He shifts his gaze and finds the dancer waiting for it. The soft *touch* returns to his skin, this time caressing down his cheeks ... his neck ... his chest ... his abdomen, his ... He grins at her. "I see."

The dance ends. After little Alexandra is congratulated and the other children are told don't-worry-it'll-come, the children wander away, hand-in-hand with adults. As they disperse, the dome of *lledri* dissipates, warmth vanishes, and the cold resumes its attack.

The dancer comes to him, gathering her veils along the way. One by one, she glances at them and then they swim through the air to her as if of their own volition.

She stops before him, and he hands her the tangerine veil. Her fair skin gleams with perspiration from the effort of her dance. She says, "I'm Vixen. Drago has told me of you." She smiles. "You're a quick learner."

She is a hottie. The definition of the word "nubile" comes to his mind. It ought to be illustrated with her picture. To turn a man on, all she has to do is stand there and gaze at him.

The young woman in the sun dress approaches. He shivers and wraps his arms around himself. He says to Vixen, "I hope I can learn the keeping-warm trick."

The woman scowls at him. "You are *elessi?*"

Glad to meet one of his new kin, he says, "I guess I am—"

She says, "Since when did Drago allow your kind here?"

Vixen says, "Get lost, Morna. Somebody oughta teach you some manners."

The woman glances above Vixen's head. "You scold me about manners? Look at you, lit up with lust like a neon sign. In front of the children!"

"If they haven't *seen* it by now, they've been living with a sack over their heads. Or aboard your ship."

"I'm going to talk to Drago." Morna stalks away.

The redhead shakes her head. "Don't mind her, she's just a crabby old bitch."

Gabe studies the trim figure walking away. "Old?"

"Four hundred if she's a day. Crotchety hag." Vixen's eyes, her irises sky-colored and rimmed with black, scan him up and down—he's never seen a woman so blatantly give the "vertical stare" men give good-looking women. Getting it from this woman creates a stir in his lower parts. She says, "Drago wants me to teach you about *touch*. Let's see just how quick a learner you are." She turns. "Come with me."

He follows, struck by her authority. Sure has a lot for a kid. But is she a kid? Thinking of how Rhianna changed her looks from a teenager to a woman, not to mention the four-hundred-year-old twentysomething "hag" he just talked to, is he seeing the real thing? It isn't polite to ask a woman her age, but he'd sure like to.

Vixen leads him to the farthest galleon, the *Fair Wind* according to the legend on its bow. By the time they reach the deck his teeth are chattering. She grins—on her it's a playful challenge that makes him think of her *touch* and what she did to his anatomy with it. She takes his hand. "I think I can help you with that."

She leads him inside, her fingers tiny in his hand and oh so warm. They pass through a large room like the one in Drago's ship. A half-dozen men and women, all youthful in appearance, lounge and drink wine. Conversations falter as Gabe and Vixen pass through to a door in the bow, curiosity plain on their faces.

When Vixen leads him into the room, the wick of a kerosene lamp flames and a warm glow illuminates a cabin of about fifteen by twenty feet. The ceiling is draped with white silk cloth patterned with green leaves and flowering vines.

Instead of a narrow bunk, a king-sized bed sprawls along one wall. He wants to be under the bed's thick, rumpled quilt, warm beneath its artful, hand-sewn hummingbirds and honeysuckle. A wood stove sits on a ceramic hearth in the corner, but there's no fire. He rubs his hands to warm them. "Don't you people believe in heat?" Then he remembers Rhianna's bare hands in the cold. Dumb question; they don't need it.

Her answer surprises him. "Oh, yes. We prefer it. But Drago has us on strict security this close to a *lessi* city."

"Those sparks I saw ... that's *lledri?*"

She nods. "Our scientists say it's energy generated by living cells. Part of that is heat, but there's this other part that we can use."

Vixen smiles. "But I like to think of it as what one of our poets calls it—embers from the fire of life."

She tosses her scarves onto a dresser and stands by the bed. With one quick, limber move, she peels her leotard down and off. She stands for a moment, letting him gaze at her nude body. The lamplight flickers, seeming to caress her curves. She's as perfectly formed as a man could wish.

"I prefer the old-fashioned way of keeping warm." She lifts the quilt, slides under and then pats the bed next to her. "Don't you?"

Her *touch* invades his clothing again and flows just above the surface of his skin like fingers made of air, creating a trail of pleasure. It circles each of his nipples and then dives to his groin. He hardens, she sits up and the quilt falls to reveal her breasts. She opens her arms to him.

It has been so long. His body wants her. Bonnie has been cold to him for most of a year. And cold is what he gives back to her, all their old heat long dissipated.

Vixen's *touch* caresses him. Her smile beckons him. He's lost. He flings his clothes aside.

Under the quilt, she comes to him, her warm body molding to his cold flesh. "O-o-o, so cold." Now her hand joins her *touch,* wandering over his shoulder and chest, two sensations of pleasure at once.

He pulls her close and runs his hand down her naked back. The scent of sex rises from her. She presses her mons to his thigh, her pubic hair soft. He couldn't be more erect.

Vixen uses her free hand on his arm to still him. "Just use your *touch.*"

He tries. He can *see* his *lledri,* but it wanders aimlessly, the control he'd had earlier gone. He senses her *lledri* settle in beside his and lead his thoughts to the *lledri* motes of light. With her help—he can't say how, it's as if she's standing next to him, putting an invisible hand over his—he guides a slow-moving finger of living energy to the surface of her skin.

His mind's eye focuses down to the point of his *lledri* probe until it's as though he is a tiny creature made of air, easing over her skin, *touching* her. Her *lledri* presses gently "down" on his. As he *touches* her, he also *sees*. She leads him toward a rise that curves upward with a gentle arch ... guides his *lledri* up to circle a brown protuberance ... and then leaves him.

He continues, on his own and in control. The protuberance stiffens as he *touches* it ... she sighs ... he realizes that it's her nipple.

He lifts his gaze to her face. She smiles and then closes her eyes. Her *touch* caresses his lips. He shifts his perceptions to his *touch* as he takes her nipple into his mouth, and he almost comes at the double sensation as her flesh meets his mouth and tongue while his *touch* flows over it. He sends his *touch* gliding down over her belly, rising and falling with its curves.

She whispers, "Gently."

He *touches* her wetness ...

Her hips lift and she murmurs, "Yes."

His skin becomes all he knows. The trail of pleasure down his back as her hands glide, the caress of her lips on his neck, and the ecstasy of her *touch* on his penis. He sends his *touch* roaming, his mouth seeks hers, sensations flood through his fingertips, his lips, his mind ...

19

The RAC walks into KB's office with the handcuffs the female Artisan left behind and drops them onto her desk. "The lab can't find any marks. The lock wasn't picked, and it isn't broken."

Maybe now he'll finally get it—these aren't ordinary bad guys. "It sure as hell wasn't opened with a key. It had to be picked, somehow." She lifts the cuffs and studies them as if they could yield an insight. "You saw the video from the cell camera. She just took it off and walked away."

The RAC lays a file folder in front of her. "Schultz's autopsy."

KB sets the cuffs aside, but she doesn't want to open the file. She looks up at him.

He says, "Appears to be natural causes."

"I don't buy it!"

He paces. "What other explanation is there? I've studied the videos. The little man makes no hostile moves whatsoever. And I'm not about to believe in some kind of invisible death ray."

Oh, yeah? What else explains it? The Artisans do things that seem ... magical. But KB isn't about to mention that word. "I just talked with Bailey at the hospital. She checked out okay and is coming in."

The RAC stops his pacing and stares at her. "Why were those windows broken?"

Guilt rushes into her, and she's afraid he'll spot her lie. "We don't know, sir. Trying to get away? Communicate with other terrorists? After all, they did escape after they broke the glass. Maybe they had a way to reach their accomplices with the glass out. Some kind of signal."

Thank God, he doesn't have a clue about what she had been doing, and Bailey will never tell.

He frowns. "How did they get help from outside fifteen stories up? How did that guy get on and off the roof? With all the satellite dishes and wires and cables, there isn't enough clear space for a helicopter."

"We'll find out, sir. I've got surveillance on Gabriel River's home and his phone tapped. We're watching his bank account and credit cards. Got an all points out for him with the cops. He makes a move, I'll know about it."

"The woman?"

"APB on her, too, but nothing yet, sir, and not on the little man, either. But we're circulating photos of all three of them pulled from the surveillance videos. We've got people at the airports and the train station, and a stake-out on the guy's truck."

KB hesitates, then rushes into what she thinks should be done. "Sir, we need a national alert."

He says, "About what? What have we got? Video of unusual infrared output from one person. An agent dies of natural causes while on duty."

"We got a jail break."

"They weren't charged with anything, and we don't have anything to accuse them of. Under the law, they are just citizens who decided to leave."

"But we have video of a guy who Bailey says looked like Schultz but that's not what the camera saw. I told you how they can change their looks." Can it be any plainer that these people are *different?* And deadly.

"What we have is an agent that passed out for unknown reasons and who could have been hallucinating."

Would it help to tell the RAC that Bailey thinks the female Artisan saved her from a heart attack? But no way does KB think that's true, and it isn't smart to muddy the RAC's little mind with contradictory reports. He'd just find a way to excuse it anyway.

He shakes his head. "I understand how you feel, Agent Volmer, but we need hard evidence."

She picks up the handcuffs. "These?"

He shrugs. "Maybe she's related to Houdini. We have a minor mystery, and it hardly warrants a national alert." The RAC goes to the doorway. "I'm writing a report." He leaves.

A report? He's writing a fucking report?

She makes herself read the autopsy results on Schultz, but they only make her feel worse. It couldn't have been natural causes! Inaction is giving her a headache. How can Gabriel River have vanished? Everything she knows says he's an amateur ... but his skill at evading her net says professional. She calls up his picture on her computer monitor. Look at the bastard—black hair, black beard. If she has ever seen a portrait of an A-rab terrorist, this is it. He has to be a sleeper planted by al Qaeda years ago, or he could be an ISIS sympathizer.

Her computer dings; it's an email from the IRS with the complete file for one Gabriel M. River attached. It takes only a minute to track down where he works and the phone number.

Thanks to the magic words "Homeland Security," she soon has an appointment with his boss.

Even though Lawrence Huntley is old enough to be KB's dad, she warms to him anyway. She likes the fact that he goes by "Lawrence" instead of "Larry." Classy. He's handsome, slim, super-confident, smiles a lot ... where does he get that tan in the middle of winter? His office is bigger than her living room and packed with antiques. The place is so tasteful she feels shabby even though her clothes are fairly new ... but they come from a second-hand store. Lawrence doesn't seem to notice, though. After the obligatory Chicago chitchat about the crummy weather and explaining that this is just a routine background check, she says, "I'm sure this is a silly question, but I'm required to ask ... has Mr. River ever been violent?"

Lawrence frowns. "Well, in a meeting last week I felt threatened. That's why I fired him."

Fired? Could be a reason for a sleeper to break his cover. "How did he take it?"

"Oh, he was nasty. But he left right away." Lawrence's shoulders go back and his chest expands just enough to notice. "I run a tight ship here."

KB bets he does. "Anybody else I should talk to? Someone who knows him pretty well?"

"I'd say Lily Whitman, his associate creative director." He points. "Down the hall that way, on your right." He stands and extends his hand across his desk. "I'm glad to be of help, officer."

When she rises and takes it, he adds, "You're sure you can't tell me what this is all about?"

KB gives his hand a shake. "Like I said, just checking, sir."

"So he's already got a line on a new job that requires a security clearance?"

She gives him her "aren't you clever" smile. "We ought to hire you as an investigator. Thanks again."

Down the hall, Lily Whitman invites KB right in. The office is about a quarter the size of Lawrence's, but still tons nicer than KB's, with a cool Grateful Dead poster on one wall.

KB estimates Whitman's age as about the same as her, but the woman is too damn pretty, slim, and confident.

Lily gives a whole different picture of River getting fired—makes it sound heroic, the working stiff against big management. She seems to like Gabe River a lot. Maybe too much? KB decides to probe River's personal life.

She takes her notebook out. "What can you tell me about Mr. River's home life?"

"I don't really know. He hasn't talked about it much since he separated from Bonnie."

Now there's some news. Could be an undercover agent breaking his ties. "So where does he live now?"

Lily gives her the address and his cell phone number. Well, at least she seems cooperative.

"You ever been to his apartment?"

The woman's gaze drops for just a second, then she says, "No. Gabe discouraged after-hours fraternization."

Little Lily has a crush on her boss, does she? KB makes a note. "He has a daughter, right? Any other kids?"

"No, Berry is it. Poor little girl."

"Why 'poor'?"

Lily leans back and crosses her legs. Too skinny, and the mini-skirt shows too much thigh. "She's a sweetheart, but she has Asperger Syndrome. That's like autism."

"I know what it is." KB makes a note.

"Gabe worships Berry. I think he'd die for her."

Interest stirs in KB. The kid could be the key to nailing this guy. She has what she needs on Gabriel River, and she's had about all the beauty and brains she can take. KB stands and extends her hand. "Thank you, Miss Whitman."

When Lily takes her hand for a shake, KB gives her an extra-hard grip. A wince shows on the woman's face. KB smiles and releases her. "Thanks again."

KB is unlocking her office door back at the agency when Bailey comes up and says, "Got a minute?"

"For you, any time." She leads Bailey into the office. "How you feeling?"

"The doc says I'm fine. Actually, better than ever."

KB sits and indicates her side chair. "Well, that's good, isn't it?"

Bailey sits, but on the edge of the chair, back stiff. "Yeah, but ..." She pauses, then says, "Somethin' you don't know. My last physical, they said I had problems." She touches her chest over her heart. "Here. Trouble in my arteries."

KB mentally kicks herself. She should have known, should have reviewed the file. It's a supervisor's duty to be informed about the physical condition of her team. Schultz had been an obvious mess, but Bailey always seemed so healthy. "Yeah?"

"They say that's what probably caused the attack—a rush of adrenaline hit my heart with more demand than it could handle, and pow! But it's better now. A lot better." She takes a deep breath, the way KB does when she has something difficult to do. "And I think it's because of the Artisan. The woman."

KB draws a breath too, but instead of yelling the way she wants to, she goes to her office door and closes it. On the way back to her chair she leans close to Bailey's face. "Are you out of your fucking mind?" Bailey shrinks from her, and KB leans closer. "They're killers."

"We don't know that she—"

"Christ, what are you, a RAC clone?" KB drops into her chair, spins and looks out the window. Her temples throb. Bailey says nothing, and KB gets her emotions under control. She faces Bailey. "I'm sorry. You've had a rough time. Maybe that's screwing with your head—"

"No." Bailey sticks her chin out. "That woman saved my life. She ain't no killer, she's a healer, did somethin' to help me and ..." A deep breath. "... and I think we ought to lay off."

KB would like to explode, but holds it in. "She is a fugitive."

"We were freezin' her to death."

"They goddam killed Schultz!"

"That's not what it looked like. She never touched—"

"I don't give a flying fuck what it *looked* like. That guy shows up and suddenly Schultz is dead and you're on the floor with a heart attack. That seem like coincidence to you?" Then they all disappear, all clearly accomplices in the murder.

She stands and opens her door. "You can go home, take a couple days sick leave, or get to work finding the perps."

Bailey stands, but she doesn't seem cowed like she ought to be. Her gaze is steady. "This is wrong. You're going too far."

"I didn't go far enough and now Schultz is toes up and God knows what those ... *things* are planning to do next."

Bailey shakes her head, then leaves.

KB goes to her window and stares out through streaks of grime. A black sense of loss fills her. She'd never have thought Bailey would betray her. The goddam Artisans. They have killed one of her people and corrupted another one.

She returns to her desk, and her gaze goes to the photo of her and her brother on Lake Michigan. He'd always teased her about how stubborn she is, but he'd also been proud of her persistence. She whispers, "I'll get 'em, Jeremy. One way or another, these terrorists are done for."

Her gaze shifts to the picture of Gabe River on her monitor. His kid. That's the answer.

20

I pull my *sight* from within Cael's sleeping body. I had thought to cure his cancer while he rested during the morning, but it has spread so far and done so much damage that the task seems impossible, although I refuse to accept that. After battling for an hour, killing malignant cells and pouring in *lledri* to help failing organs, I spent another hour searching for his *key*, the direct descendant of the original cell that had begun his life in my womb. It's a search I have made almost daily since he was in his thirties and it became clear that he was one of the rare clansmen who might be unable to find it. But he has to have one, all clansmen do.

I know it is useless to try—no one has ever been able to find the key cell of another. There are so many millions of cells, and, so far in clan history, only the individual has been able to recognize the unique resonance of his beginning. But I have to keep looking. If Cael can find his *key*, he can trigger the reaction that washes *lledri* through his body, cell by cell, cleaning out toxins and disease to renew his body's life and function. It will, at long last, slow his aging to one day a year. He will always be an old man, but isn't that better than being no man at all?

Cael's eyes open, and I see his father in the sharp intelligence that shines out. "Hello, Mother. I thought you'd be here."

"Do I spoil you with my attention?"

His grin is wry. "No, and I prefer to think of it as indulgence."

"Ah, the curse of the only child." I help him sit up, position pillows behind him, and hand him a glass of fresh water from the table beside his bed. Forcing cheer into my voice even though I know he will see my true feelings in my colors, I say, "Given time, I can beat this. You will be fine again."

He shakes his head. "I haven't been fine for many years."

"But every moment of life is worth living." This from me, still drawn to the peace of death and its release from loss. What a hypocrite. But I will not abandon hope for my child.

He studies me. "That's not true, and I think you know it. How has your life been since Dad was killed? You came to see me for a few days, never went near your rooms, and then pain drove you away."

I shift my gaze from him, unable to speak of that even with Cael. His cold, bony fingers curl around my wrist, and he says, "I'm sorry. My bitterness gets the best of me now and then."

I turn back to him, take his hand and wrap it with both of mine. It feels as if I could crush it like a bird. But I am a healer, and I have never walked away from a fight to help another. I release him, stand and smooth his hair. "We'll talk about this after breakfast."

He grimaces, and I see the color of pain blaze from him. Filling a syringe with morphine, I give him relief. "You won't need this after I rid you of the cancer."

The weariness in his eyes troubles me. He says, "Please, just let me go."

"We'll see." I mean "never," and he knows it.

I close his door behind me, and I'm relieved that no one is in the family room. I hate the stares that blaze with curiosity from friends and kin too polite to speak.

Facing the stern of the ship, I gather my courage and go to a familiar door. But I cannot immediately enter the quarters Graeme and I shared for more than a hundred and fifty years. I know every inch of the two rooms intimately, every bit of grain in the paneled walls, every twist and turn of the patterns in the Oriental rugs. Even though I have not been inside since Graeme died, I know the comfort of the old feather bed that cradled our sleep and embraced our love-making. I don't want to go there now, but if I am to have an effect on Cael, I can't avoid it. As long as he sees me refuse my life, he will not listen to me about saving his.

Drawing a deep breath, I enter the sitting room. A quick survey pauses at a daguerreotype on the wall—our honeymoon trip to Niagara Falls. On a lamp table sits a photo of Graeme on the floor with toddler Cael, the two laughing as they wrestle.

And then I'm awash in Graeme's presence, a sense of his persona emitted by his *lledri* embedded in the very walls of the room over our many, many years together. My throat tightens, and then my gaze settles on Graeme's blue-gray plaid flannel shirt, tossed onto a rocker. It makes me want to call his name.

My mouth opens to do so, and my heart quickens in anticipation of hearing his voice, but the word chokes me. I go to the rocker and pick up the shirt, his favorite. I drop into the chair and lift the wrinkled fabric to my face. Oh, help me, his scent is still there.

I bury my face in the cloth and great sobs wrack me, bending my body, cramping my belly. I cry as I have not been able to in the months since his death.

When I can breathe normally again, I sit back and close my eyes to the memories that surround me. That does no good, of course, and they continue to tumble in my mind.

A selfish resentment of my son's illness surfaces. Why must Cael need me now, when all I want is an end to this pain? Will I ever break free of these cruel chains?

Shame joins my guilt.

~

Gabe wakes with sunlight from a porthole bright on his face. He's on his back, alone in Vixen's bed. His gaze travels across the flowering vine pattern of the silk draping that covers her ceiling. His body feels at peace, more rested than in months. His thoughts go to Berry. How is his daughter? Has she even noticed that her father hasn't called? Then he pictures Rhianna as he last saw her, handcuffed and being shoved into a cell, her chin high, shoulders back, her fear when they were captured fresh in his memory. Why hadn't she wanted to escape when Drago came?

The cabin door opens and Vixen slips in as if taking care to make no sound. When she sees him awake, she smiles. "Good morning, Gabriel."

Her curly mane of russet hair is pulled back into a low ponytail at the nape of her neck, accentuating her face— her blue eyes seem larger and even more striking, her features more delicate, yet her chin stronger. Her tank top and low-slung jeans reveal a delightful amount of the flat belly he had explored the night before. Morning light glints from the delicate gold flower that pierces her navel.

His thoughts dive to what lies south of the flower, then a rush of guilt hits him for seducing a teenager. But she'd been the one doing the seducing and, as for her being a teenager, who knows with these people? Like with Rhianna, he senses many years of living behind Vixen's cool gaze, a mind filled with roomfuls of experience. Not that her expression was always cool. Last night had definitely been in the category of inflammatory.

She sits on the bed beside him, and he becomes aware that he sees colors around her head. Just as when he saw the color of deception, it's as though the air is tinted with streams of Easter-egg dye. There are brief hints of several hues, but the dominant one is a buttery yellow, the same color he glimpsed coming from Berry when Rhianna was caring for him. He passes his hand through it. "I see ..."

She grins. "A soft yellow?"

He nods.

"You make me happy. It seems our ..." She smiles, and her eyes crinkle. "... *lesson* has awakened you." She tugs on his beard. "This tickles. But in a nice way." She leans over him and places a soft kiss on his lips.

She makes him happy, too.

"You are a *very* quick learner, master *elessi*. And remarkably talented. I've never had an experience quite like last night's love-making, not even with a pure clansman."

Feeling not a little prideful, he runs a hand down her slender arm. Her flesh is firm, taut with youth, not slack in places like he's noticed in Bonnie. "You know how you said that woman last night was, er, four hundred years old?"

"And you want to know about me." She rises and starts picking his scattered clothes from the floor, tossing them his way. "I don't keep track, a useless thing to do. Must be ninety-something by now."

Holy shit. He'd thought he was a cradle robber, but now he's a grave robber. Except that her body—and what she does with it—is a lo-o-o-ng way from the grave.

But Drago's housekeeper had seemed much older. "Emmaline?"

"Forties. She just found her *key* a year ago. It's different for everybody."

His jeans land on his face and he sits up. On the way out she pauses at the door. "Breakfast is ready, and then Drago wants to see you. The head is two doors to your left." He regrets it when she closes the door behind her; there are few things more pleasurable than watching a finely turned female body. Yeah, he knows he's not supposed to "objectify" women—but they, and men as well, *are* objects, aren't they?

As he dresses, he makes a mental note to ask Drago about getting to his apartment—he needs clothes, his laptop. He needs to somehow straighten out this Homeland Security mess. He pockets his dead cell phone—he needs the charger, too, although he wonders if there's a place to plug it in on a pirate ship. He feels sure that Berry is okay ... but he needs to know. And he just wants to hear his daughter's voice.

Refreshed after a hot shower—he asks Vixen how they manage that, and the answer is solar panels, not *lledri*—he has breakfast with Vixen and a half-dozen of the ship's occupants.

She introduces her mother, brother, and a cousin, all twenty-ish on the surface. The talk is of when Drago would finally decide to head south. The children are finding the constant snow and cold boring, and the adults agree. It isn't like they can ski in flat Illinois. He thanks the cook—Vixen's mom—and leaves for Drago's ship.

Once outside, the cold isn't boring to Gabe, it's frostbite. He runs for Drago's ship and finds him on the deck, in shirtsleeves, feeding a couple of blue jays that seem quite tame.

Drago says, "Fine morning," and leads the way into the quarterdeck cabin, Gabe rubbing his hands to warm them.

Drago glances his way and says, "Here, let me help." Warmth flows over Gabe's skin as it had the night in the cell.

"Thanks. I wish I could do that."

Drago says, "Vixen tells me that ye have excellent *touch*. If your other abilities match that, she should be able to teach ye how to hold your body heat. She can work on that after we're done here."

"Done with what?" Gabe would love to have something specific to focus on doing, especially to repay Drago ... and he yearns to be one of these people.

Drago gazes at him. He strokes his mustache. "I'll be honest with ye, Gabe—"

"Rhianna says you people never lie."

Drago smiles. "When even an untrained *elessi* can see a lie in the making, why bother?"

"What can I help you with?"

Drago walks to one of the carved panels that line the walls. "This is my ancestor, Merlin, working with King Arthur on a problem that has plagued us for centuries." He looks to Gabe. "A problem that troubles every human, one way or another."

"Merlin was one of your ... our people?"

"Yes. The round table was their effort to bring peace to the *lessi*, er, human world. A noble failure." He leaves the panel and sits on a bench before an elegant harpsichord. "I think I've found the means."

Gabe forces his thoughts away from being part of a people that included wizards and mythical kings. "And I can help?"

"By linking your *touch* with Vixen's, maybe so." He plays a single minor chord and rises. "Come with me to my lab."

As they pass a garden on the deck, Gabe touches the leaf of a shoulder-high corn plant. "How do you do this?" Wait a minute. Dumb question. *Lledri*. But still ...

Drago seems to understand. "We can infuse *lledri* into the deck planks because the wood was once living matter. The *lledri* then radiates to warm and nourish the plants." He examines the plants. "I'll have to get Emmaline to replenish it soon." They move on, toward the forecastle cabin.

Inside, a smell like a veterinary clinic hits Gabe. He passes cages containing monkeys, rats, and white mice. Through a door and they are in a laboratory. Gabe scans the stainless-steel tables, microscopes, beakers and other chemistry gear. "A lab? I thought you—I mean, we—are like, uh, wizards."

Drago laughs, and it gives his sober storekeeper's face a boyish appeal. "We must deal with the laws of physics just as everyone does. And science is still the best way to learn things."

"No Harry Potter? I don't get issued a wand?"

Drago grins. "That would be marvelous, but no. There are no spells, no incantations, no pentagrams, no hexes. It all lies within the realm of ordinary physics." He rests a hand on the electron microscope. "There is nothing supernatural, it's just that we know about a force that the rest of the world is blind to, and we have inherited the mental equipment to manipulate it."

Gabe puts a hand over his head. "The colors?"

"Different emotions excite different neurons. They radiate *lledri* at different frequencies. We perceive it as colors."

Gabe eyes the scientific instruments—he hasn't been in the presence of a microscope since high-school chemistry, and he'd gotten a C in that. "If it's science you want help with, well, I'm a whole lot better with words."

"I'll handle the science. It's *touch* ye can lend a hand with. You see, it's a tool I can use to create—" He pauses gazes at a portrait of a young man on the far wall. "To achieve freedom for us —" Drago shifts to Gabe. "For Magians, and peace in the world."

"Seems like a tall order." Gabe gestures at the lab. "What can you do here that—" Wait a minute. Monkeys, mice, rabbits … all critters labs use to test stuff on. "A drug?"

Drago steps close to a caged monkey. The animal shrieks at him and backs to a corner. "A biological agent."

"That does what?"

The little man turns to Gabe and strokes his mustache. "The biggest problem the Clans face is the swarm of *lessi* fouling the earth and persecuting us whenever they learn of our existence. Ye have experience with that."

A flash of anger at Agent Volmer and what she'd done to him rises in Gabe. "Yeah." He's afraid she isn't through with him. He's on the run, and he could end up back in that cell, freezing to death. "Too much experience."

"The insane breeding and greed of the *lessi* are the causes of war, famine, climate change, all the curses that trouble the human race."

"So you stop this how?"

"My biological agent will instill a fundamental change in the *lessi* that causes a population decline. Famine and hunger will vanish altogether. There will be no need for war."

"You think you can do all that?"

"There's even more, if things work the way I've designed them." Drago glances at the portrait again, then spreads his hands and smiles. The smile doesn't rise to his eyes. "Imagine a world without terrorists blowing up innocent children. A society without corruption draining its strength. A time when the stupid and the arrogant cease to trouble us."

Lawrence's smug face comes to Gabe's mind. "I'm for that. But what about ... us?"

"The Clans will remain as they are."

Gabe studies Drago's colors. No green of lies. "My daughter ... ?"

"Rhianna says she has your potential."

"I guess so. She sees the colors."

"Then what is there to worry about?"

"My wife ... his mother."

"She will live out her life in a peaceful world. Can anyone ask for more?" Again, no green appears in his aura. Drago moves to a machine on a lab bench that has an eyepiece like a microscope. Stroking it, Drago says, "Ye do want my help in bringing ye and your daughter into the Clans, don't ye?"

That's a dumb question. Then he sees how Drago appraises him, his gaze cold. Does that mean he might not help? A spike of fear strikes Gabe. He thinks of returning to his old isolation with Berry left forever confused and silent. No, he can't do that. He answers, "I'll do anything I can to earn it."

The door bursts open and Vixen strides in. "Well, I'm here. Not that it's going to do you any good."

Drago opens his arms to her. "First things first, dear Vixen. I want to apologize for my behavior the other day."

She cocks her head and eyes him. It strikes Gabe that she must be examining Drago's colors for a lie. He doesn't see the nasty color coming from him, so he must be telling the truth. It's hard to imagine living with people who never lie, but it would be nice.

Vixen says, "I'm still not going to do this ..." She waves a hand at the lab. " ... this whatever it is. Besides, I can't."

Drago steps close to Gabe. "Ah, but I think perhaps, together, ye and Gabe can."

Her surprise is clear in her expression, and there's a blue-white flash in her colors. The color for surprise? She says to Gabe, "You're going to help him?"

Damn right. He owes Drago bigtime. He wants to be part of these people, and this looks like the way in. And what Drago wants to do would bring peace and prosperity, and people could live good lives. "I want to try."

Drago slaps him on the shoulder. "Rhianna was right about ye."

Vixen's brows rise. "You know Rhianna?"

"Yes. She was helping me and my daughter when we were arrested."

"And you understand what Drago wants to do?"

Drago walks to a switch on the wall. "I explained it to him." He flicks the switch and a generator starts up outside.

"Oh, sure, you explain it to *him*." Gabe sees a purplish red flare in Vixen's colors. It matches the harshness in her voice. Anger? She says, "I don't think so," and turns for the door.

Drago says, "But this is for the good of us all. How can ye not do your duty?"

She turns back. "How do you do it? I'm sure you're not telling the truth, but I don't *see* a lie. What are you leaving out?"

Gabe says, "Please?" He steps close and studies her. Her features are still pretty to see, but her expression looks like a punch about to be delivered. "You won't understand, but I've always been an outsider. This is my chance to be ..." To be what? He reaches out and runs his fingers across her shoulder. "To be kin."

Her face relaxes, and she nods. "All clansmen know what it's like to be outsiders ... though not so desperately isolated as you." She goes to the monkey's cage, and he *sees* a stream of *lledri* flow into its head. The monkey comes to her and she pokes a finger through the bars to scratch its head.

Turning back to Gabe, she says, "All right. If Rhianna trusts you, so do I. And I like you." She says to Drago, "Okay, trot your little nasties out and let's see what we can do."

21

In Drago's quarterdeck study, the grandfather clock chimes four in the afternoon. Drago looks up from his journal—eight hours have dragged by since Gabe and Vixen appeared to have successfully inserted the last gene into his combined whooping cough and botulism bacterium. There has been time enough. He finishes his morning entry with a question: "Is it viable?" The answer is in his laboratory.

When he steps onto the galleon deck, the afternoon sunlight is pallid, weakened by the constant grayness overhead. Chicago winters are such monochromatic misery. He heads for the laboratory in the forecastle.

Inside, he dons a surgical mask and latex gloves and stares for a moment at the petri dish where the hybrid bacteria have been incubating at 30° centigrade. He's pleased to see that healthy colonies of the creatures have spread across the medium. But are they what he hopes to breed? His hands tremble when he prepares a slide.

He increases magnification to its limit. Bacteria twitch and wriggle with deadly life until the vacuum kills them. All the right genes appear to be in the right places. Drago whispers, "I christen thee *b. Dragonum.*" If the recombinant DNA he has created does what it's supposed to do, ohhhh, if it works ...

His gaze lifts to the portrait of Graeme on the far wall and says, "The future is ours, my son."

He shares the future of his cure with his son. "We will see a wave of what seems to be ordinary whooping cough sweep the world. Immunization shots will fail because of the hybrid nature of *b. Dragonum.* Antibiotics might be found to eliminate the bacteria, but not in time to stop my cure before it spreads, person to person, across the globe. The Covid pandemic is a toddler compared to my giant."

Graeme's painted gaze seems to send approval. Encouraged, Drago says, "And then the botulism component will produce thousands of prions in every bloodstream, and antibiotics don't affect proteins. The prions will cause proteins to misfold and spread, creating holes in neurons. The brains of the lessi will become tatters, and soon the barking of whooping cough will be followed by the silent creep of dementia."

He can hear Graeme as if he were here. "But won't they suffer, Father?" Sweet boy. Always thinking of others, like his mother had. And that damnable Rhianna.

The habit of truth is difficult to break, even when talking to a memory. "Perhaps for a short while. Insomnia, depression, and confusion will strike. Problems with memory, coordination and sight. *Lessi* will become unable to drive cars or fly planes, perform surgery or operate computers. As the disease advances, involuntary, irregular jerking movement will appear. People will stagger and fall, unable to rise. Problems with language, sight, muscular weakness, and coordination will worsen."

Drago glances at the portrait, seeking approval. "After the murder and ruin they have wreaked on us and themselves, it's no more than the *lessi* deserve." What a fine vengeance this will be. But the face in the portrait seems cool to him. Disapproval? "It's to save our children, Graeme."

He continues. "In the final stage of the disease, the *lessi* will lose all mental and physical functions—it will be as if the population of the world was struck with the final stage of Alzheimer's. They will not suffer then, not as we understand it. *Lessi* society will stagger and fall, never to rise again." Pride wells in his chest. "We will be free." He doesn't think Graeme would want to know that many will starve to death. But at least they will likely be comatose when it happens.

Graeme's voice sounds in his mind again, tinged with concern. "But our people ... will our healers be able to keep the Clans safe from this terrible curse?"

"I don't think of it as a curse, son. It's a blessing. And I'm sure the others will come to feel that way too, once we're free to roam and live as we wish, as we were born to do."

He gazes at the portrait with affection. His son has always been so bright. "But ye are right to ask. We and our kin will survive. The ability to turn our *keys* will cleanse our bodies of the disease and the toxins. And then we will claim the world for ourselves to rebuild a superior human race. And I will have avenged your death."

"I don't want a holocaust created in my name."

"Ah, Graeme, ye were always too idealistic for your own good."

Enough about what might happen. The monkey chatters at him from its cage. Probably hungry. It's time for the next stage.

Making sure his mask is secure, he inoculates an atomizer bottle of .1 percent peptone water with colony-forming units of living bacteria. Attaching the atomizer top, he lets the brew sit while he isolates the rhesus monkey in an airtight glass box and initiates the pump to lower the air pressure inside. He activates a slow infusion of oxygen.

Then it's quick work to atomize the liquid through a valve, spraying the bacteria into the cage. The spray simulates the result of a whooping cough. The monkey, pacing and protesting his imprisonment with shrieks that are thankfully muffled by the glass, inhales the aerosolized bacteria. To calm the monkey, Drago slips a fresh carrot through a valved opening. The creature munches with contentment, unaware that he might not have long to live.

Drago is tempted to wait until he can be sure the monkey has taken in enough of the atomized bacteria, but he needs a true test, and bacteria from a person's cough will dissipate quickly in the air. After a minute passes, he turns on an exhaust fan to evacuate the contaminated air through a biofilter.

Once the air in the box cage is clear of disease, he dons heavy gloves—the beasts have teeth like needles—and moves another monkey into the cage to test whether the bacteria will be sufficiently aerosolized by the first monkey's coughing to infect the second one. Now comes the most difficult part, waiting. His hope is that the botulism component of his new bacterium will create a full-blown infection within hours instead of the week the pertussis component normally takes to develop whooping cough. Even then, will the toxin-generating genes of *b. Dragonum* produce prions as planned? Only when his cure has reached full potency in the blood of a test animal will his creation reveal its capabilities.

He exits and locks the forecastle door. An exterior cabinet beside the door has sterile masks and gloves to use when he returns to check on progress; he prays to Merlin's ghost that his long-sought remedy for the burden his people have borne for centuries will work. Oh, for a life of freedom again, in a world unsullied by the poison that spews from what the *lessi* murderers erroneously call "civilization." He and his clan had once roamed freely across colonial America, and now they huddle in forests and swamps.

He finds Emmaline searching for weeds in the amidships garden. She pauses at a tomato plant, reaches in and plucks a plump red fruit. "We'll be havin' a fine salad tonight. How's your work going in there, Drago?"

He tries to still a rush of excitement at the mere thought of his "work," but knows she will see the spike of emotion. So he shrugs. "I can only hope it's going well."

"So the new lad was of help to you?"

"Aye. Teaming him with Vixen seems to have worked."

Emmaline laughs. "Yeah. That Vixen is good at teamwork, all right."

Not caring for references to Vixen's slatternly behavior, Drago says, "I noticed aphids on the mums." He had been tempted to use *lledri* to send the insects up in smoke, but, with his lack of finesse, he'd have been just as likely to incinerate the flowers as well. "And the *lledri* in the deck planks needs to be refreshed."

"Sure, and I've been doin' that while I work. And, if you were to look, you'd have trouble findin' any aphids now."

Just once, he wishes, the woman would not be ahead of him. But then, all she has to do is concern herself with domestic issues while he's dealing with world-changing events. "Good work." Drago heads for his study in the quarterdeck cabin. Well, let Gabe River enjoy Vixen while he can. Perhaps she will keep him occupied until Drago is ready for the second test of *b. Dragonum*.

If it works on monkeys, it should work on an unskilled and ignorant *elessi*.

~

KB wipes fog from the inside of her car window to clear her view of the modest triplex apartment house on Magnolia Street. Even though it's late afternoon, lights are on in the top and basement apartments. There's been no activity from Gabriel River's place in the middle. She doesn't expect any, either. In her opinion, the guy is avoiding her net too effectively for an amateur. The hell with it, watching an empty apartment is useless. She needs to get a feel for him.

She gets out and takes a shopping bag from her back seat, kept there just for times like this. KB crosses the street and strides purposefully up the sidewalk as if she lives there and enters the building. The best way to avoid being noticed is to behave as if you have every right to be where you are and doing what you're doing.

In the foyer, rap music from above wrestles with big band tunes from below, and the conflict covers the clicks and rattles of picking the lock. Once up the stairs, Gabriel River's apartment is even easier to break into. Just in case he's sneakier than she thinks, she takes out her weapon, flicks off the safety, and enters.

She stands in his living room and opens her senses. It smells ... clean. Not at all like where her father lived after he deserted them, the whole place reeking with stale male sweat mixed with the sweet-rotten stench of spilled beer. She explores.

A child's room is tidy except for a mussed bedcover and an open backpack on a chair. The other bedroom is a typical male mess, strewn with clothing and the bed unmade. But, still, clean-smelling. Well, what kind of a sweat would a guy in an ad agency work up while inventing clever little lies? As far as KB is concerned, the guy *is* a lie.

The kitchen is empty, so she holsters her gun. A jar of Ovaltine sits on the counter, and she finds three dirty cups in the sink. She smiles at what a treat Ovaltine was when she was a kid. When her mother could scrape together enough to buy it, that is.

There's milk in the refrigerator. It'll spoil. She's been raised to never waste anything. Her mom had washed dirty baggies and aluminum foil to use again. What the hell, she has just spent hours in a cold car. She finds a clean mug in a cabinet and then uses the microwave to make Ovaltine. It smells and tastes as good as she remembers.

She takes her drink to River's computer set-up in the living room, sits and jiggles the mouse. The monitor comes to life. The guy doesn't have the sense to password-protect his computer. She explores, but there's nothing except a browser and a bunch of Word documents. Some are research on autism and Asperger Syndrome, which backs up what she's learned about his kid.

She digs further. Looks like he was working on a novel, something about vampires. Now that's dumb; why make up evil when there's plenty of real horror in the world? She turns to a stack of mail on the desktop.

An opened envelope attracts her eye. The return address is for the Oak Creek Senior Home in a western suburb, Naperville. Inside is a bill for the care of one Melissa River. Has to be his mother. Weird that a terrorist would have a mother in a nursing home—but it could be part of his cover. Maybe she's his control.

KB will find out.

22

Shivers wrack Gabe from scalp to soles as he stands beside Vixen at the edge of the meadow. Lines of footprints in the snow crisscross as three teenagers dash about, playing catch with a Frisbee. Gabe hopes Berry will someday laugh and play like this. It sure would be fun to get out there and—

Vixen says, "Gabriel, you're not focusing."

He's never liked his full name, but the way she says it feels good. Sort of intimate. Intimacy isn't enough to keep him warm, though. He concentrates on the *lledri* energy radiated by his body and forces it to circle his middle, just above his skin. He guides it around and around his body.

Just as Vixen told him, once he gets the flow going it continues mostly on its own, with just an occasional *push* to keep it close to his skin. She says it becomes automatic, like breathing; she hasn't had to think about how to do this since she was a child. Well, if a child can do it ... A delicious warmth wraps his midsection—and then a Frisbee sails directly at him.

He reaches to catch it but then, impossibly, it curves away and heads for a girl, the one who played the flute at the calling-out ceremony. The kids' laughter peppers the chill air.

He loses control of his *lledri* and cold strikes his belly. Screw that, he knows how to stay warm. He runs into the meadow, waving to the kids and signaling to join the game.

They have some skill, but he thinks he can show them a throw or two. He'd been pretty damn good when he was a handler on his college Ultimate Frisbee team.

The girl sails the Frisbee at him but, just as it's about to smack into his hand, it lifts over his head and curves to a long-haired boy on the meadow's far side. Okay, it's keep-away, and they're using *lledri* to control the Frisbee.

The next time the disk comes his way he reaches out with his *touch* to steer it toward him, but, clumsy like a toddler just getting the hang of walking, he misses and it flashes past, though it does wobble.

The kids circle, throwing close to him but using *lledri* to keep the Frisbee safely out of his grasp. Vixen joins the fun, and they taunt him, zinging the disk closer and closer.

Fifteen minutes of dashing and leaping warm him up, but he's getting pissed. Time for a little deception and, with luck, the layout he perfected in college. A throw comes his way, but this time he turns his back on it and walks away. The second he sees it in the corner of his eye on the way past him, he leaps, dives, and, with his body horizontal above the snow, snatches the Frisbee. "Ha!"

He twists in the air and throws it on a dead straight flight to Vixen. Then he slams into the frozen ground with his shoulder, and the impact forces the air from his lungs. He rolls onto his back in the snow, laughing and gasping for air at the same time. Victory!

Vixen runs to him, the Frisbee in her hand—damn, she's pretty, her fair cheeks rouged by the cold, her eyes bright with amusement. And respect, he thinks, when she says, "I've never seen a move like that."

The kids gather around them, and the long-haired boy says, "Nice. But the crashing-on-the-ground part wasn't too cool."

Gabe starts to ask how he'd avoid the crashing-on-the-ground part, but the answer is obvious—you *push* up with *lledri*.

That's probably how Drago flies the skimmer he used to rescue Gabe. The *lledri* thing is very useful, if only Gabe can get the hang of it. "I'll work on that."

Vixen holds a hand out to him. He takes it, she pulls and he springs to his feet. She says, "Let's go in and warm you up."

He takes the Frisbee and tells the long-haired boy, "Go long."

The boy runs and, about thirty yards away, turns and stops. Gabe signals him to keep going. The boy runs, glancing back over his shoulder every few strides. When he's fifty yards away, Gabe cocks his arm and hurls the hammer, the overhand throw that slices the disk through the air vertically, in a long arc, hard and fast. It looks as if it will crash, but it flattens out enough to curve to the boy who, even then, has to leap to catch it.

Vixen laughs. "It looks like we may have a few things to learn from you, too."

Inside the galleon's family room, weakness sags Gabe's knees and he plops onto a love seat. At a table in a corner, two guys who look to be in their twenties frown at a chess game, and at a porthole a plump woman works on a delicate watercolor of the winter scene outside. A boy about Berry's age sails a balsawood glider across the hold.

Gabe rubs an ache in the shoulder he landed on, remembering the dislocation he'd gotten making that move in his senior year. He looks up at Vixen. "I'm going to pay for that catch."

She perches next to him on the edge of the love seat and studies his face. "I wish our healer was here. You're exhausted."

Yeah, he is. Working *lledri* with her in Drago's lab for hours had been real labor, and his tank is empty. The boy's glider bounces off his chest and lands in his lap. The owner runs up and says, "Sorry, sir."

Gabe smiles. "No prob, Bob." The kid laughs, Gabe launches the glider, and the boy dashes to retrieve it.

What's Berry doing? Gabe pulls his cell phone from his pocket and opens it, hoping to discover that a little life has returned to the battery. Nope. He slumps. Maybe Drago will take him into town with his skimmer.

Vixen's delicate fingers take the phone from him. "I can recharge this for you."

"What can't you people do with your *lledri?*"

She laughs. "Recharge cell phones, for one thing. We have batteries that store solar power for that."

There's so much to learn. So much to do. His eyelids close.

Vixen's touch on his shoulder brings his eyes back open. He says, "Sorry."

"I'm the one who should apologize for not seeing how drained you are." She holds out a hand. "Come with me."

"I don't have enough juice left to—"

Her smile is sweet, not lascivious. "No, not for that. Come."

She leads him to a door next to her room. It opens into a small bedroom with a single bed. A patchwork quilt promises warmth. "This is yours to use as long as you need." She winks. "And so is the room next door."

The bed is irresistible. He sits on it, then lies back. "Maybe if I just rest for a minute ..."

The aroma of bacon wakes him. It's dark outside the porthole. The quilt covers him, and he still wears his clothes.

Vixen stands next to the bed, holding a plate from which food fragrances flow, and his stomach lets him know it has been empty for too damn long.

With a smile, she says, "Your minute of rest has been hours, and I figured you'd be hungry." She takes the plate into the family room, and he swings out of the bed and follows.

She sets the plate on a table and he takes a chair. The plate is loaded with scrambled eggs, two slices of toast that are a little burned around the edges, and crisp bacon.

"I'm not much of a cook, and eggs are pretty much all I do. I hope this is all right."

The bacon has his mouth watering. He swallows. "It's perfect."

"Coffee?"

"Please."

She takes his cell phone from her jeans pocket and places it on the table. "This is good to go." She heads for the galley.

After a few bites throttle his hunger down to a bearable level, he opens the phone. Pleased to see a full charge and three bars, he dials Bonnie's number. "Hi, it's me."

Her voice holds concern instead of the irritation he expects. "You didn't call. Are you all right?"

"Had a problem with my phone. How's Berry?"

She sighs. He visualizes Bonnie, probably swirling red wine in a goblet at this time of day. "The party wasn't a good thing to do. I had such hopes, the way she was acting when you brought her home. But she shut down completely. Frankly, with all those screaming kids, I felt like doing the same thing."

"Is she okay?"

"I guess. She's back to her usual withdrawal. Who's 'Rhianna'?"

His gut clenches. "Where'd you get that?"

"That's about all she says, that and 'Daddy.' So who or what is that?"

He sips his coffee while searching for an answer. He won't lie, and getting into Berry's relationship with another woman was no place to go with Bonnie, so he uses Drago's dodge. He tries to put a little shrug in his voice. "I can't say. Can I talk to her?"

"I'll see if she's still awake. She was really upset when you didn't call or come back to take her to dinner." Now her voice hardens. "I don't want that to happen again."

"Believe me, I don't either."

After a pause, she says, "Here she is."

Silence from the phone, but that's to be expected. Berry has an even harder time talking on the phone than she does face-to-face. It drives her grandparents in Arizona crazy. Gabe says, "Hi, honey. How are you?"

No answer.

"I miss you."

So soft it's barely audible, a word comes. "Rhianna?"

Wow, she must have really made an impression. "I'm sure she's thinking about you right now, Berry."

Silence comes again. Gabe knows that to break it might cut off whatever thought Berry is laboring to get out, so he waits. At last it comes. "Hot chocolate."

That brings a smile. "Yeah, I hope we'll have more hot chocolate with her soon."

More quickly than expected, a response. "Good."

Another moment of silence, then Bonnie's voice. "How do you do it? That's more than I've gotten out of her in days."

"Just lucky, I guess."

"She needs you, Gabe."

He has no response to that. The thought of going back to live with Bonnie had been difficult before, and it seems impossible now that he's found the Clans. And, to be honest, Vixen. But he can't abandon Berry. All he can manage is a limp "Yeah."

"Next weekend?"

Oh, if only he can. "Sure. I'll call later and we can set it up."

"I'll tell Berry. See you."

He ends the call and sips coffee. God, his life is a mess.

After he downs the last bit of bacon and sits back, Vixen says, "You say Rhianna was helping you with your daughter?"

"Yeah. Berry." He tells her about Berry's problem and what Rhianna did.

Vixen nods. "Rhianna is a wonderful healer, and she can't resist trying to help anyone and everyone. I've seen her heal a moth that brushed too close to a candle flame." She shakes her head. "But she can't do anything for her son."

"She's got a boy?"

Vixen laughs. "Her 'boy' is older than I am." Her expression sobers. "An old, old man. He never got the hang of rejuvenation, and it just kills Rhianna. I've gotta tell you, I'm glad

I never had kids. Never wanted one." She places her hand on his thigh. "Too much fun to be had."

Gabe shakes his head. "You don't know what you're missing. When my daughter hugs me, well, I'm a writer and I can't even begin to describe the joy of it." He looks around. One day Berry will be here, sitting in the belly of a ship in the middle of a forest with her people, happy and free, thinking that what she is and can do is all quite natural. "Thanks to what you're teaching me, and to Rhianna and Drago, being a father will only get better."

"Drago." She stares in the direction of Drago's ship. "What do you think he's really after with his bugs?"

"He says peace and the elimination of poverty and hunger."

Frowning, she turns back to him. "How, exactly?"

Gabe tries to recall what Drago said. "His 'biological agent' will change ordinary people, I guess you call them *lessi*. Population will go down, and he says we won't be bothered with stupid and arrogant people anymore."

"He's killing off the *lessi?*"

"He didn't say that. He says they'll live out their lives in a better world."

"He didn't *say* he was killing them. Drago is the master of leaving the truth unsaid and the lie invisible."

"But if you can see lies, don't you have to believe what he says?"

She shakes her head. "Not when he deceives by omission. What's he leaving out of this wonderful scenario? Did he assure you that no one would suffer?"

He shakes his head. "I didn't think to ask. I assumed not."

She puts her mug down, stands and paces, nailing him with her gaze when she speaks. "Did he say exactly how his 'cure' will change people?"

"No. I just figured it would be good for—"

"With Drago, you can't assume anything. Look at the facts. We helped him alter the genetic makeup of bacteria, right?"

He nods. Then patted his belly. "But bacteria can be beneficial."

"Did you see the color of those germs?"

He has to think about it; he'd been concentrating so much on *touching* the DNA material. Yes, there'd been tiny bits of color. "Black?"

"That's disease." She sits beside him, frowning, her body rigid. "So Drago intends to sic a disease on the *lessi*. What makes you think it's going to be all fun and games? Drago has always hated the *lessi*. " The color of her aura is mostly a purple red.

Then her eyes widen and she puts a hand to her mouth. "Oh, no." A streak of thin yellow with greenish undertones flashes through her colors. Not a lie, though. Fear? She gazes into his eyes. "Your daughter."

"But Drago said ..." What had Drago said? Something about Berry's potential, and then he'd asked what there was to worry about. Drago had avoided saying that Berry would be all right. Or Gabe, either. Oh, he'd said the Clans would be okay, but then Gabe and Berry aren't members of the club yet, are they?

He sits back and replays his conversation with Drago. He sees holes in what Drago said, leaving much unsaid, and how what he said was designed to lead Gabe to go along. And Gabe had been like a tail-wagging puppy begging for a bone.

Vixen stares in the direction of Drago's ship. "I can't let him do this."

The risk that she's right is too much to take. Gabe stands. "This is my responsibility. I'll get him to stop."

23

I rest my gaze upon Cael as he lays asleep, morphine subduing his pain. How can my sweet boy have turned into an old man, his cheeks sunken, his nose beaked? I realize that I have not really looked at him for many years, seeing instead his personality—his bright mind, quick humor, and gentle nature. Well, he will have many more years if I have anything to do with it.

I ease my *sight* into him to hunt cancer. In the past day I have scoured the disease from his bones, streaming *lledri* into the marrow to revive it, but there is more throughout his body. I find a colony in his left lung and kill it. His heart still beats strongly, and the residue from the dead cancer cells will wash away in his bloodstream to be eliminated by his kidneys.

I move my *sight* through his chest, alert for the darkness of disease, for anything unusual. As I pass his heart, I glimpse an exceptional brightness near the aortic valve. Moving toward it, I come to a glow. My breath catches. I have seen a gleam like it once before, the day I found my original cell. My *key*. I come to a cell deep within his heart that radiates the essence of Cael. Joy blazes through me. I have found his *key*. I scan the tissue around it and commit its location to memory.

Sitting back, I treasure the possibilities. Yes, he will always be an old man, but rejuvenation will stop his aging, and he will be healthy. There's no one I would rather spend my days with than my son. Perhaps life is worth living after all.

Choked with emotion, I can manage no more than a whisper when I say, "Cael. Son." I stroke his brow, and then run my fingers through his hair the way he likes. He stirs. "Wake up, Cael. I have wonderful news."

His eyelids tremble, and then open. I catch the faintest flash of resentment in his colors. Not at me, I suspect, but at being still alive. Still suffering. Well, that will end now that he can turn his *key*.

The wrinkles of a face furrowed by time emphasize his expression of derision. "Mother. Still trying to bring the half-dead to half-life, I see."

I smile with happiness I haven't felt in many months. "I found your *key*."

His eyes widen. "That's impossible."

"Follow my *sight* and I will lead you to it."

He nods, then surprises me when the thin yellow of fear streaks through his colors instead of the gold of hope. Well, that will change.

Cael has inherited my skill with *lledri*, and it's easy for him to follow me to that glowing, special cell. I watch his face as he focuses inward. His features soften and relax. Finally, I *see* the joy I expect in his colors.

He says, "At last."

"Now you can be well and whole. I will teach you how to stream *lledri* through your *key* to flood your body, destroying disease, toxins, all that does not match the fundamental pattern of your tissues. You'll be cured of cancer."

He lifts his gaze to me, peace in his expression. At last I *see* his aura ripple with the golden hue of hope. I am so happy for him. Suddenly, life is good.

He says, "Oh, no, Mother. I can do better than that. Teach me how to do the Final Fire."

Shock rips through me. "How can you find life at last and in the same moment reject it? No! Never. I will not allow it."

He stiffens, then struggles and sits erect. His mouth firms, his lined face is set for a fight. "Then you and I have nothing more for each other. This clan is my family as well, and I will ask them to help me."

Night cloaks the lake, but campfire light dances red and orange on the beach sand. I have no need of the warmth, at least not for my body. My soul, though ...

Cael, Mary Fay, and the three other members of the Deverell clan council gaze at the flames. Across from me and next to Mary Fay, Cael shifts his body, discomfort in his aura. He props himself up with an arm and stretches his legs stiffly to the side. He avoids my gaze.

His Aunt Martha, my sister and a sweet woman overly fond of chocolate-chip cookies, relaxes next to him in a beach chair. Una and Britt, the same age as Cael and once his constant companions, flank me. Memories of them growing up together flit through my mind. Playmates and best friends until they found their keys at the height of their vigor—Britt in his middle twenties and Una just as she turned thirty—Cael has become so crushingly unlike them. Since then they have aged only one day for each year that has passed, while Cael's body suffers every daily insult and injury of his hundred years and ten.

Britt sprawls on his side, lean and tanned, wearing only swimming trunks. Una, in a T-shirt and bikini bottom, sits

"Indian-style," her limber, slender legs crossed before her. Cael's physical discomfort makes me realize that I, too, sit easily on the sand, legs crossed as Una's are. And I don't look a day older than her.

Mary Fay says, "I've called this council for two reasons. A request by Cael and because of a new threat from Homeland Security that Rhianna has learned of. " She nods to Cael. "Please express your wishes, Cael."

He straightens as best he can, his back bowed by the burden of his years, and scans the faces of the council. At last he comes to me and holds my gaze. "I have found my *key*—"

Martha claps her hands. "Oh, how wonderful!"

"And I want to find peace with a Final Fire."

I wince inside at his words, and the air seems to leave Martha. Britt and Una glance at each other, mouths agape.

Cael says to Mary Fay, "I know I don't need the clan's permission to do this, but I wish it to be a formal ceremony. I need help." He looks to me. "And instruction."

All faces turn my way. I say, "I oppose this with all my being. Please do not help my son leave before his time."

Cael's laugh is a cry of pain. "Before my time? Mother, my time is long past." He points to Una. "The time since a woman would look at me is long past." He shifts to Britt. "The time since my friends came around is long past."

The two cast their gazes into the fire, and the bruised gray-green of shame streams into their auras.

"I can't blame them. Who would want to be with a doddering old man? Not I."

His gaze goes from face to face. "My mother has mourned the loss of my father for many months, and I understand. I have mourned the loss of my birthright for a century, and she has no grasp of the pain."

Now it is I who sends my gaze to the fire. Have I been so selfish, so unseeing as to have missed his misery? Or has he been a master at hiding it?

He says, "I pretend, for the sake of us all, to be content. It's not quite a lie—call it acting."

My heart weeps for him, but still ... I lift my gaze. "But life ... life is so precious."

His voice is strong. "How precious is life when, no matter what your health, it is lived in isolation? With no friends to share your hours? No love to look to the future with? Tell me how precious a life like that is after you have lived it, you who have been a vital young woman for almost three hundred years."

His anger towers, and I retreat from it. How has he kept it hidden?

Cael scans the rest of the group. "I am trapped, wrapped in a never-ending shroud of old age in a society that does not know aging. Can you imagine?"

I can't, but I hear the anguish in his voice. Who am I to demand that he continue to suffer, and suffer, and suffer?

He isn't through with us. "I have thought of going to live among the *lessi,* where I would be just one of many 'elderly.' But how would I live? In the *lessi* world, there is no work there for someone as ancient as I. No companions who share my history. I could not talk of my life in the Clans. And when the cancer that my mother has been cleaning from my body blossoms and consumes me, I would die in pain." He looks to me. "No. I want to find peace with my Final Fire." To Mary Fay he says, "It is up to you whether or not I do it alone."

She gazes at me, the ashen gray of sadness in her colors, and then at Cael. "It is your right." She takes his hand. "I came from the *lessi* world, and you're correct. It's no place for the old and infirm. You are a marvelous actor, Cael, but I've caught glimpses of your despair. I will do everything I can to help you."

Cael opens his mouth to speak, but then simply nods and wipes at a tear.

Mary Fay says, "When?"

Cael finds his voice. "Tomorrow."

I raise my hand in protest. "Oh, no. Can we not have time to ready ourselves?"

"Do you mean time to try to dissuade me?"

"It's not that, I—"

To Mary Fay he says, "Tomorrow? Before I lose my courage."

She nods and looks to Britt and Una. "Will you two see to the building of a raft?"

Britt gazes at Una, who nods. He has to clear his throat before his voice will work. "Yes." He says to Cael, "And we will teach you how to create the Fire."

I say, "You love Cael, how can you do this to him?"

Una gazes steadily at Cael. "We do this *for* him because we love him."

Cael looks away, out toward the dark lake. The gold of hope infuses his colors.

I need to scream and weep, but not here. As I move to rise, Mary Fay says, "Please, Rhianna, don't go. We need your help to learn what kind of trouble your sxperience in Chicago means for the Clans. We must go there and—"

"I've told you no."

"Mother," says Cael, "why not? There will be nothing to hold you here."

"Don't speak to me of that." Then a desperate ploy comes to me. "Unless you will wait until I return."

The fire's crackle tempers the long silence that follows. I know I should feel shame, but, by all that is sacred, this is my *son—*

Cael says, "I know how deep and painful your grieving for Father has been. If I were to ask you to bear it beyond your limits, what would you do?"

"You know what I would do."

"Well, I can't." My heart tears at the sorrow on his face and in his colors. His voice breaks. "I am just so damned weary."

He pushes himself up on shaky arms and gets to his knees. He tries to stand, but topples. Mary Fay catches him and helps him up. He says "Tomorrow" and shuffles into the starlit darkness.

The others turn their gazes on me. I don't need *lledri* to see their scorn. I spring to my feet—and can't help but contrast my easy strength with Cael's fragility. Heading opposite the direction Cael took, I stride into the night, wanting to walk away from my hurt and knowing that I can't.

24

The night is clear when Gabe walks with Vixen to Drago's galleon, the stars and moon making the snow bright, the cold making it crunch. Faint strips of light escape curtains from a window in the forecastle lab and from Drago's study in the quarterdeck cabin at the rear of the ship. Gabe tries the door to the laboratory, but it's locked.

Vixen steps in front of him. "Let me see." She focuses on the lock and a few moments later he hears a click. Working the knob, she pushes the door open and leads the way inside.

She takes a kerosene lamp from a hook in the first room and ignites the wick. The animal smell is as strong as before, and the animals in the cages still wait for their fates. Gabe calls, "Drago?"

When there is no answer, he takes the lead through the door to the laboratory. An electric lamp shines there, and somewhere a motor hums. No Drago, but two monkeys pace in a glass box. "He must be in his study."

One of the monkeys doubles over in a paroxysm of coughing. Though muted by the glass, its cough sounds deep and painful. Vixen goes to the cage. "Poor thing."

Gabe joins her. The motor hum comes from an attachment on the back of the box. A tube connects the attachment to the wall. To a vent? The monkey's spasm ends and Vixen opens a latch on the top. "Maybe I can help it. I know a little of healing." She pushes up on the hinged lid, but it resists. "It's stuck."

Gabe lends a hand and lifts. The lid gives with a sucking sound, and air rushes over his hand and into the box.

Vixen flinches back. "My God!"

Motes of black color stream from the two monkeys and out of the box. The coughing monkey spasms again and Vixen reaches for it.

The animal offers no resistance and lies limp in her hands. She sets it on the lab table and focuses on it. Gabe stands close and manages to use his new *sight* to follow her *lledri* into the monkey, but he doesn't understand what he sees in a chaos of cells and tissue. The monkey coughs at them, a cloud of blackness shoots from its mouth, and Gabe turns his head away.

Vixen's eyes widen and her gaze shifts to Gabe. "Its lungs and blood swarm with those bacteria we helped Drago make."

Drago's voice startles Gabe. "What are ye doing?"

They turn. Drago stands at the open door, wearing a surgical mask. Latex gloves protect his hands. He slams the door and rushes to the table. Shoving Vixen out of his way, he scoops up the monkey and drops it into the glass cage, slamming it shut. Its limbs clumsy, its movement halting, the monkey gets to its feet. It staggers two steps and then collapses.

The fallen monkey contorts with another coughing fit, which is echoed by the other monkey. Drago's eyes crinkle above his mask as if he smiles. Gabe sees the butter color of happiness in his aura.

After Drago latches the lid to the box, he turns to Gabe and Vixen. His gaze shifts back and forth between them. "Ye have no business here."

Gabe points at the sick monkeys. "That's what your 'biological agent' does?"

Spreading his hands, Drago says, "The process isn't complete."

"What happens next?"

Drago shrugs. "I can't say."

Gabe *sees* the green of a lie seep into his colors. "You mean you won't say."

"That's correct. I won't."

The streams of black motes from the box had ended when the lid closed, but Gabe feels as if they're still in the room. "We've been exposed, haven't we?"

"Perhaps. Only time will tell."

"How much time?"

"I honestly can't say." He turns his gaze on Vixen. "But I don't think ye have anything to worry about. You have your *key*." He indicates the door. "I need to decontaminate this room. Please leave."

Vixen says, "You have to stop this."

Drago studies her, his eyes intense above the mask. He looks to Gabe. "I'm not sure that I can any more. Or that I would if I could."

He turns to face the monkeys. "This is the beginning of freedom for the Clans." He turns to Vixen. "And the children ye dance for."

Both monkeys cough. Vixen steps close to Drago and glares into his eyes. "I won't let you do this."

Pain lances in Gabe's chest. It feels as if a hand grips his heart, squeezing. It's hard to breathe. His legs give, and he falls to his knees.

Drago says to Vixen, "If ye try to harm me, I will crush his heart."

She kneels beside Gabe. He croaks, "Hurts ..."

Glaring up at Drago, she says, "All right. Release him before you do real damage."

The pressure leaves, and with it the pain. Taking deep breaths, Gabe feels his strength return and gets up. Clenching his fists, he steps toward Drago. "You son of a—"

The pressure grabs his heart again and he staggers. Vixen steadies him and cries, "You harm him and this lab goes up in flames."

The grip on Gabe's heart releases, and Drago says, "Fine. Get out. Vixen, you are banished."

"Good luck wilth that." She takes Gabe's hand and leads him out. On the deck, she stops him. "Hold still."

She concentrates on his chest. After a moment, her eyes widen, and the pale, nasty yellow that he'd *seen* when people are afraid streaks her colors. Her eyes narrow into a squint and seem to lose focus.

A moment later she gazes into his eyes. "I see the germ in your lungs, and in mine." She places her palm against his chest and focuses there. A frown furrows her forehead. After a long minute her gaze leaves his body. "I just tried to kill it, but it reproduces faster than my skill can destroy it." Her frown deepens. "We need a healer. Maybe Rhianna is still in Chicago."

"How do we find her?"

"The clan leader—Mary Fay—should know."

~

KB wrinkles her nose at a hint of a smell in the lobby of the Oak Creek Senior Home that she's encountered before. In her mother's hospital ward at the county hospital, where she lies dying of cancer. Sort of a combined medicine and outhouse odor. For KB, it's the smell of death.

Big Ficus trees, fancy-looking area rugs on the beige linoleum floor, and overstuffed leather furniture make the place look plush. The ad business must pay well for River to afford this. Maybe there's terrorist money, too. A middle-aged couple with a child of about ten sits with a wrinkled woman whose gaze darts spastically around the room. The visiting family's faces are glum, but they keep talking, forcing smiles now and then.

The shift supervisor is friendly and young and super-helpful once KB gives her the background-check story and a look at her Homeland Security ID. She leads KB down a long hall lined with doors, most of them standing open. "Mrs. River is one of our nicest residents, so lively, and quite lucid most of the time, although she has some wild stories. She has come a long way since her stroke, almost completely rehabilitated. And her son is very charming. He visits at least once a month, but usually more than that. I wish all our residents' children were as faithful."

They pass a bent old man who makes his way down the hallway with a walker. He lifts the walker and sets it a step ahead of him, then leans on it, slides one foot forward, and then brings his other foot up. He straightens, and then he moves the walker ahead one more step. KB wonders how many hours he's been at it. The supervisor says to him, "Mr. Swenson, how are you today?"

The old fart doesn't even glance at them. He just works on taking another step as they pass.

The supervisor says, "Mr. Swenson isn't the talkative type. But I'm glad to see him up and moving."

KB glances back. She calls that moving?

As they pass open doorways, KB notes that the furniture in each room isn't all hospital beds and metal chairs like she expects. Each is different, some rooms crowded with elegant stuff, others sparsely furnished with crap that looks as worn and tired as the occupants.

The supervisor stops at room number twenty-six. Even though the door is ajar, she taps and calls, "Mrs. River?" But she doesn't wait for an answer before pushing the door open and entering. KB follows.

Habit and training send KB's gaze roaming over the room. A braided oval rug in shades of blue hides much of the linoleum. Early American furniture shows wear, but it's clean and respectable.

The medicine smell isn't so strong here, maybe counteracted by a dish of potpourri on a lace doily atop a dresser. Photos on the dresser depict Gabriel River and his kid and wife. She sees nothing of a little old man or any other hint of a Mr. River.

A petite, plump woman with salt-and-pepper hair sits in a rocker. Her hands move knitting needles in a skilled rhythm, creating a red scarf. Where does Gabriel River get his height? The woman looks up and says to the supervisor, "Oh, hello, April dear."

The supervisor says, "Mrs. River, this is KB Volmer. She is with the—"

KB cuts in. "I'm a friend of Gabe's." No need to reveal more than necessary. "I was out here visiting my aunt and thought I'd say hello."

The supervisor gives KB a questioning look, but then lets the story stand and nods. "I'll leave you two to get acquainted." She pulls the door almost shut when she leaves.

Gabe River's mother rests the scarf and her needles in her lap. Her smile seems genuine. "Hello, dear." She indicates an armchair beside her. "Please sit."

KB obliges. The woman is clearly happy and content. Resentment rises in KB—the crowded Cook County hospital ward her mother lies in echoes with moans and stinks of soiled sheets. She tries to keep the edge out of her voice when she says, "Hi, Miz River." She gestures at the photos on the dresser. "Nice pictures. But I don't see Mr. River."

Miz River chuckles. "Oh, that's a story."

When she doesn't continue, KB smiles. "I love a good story."

"Oh, no. I can't. It's a secret."

Letting her smile die as if she's disappointed, KB says, "My favorite thing about talking to my mother was her stories about how she and Daddy met. You know how girls love to hear that." Her lie is so far from the truth that she hopes it doesn't show on her face.

"Oh, I don't know if I should."

"Well, if it wasn't a happy time ..."

Big smile. "Oh, far from it." She opens her mouth, shuts it, opens it again—she's itching to tell, KB feels it. Miz River glances at the door. "Can you shut that all the way?"

"Sure."

After the door is closed and KB returns to her chair, Mrs. River says, "You promise not to tell Gabriel that I told you."

"Cross my heart."

A twinkle of mischief lights up Miz River's eyes. "Well, there wasn't exactly a Mister River."

"Oh, I'm sorry—"

"But there was my angel, Gabe's father." Miz River's gaze drifts and loses focus as if she looks at another scene. "That's why I named him Gabriel, you know."

Okay, so she's a dingbat, and Gabe River is a bastard.

Miz River's gaze skips from her memories back to KB. "Oh, I know what you're thinking. My son is a 'love child.' But I ask you, what could be better?"

Thinking of River's black beard and hair, KB wonders if the "love father" was Muslim, and that's how River got into terrorism. "How did you and his father meet?"

"I was eighteen, and a bunch of us were partying in the forest preserve the day before graduation. There was a lot of beer. When it got dark, we built a big campfire, and things were fun until Johnny Bledsoe started after me." She laughs. "It seemed like he had at least four hands."

KB makes a mental note of the name. You never know what will lead where. "Then what happened?"

"Well, I thought if I got out of sight he'd leave me alone, so I walked into the forest. Lordy, it was dark." She giggles. "It didn't help that I'd been drinking."

She smiles at KB. "Do you know, that was the last time I ever drank like that?"

Not wanting her to wander away from River's history, KB says, "So then what happened?"

"I wandered around, singing and dancing. But then the dark got scary and I decided to go back to the party. I figured I could find a way to keep Johnny's hands off me. I couldn't see the campfire, but I heard music, so I aimed for that. As I got closer, I realized it wasn't the rock and roll we'd been playing. It was guitars and violins and flutes, but it was happy music." She smiles. "I'm afraid you won't believe what happened then."

KB fakes a smile. "Try me."

"Aren't you sweet? Well, at last I came to a campfire that lit up people having a party in front of a pirate ship."

And what kind of happy weed had she been smoking? KB says, "Imagine that, a pirate ship. So there was a lake?"

"No, it was in a meadow, and I don't think it was really a pirate ship, that's just what it looked like to me. Only it didn't have sails, and long wooden poles propped it up."

KB makes another mental note: hallucinations at party. "Weren't you afraid of the pirates?"

Miz River laughs, a light little flutter of a sound. "Oh, they weren't pirates. I stopped beside a big oak tree and watched them dance and chatter. And then a young man floated down from above me. Really. He floated. Like an angel."

She smiles at the memory. "He bowed a real bow and said, 'Welcome to the Clan Deverell.' Tall, he was, with long black hair like a hippie, just a little older than me. It was Riverbank."

"Pardon?"

"Riverbank. That's what he told me his clan's name meant. From the riverbank. That's where I got the name River, to honor Gabe's father."

This is getting weird. It irritates KB to have to sit through hogwash. But maybe there's a lead here somewhere, so she says, "What was your name then?"

"Santorini." The old woman gazes out the window, sighs, and settles into silence.

KB notes the name. "Then what happened, Miz River?"

"Dylan—that was my angel's name—took my hand and led me to the fire. They had a wonderful wine, much better than beer, which I never liked all that much. We danced and danced, and then he led me to the shadows behind the pirate ship and kissed me. It was the most amazing kiss. It seemed to flow over my skin and down to my ..." She raises a hand to her breast. "Well, anyway, that was how Gabriel got started."

KB decides she's wasted enough time. She stands, pulls out her ID, and shoves it in front of the woman's face. "That's enough happy crap."

Miz River squints at the credentials. "Homeland Security? What's that?"

Yeah, like she's never heard of Homeland Security. KB hates to be lied to, and she lets it show in her voice. Louder, and with an edge, she says, "Who does River work for?"

The woman flinches back. Good, she's a little scared now. KB has no sympathy for terrorists, and this woman is trying to cover her terrorist son with her batty story. Give me a break.

Eyelids flickering, which KB's training says is a sign of someone dodging the truth, Miz River says, "He's a writer at an advertising agency."

KB puts her ID away, plants her hands on the arms of the rocker, and leans close to Miz River's face. "Give me a name. Who's in his cell? Tell me, you old bitch."

Miz River gasps for air, and her hand goes to her throat. Nice act, but not convincing.

KB leans closer and laces her voice with the venom she feels in her heart. "Tell me."

The woman's eyes roll, her head falls forward, and she slumps. Okay, now that looks real. KB draws back, puts her hands on the woman's shoulders, and shakes her.

Miz River's head lolls from side to side, her eyes stare, her mouth sags open. Spit drools from one corner.

Oh, shit. What did the old lady do, blow a fuse? KB straightens and glances behind her, but the door is closed and no one could have seen.

Miz River doesn't move or twitch, but her chest rises and falls. KB pinches her arm, hoping for a response. Nothing. Maybe she just fainted.

Christ, she's just an old lady. Guilt wells up to choke her throat, and shame too. "I'm sorry. I didn't mean ..."

Hold it. Settle down. Pushing her emotions away, she pulls on the armor of her training. It's collateral damage. Unfortunate, but necessary to the mission.

KB goes to the door and peeks into the hallway. Nobody there but Speedy, still creeping down the hall. She steps out, closes the door, and heads for the exit. Now she wishes she hadn't shown the supervisor her badge and given her real name.

Just as she reaches the lobby door to the outside, the supervisor steps from an office. "Did you have a nice visit?"

KB pulls on a smile. "Oh, yeah. But she said she was feeling a little tired, so I left her resting. Thanks for your help."

"No problem. Come back and visit again."

KB leaves. This isn't going into a report. The RAC would shit a brick.

25

The noon sun bathes me with warmth, and an easy breeze from the lake tries to soothe me, but all I feel is the chill of loss, both from the past and that to come.

Clan Deverell stands strewn along the beach that borders the lake, nearly one-hundred-fifty of us together at the same time, a rare occasion. Another hundred or so are scattered around the world, roaming as we do, too far away to get here in time. Most would be here if they could, I'm sure. Our long lives and isolation enhance kinship.

Cael stands next to me, gazing at a raft that floats in the shallows. Made with stout cypress logs and about six feet square, it's his transport to where there is no pain.

At least that's what I believe awaits him. As far as I have been able to observe, when life passes, when the matter of flesh and the living energy of *lledri* that make up a person scatter and become part of the world, there is no coherent entity remaining that could enter some kind of afterlife. I have seen many people die, both *lessi* and clansmen, and it's always the same. But I am willing to be mistaken. At times like this, I hope I am.

White sheets stretch from poles at each corner of the raft to enclose it with fabric walls. The Clans are taught that the intense energy released by a Final Fire drives children mad. I suspect that's just an old wives tale, but to risk it would be foolish. The Fire will consume the walls, but they will last long enough to deflect most of the *lledri* harmlessly upward.

On Cael's other side, Elathan, the clan's eldest, a strapping man who looks to be thirty despite his nearly six hundred years, says to Cael, "Are you ready?"

"I am." Cael turns to me. Once, in the fullness of his youth, he would have looked down at me, but this bent old man is eye to eye. "Mother ..." He sinks to his knees before me and gazes up. "Give me your blessing?"

His eyes. My baby's eyes hold that little-boy-lost look so like his father's. Another face bearing that expression ghosts into my thoughts—Gabe's daughter, Berry.

Oh, how can I bear this? How can I let it happen? This is my child. I want to care for him.

The pain in Cael's expression and his colors flood my senses. My child is tortured. How can a mother forbid her child relief so that she keeps him alive for *herself*? I am shamed by my greed, my selfish wish for him to turn his *key* and live on.

I place my hands on the sides of his face and gaze into his eyes. I know that tears well in mine, but I offer him a small smile. And I mean it. I don't want him to go to his end believing that I condemn what he needs so desperately. My duty is to comfort my child.

I kneel, my hands still embracing him. "I love you, Cael. I always will. You will be with me for all of my years, and I wish you well on the journey you take today."

He hugs me to him. He whispers in my ear, "I love you, Mother." He pulls back and gives me a quivery smile. "Soon I will be laughing with Father, just like old times."

Oh, I would that it were so. I stand and pull him to his feet. He takes my hand, and then his face and body change to a *glamère* of a youthful Cael of twenty-five years, lean and strong.

I choke back a gasp, and he says, "I want you to remember the *real* Cael, the 'me' that I am inside." I nod and offer a shaky smile, and then we wade into the warm water.

I steady the raft as he climbs aboard. Una and Britt have made a pallet of blankets. He lies upon it and settles, his gaze aimed up at the blue sky.

Whispering "Goodbye," I give the raft a push to start its journey toward the center of the lake. There, the flash of the Final Fire will be distant enough to do no harm. I have seen this five times before at this place, and a half-dozen other times around the world.

I join Elathan on the shore. My old friend offers a brief, warm embrace, and I am glad for it. Mary Fay steps beside me and puts an arm around my waist. I slip my arm around her, grateful for her strength.

Elathan calls out, "We wish you well, Cael. Find peace until we meet again."

Like a whisper of wind, his reedy voice comes. "Goodbye. I love you all."

Guided by the combined *lledri* of the clan, the breeze turns toward the raft. Each member helps push against the raft's fore and aft sheets, which fill as if they were sails.

Silence embraces us. Slow minutes later, the raft reaches the center of the lake. The artificial breeze dies and the raft floats, becalmed.

I know what Cael is doing. Gathering all of the *lledri* he can grasp, he streams it into his *key*. By using some of the energy to contain the *lledri* pouring into his original cell, he builds tremendous power and pressure.

A flare of *lledri*, a fountain of sparks invisible to ordinary vision, shoots upward. Cael has reached the point where he can no longer contain the *lledri* and it has burst from his *key*, consuming him in an instant. Most believe the Final Fire is without pain. It is so swift that I think that they could be right. I hope.

As it streams upward, the *lledri* spreads and becomes a bouquet of living energy returning to the world, its leading edge vanishing into sky blue. The sheets burst into flame and their ashes join the vortex of heated air that flees into the atmosphere. The flow stops, the energy thins and dissipates.

Not all of it goes upward. A wisp of *lledri* enters my mind. Its flavor is Cael. My last *touch* of him.

Within seconds, all that remains of my son and his century of life are smoldering bits of cypress drifting on the lake. And memories.

We stand in silence, except for the smaller children, who live only in the moment and must be moving, talking, living. Each adult, I am sure, thinks of their mortality. How could they not?

The clan disperses in fits and starts, the children leaving first, no doubt eager to return to their laughter.

Soon all but Mary Fay and I have gone, Mary Fay's sturdy body the only reason I can stand.

Goodbye, Cael.

By midafternoon, I have gathered Cael's things and put them into storage to be used by others. Biting back my tears, I finally yield to reality and do the same with Graeme's. I cannot surrender his plaid shirt. I set it aside to be sleepwear to warm me on a chilly winter night.

I stand at the rail on the deck, gazing at the lake, my mind as adrift as Cael's raft had been.

My heart beats, but to no purpose.

My lungs breathe, but to no end.

Footsteps sound on the deck behind me, and Mary Fay's voice comes. "Rhianna."

Is she going to pester me again about the trouble in Chicago? Anger kindles in me at Mary Fay's interference with my misery. I need to wallow in it so I can once again find the strength of cowardice to escape it forever. I ignore her.

Mary Fay holds a cell phone where I can see it. "I just turned this on and found a voice mail you need to hear." She presses a key and then hands the phone to me.

Resenting the curiosity that I feel—curiosity is a sign of life, and I want none of that—I put the phone to my ear.

"Mary Fay, this is Vixen. I need a healer, fast, and I'm hoping you know if Rhianna is still in Chicago. It's this germ Drago created to kill the *lessi*. I'm infected, and so is Gabe River, the *elessi* Drago brought here. It grows so fast that my limited skills hardly slow it. The disease is terribly infectious—we were exposed for only a few minutes. I didn't want it to spread to the clan and the *lessi*, so I'm taking Gabe to the safe house in the city. I'll fight it as long as I can, but please tell me how to find Rhianna."

Closing the phone, I stand silent for a moment and the shock of Drago's monstrous deed slams around in my mind. So this is the "cure" he has been so intent upon finding.

I go to missed calls to find the number and call back. I'm surprised to hear Gabe answer.

"Hello?"

"Gabe, this is Rhianna."

"You're safe?" I hear a smile in his voice. "That's great. Where are you?"

"Florida, but I'm coming to you. Where are you now?"

"Vixen and I are—" He breaks off for a heavy cough. "We're in an apartment in the Marina Towers in downtown Chicago."

I visualize the round high-rises beside the Chicago River, ringed with balconies that make the buildings look like corncobs standing on end. "I can be there in a few hours." I hear a cough in the background. "Berry's not there, is she?"

"No. She's safe with her mother. For now."

"Can I talk to Vixen?"

I don't know Vixen well. The woman has always seemed to be just a high-living girl who treats life as a party, even though she has served the Clans well with her knack for helping children come into their ability to use *lledri.*

Her voice sounds thin. "Rhianna, you're coming?"

"Yes. Tell me what's happening?"

"So far the only symptom is this terrible cough, but I can see the bacteria in our blood and some other nasty-looking things gathering in our brains." Worry is clear in her voice.

"Aren't there any healers nearby?"

"Drago's clan healer is down in Louisiana, and I couldn't find the one with Clan Bryth where they've gone to ground somewhere in the Rockies."

"I'm coming. Do your best."

"Hurry. I'm not worried about me, I can always turn my *key*, but that would leave Gabe without my help for too many hours. He would surely—" His cough sounds in the background. "—die. And I don't want to reach the point where I have to choose between my survival and his." She coughs. It's the sound of agony.

"I'm coming."

I end the call and tell Mary Fay about it.

"A disease to wipe out the *lessi*? Do you think in retribution for the killing of Graeme?"

"It's deeper than that. He's always hated them."

Mary Fay scowls. "I'll call the clanmasters and have a summons sent to Drago to attend a Grand Council. Meanwhile ..." she trails off and raises her eyebrows at me.

"I need to go to Chicago." I hand the phone back. "Charter a plane for me at the Miami-Dade Airport. I'll use a skimmer and should be there in two hours."

"Take Una with you. She's a powerful *mover*. You'll get there faster, and she can return with the skimmer."

"Done." I gaze out at the lake. All external signs of Cael are gone, but I feel as if my sorrow is enough to fill the sky with teary memories.

Cael does not allow me to drown myself in them. His voice comes to my mind. "Go, Mother. You are a healer. Do what you do. Give life."

I can hardly resent the words of my son, can I? My lips curve up at the irony of the dead spurring me to keep living.

~

Drago stands before the glass box that holds the two sick monkeys. The first test subject sprawls in a coma, spittle trailing from its open mouth. The other, unable to stand, exhibits the involuntary and irregular jerking movements of *myoclonus*.

B. *Dragonum* has proved to be far swifter and more deadly than nature's version of mad cow disease.

The second monkey's condition assures Drago that the disease is virulent and airborne. He had thought he'd seen signs of infection in Vixen and the *elessi*, and the message from the clanmaster of Clan Deaghadh in Colorado confirms it.

Going to his lab bench, he rereads the summons delivered by a blue jay.

"Clanmaster Drago, be informed that the Grand Council summons you to the Chicago safe house on 27 January to answer charges of creating a plague deadly to human beings."

Does that mean the *elessi* is already dead? Has Vixen fought it off, or succumbed? Gauging by the disease's progress in the monkeys, that they would already be dead seems unlikely, especially considering a human's much larger brain mass. Still, they must be exhibiting symptoms threatening enough for the clanmasters to conclude deadliness.

How dare they order him to a Grand Council? Drago answers to no man, especially when his mission is so necessary. But there is little doubt that they plan to stop him. The Clans' policy of no interference with the *lessi* has grated on him for more than a century. Well, soon enough there will be no need for it.

With parental care, he transfers *b. Dragonum* from the petri dish to a liquid growth medium. A few hours and millions of bacteria later, he will transform them into spores.

He stands before the portrait of Graeme. "Soon, my son, your killers will receive the retribution they so well deserve for all of their crimes, but most of all for your ..." The next word swells in his throat, and he can't finish.

Going to his computer, he pauses for a moment to enjoy the photo of the Seattle Space Needle on the screen, atop it a giant flag streaming in a strong westerly trade wind. He launches a browser and goes to weather.com. Yes, the jet stream still flows directly over Seattle and into the heart of the country, and is expected to remain there for at least a week. Time enough.

He moves on to u-travel.com to book a flight to Seattle. His flight doesn't leave until five in the morning, but that's fine. He'll arrive in time to have a nice brunch at the Edgewater Hotel and perhaps shop in Pike Place Market before initiating his cure. After all, once the *lessi* are gone, those pleasures will no longer be available.

A knock on the outer door sounds. Although confident that the lab is now sterile, he doesn't want anyone to see the dying monkeys, so he hurries out to the animal room and secures the lab door behind him. After stripping off his latex gloves and surgical mask, he opens the outer door. Emmaline waits outside.

"Your lunch is ready." She peers at him. "Somethin' troublin' you?"

"No. All is well." He steps out and locks the door. "Why?"

"Oh, it looked like your eyes were tearin'." She heads for the door to the hold.

He wipes a finger at an eye, and the tip comes away wet. As the air takes the moisture away, he whispers, "A thought for ye, my beloved son."

26

Gabe doubles over with a wracking spasm of coughing.

Next to him on the couch, Vixen places a hand on his back, a sympathetic touch she has often given him during the hours since they talked to Rhianna.

He collapses back into deep cushions. The teal corduroy couch is plush and designed for comfort, as is everything in the clan apartment. Vixen told him that the place, connected to a second unit, provides six bedrooms and living space for clansmen who visit the city.

The closets are filled with clothing of all styles and sizes for both genders; his clothes were getting pretty grubby and, at Vixen's urging, Gabe helped himself to jeans and a clean gray flannel shirt. If he weren't so damned sick, he'd be enjoying the deep white plush carpet and the paintings that beautify the walls.

Vixen, despite her *lledri* energy resources, slumps as well, dark circles under her eyes. Then she too doubles over with coughing.

When her fit eases and she leans back, he studies her. She's so small, but her strength amazes him. He's read that women have more endurance than men, and now he's convinced of it. As for him, he wishes he could be a kid again, huddled under the covers with his mother bringing a glass of ginger ale and her soothing touch.

He gazes out the window at downtown Chicago from the top-floor apartment. The sunny, mild day, rare for winter, is dimming into dusk. Rhianna had better get here soon. Vixen has slowed his sickness, but she can't stop it. He suspects that she has neglected herself, focusing most of her *lledri* on destroying the bacteria in his body rather than hers. It's always been hard for him to express his feelings, but he has to say this. He looks her way. "I can't thank you enough."

She shrugs.

"Why? I mean, you don't really know me."

She grins. "Except biblically."

He'd laugh, but that could bring on more coughing, so he waits.

"Honor." To Gabe's raised eyebrows she says, "Yeah, that surprises me, too. But the Clans did this to you, and that includes me. We still talk about honor and teach it to our children, and it was important when I was a kid." She rests her fingertips on his forearm. Her expression softens. "Besides, I like you. A great deal."

His cell phone rings. He doesn't recognize the number. *Please let it be Rhianna.* "Hello?"

"Mr. River?"

He doesn't recognize the woman's voice. "Yes."

"This is April Messner, the director at the Oak Creek Senior Home. I'm afraid this is not a good call."

Vixen says, "Rhianna?" He shakes his head.

"Mr. River?"

"What's happened?"

"Your mother has suffered a stroke and she's in a coma." A pause. "I'm so sorry. She was fine when I left her with her visitor."

He'd thought there might be another stroke, but he's unprepared for this. His throat tightens. "Who was that?"

"A nice young woman from Homeland Security. She wanted to talk to your mother as part of a background check for your new job."

Agent Volmer? "Stocky? Heavy black eyebrows that meet in the middle?"

"So you know her. I'm so sorry, Mr. River. We're taking good care of Mrs. River, and surgery has relieved the pressure on her brain. There's hope."

"I'll come ..." He fights back a cough. "... as soon as I can."

"Please call any time. I'll let you know if there's any change."

He ends the call and tells Vixen about it.

She says, "The same agent that took you and Rhianna in?"

"Has to be." He's seen Agent Volmer at work. Torture is her game. The floor falls out from under his mind. His mother. God. Damn.

He doesn't know how or when, but Agent Volmer will pay for what she has done.

The front door opens and Rhianna walks in.

~

KB stares out her office window at the darkening sky. Where are the Artisans? She has watchers at the airports and at the train and bus stations. She has facial recognition software running on the output from airport security cameras. She has phone taps. She even has a stakeout at the wife's house. The

Artisans are skilled at evasion. Highly trained. Violent. Her phone rings.

"Yeah?"

It's Bailey. "Got a hit on Gabriel River's cell phone. They're emailing me a sound file now."

"I'm on my way."

When KB gets to Bailey's cubicle, she plops down in a side chair. "Let's hear it."

Bailey clicks an icon on her monitor screen and KB listens to a call from the manager of the old folks' home to Gabe River about his mother's stroke. She winces inwardly at her unintended "collateral damage."

River sounds weak. There's a woman's voice in the background with him. The Artisan female who escaped? When the call ends, KB says, "Where is he?"

"Call wasn't long enough to pin it down, but in the Chicago metro area."

KB stands. "Good. Keep on it."

Bailey gazes up at her, anger in her expression. "I seen what you do. Freezin' those people. It was you made the old woman sick, right?"

Bailey can't know anything. KB shakes her head, "I just talked to her, no reason for her to blow a gasket. I'm sorry for her." She steps toward the doorway, but Bailey's words stop her.

"What did you do?"

"Just showed her my ID and asked some questions." That's the truth.

So why does she feel guilty about it?

"You go too far, KB. Gonna come back on you one of these days."

Now that pisses KB off. She lowers her voice so Bailey's cube neighbors can't hear. "Listen, when it comes to nailing terrorists, there is no 'too far.'"

"They passed a law against torture—"

"I'll take care of my job." KB leans closer. "You just do yours and find me the Artisans."

She stops at the doorway and turns back to Bailey. "You go to the RAC about torture, I'll make sure you're in for a world of hurt."

Bailey gives her a long, cold stare, and then swivels away to face her monitor.

On her way back to her office, KB does her best to recall something from her leadership courses on how to handle the Bailey situation, but comes up clueless.

Well, it doesn't matter. She's closing in on the Artisans, she can feel it. Something is gonna break loose. And then nobody will care how she got the job done. Until then, she'll just have to live with it.

~

When evening comes, Drago finds cause to celebrate—*b. Dragonum* has increased a million-fold in the growth medium. He transfers it to an oven and stresses it with a sudden increase in heat.

The bacteria, fearing for their tiny lives, transform into spores, generating protective protein coatings designed to preserve life in extreme conditions. Millions of the carriers of his cure will revive when they find a benign environment. Like warm, moist *lessi* lungs.

While he waits for the transformation to complete, he readies an inexpensive plastic thermal bottle, a gaudy yellow thing with a red cap. With the addition of a sealant on the threads, it will do nicely for transporting the spores until he can send them on their mission. As cheap and flimsy as it is, it will provoke no interest. Who would hide anything valuable in such a place?

When the sporing process is finished, he places the spores and the thermal bottle in a hyperbaric chamber and then lowers the air pressure so that atmospheric pressure will prevent any leakage. Using remote-controlled arms, he fills the thermal bottle with what appears to be a fine powder. Perfect.

Then he increases the pressure to five atmospheres and screws on the bottle top. Now the pressure inside the bottle is sure to provide excellent dispersal when the bottle blows wide open. All it will take is an impact against something hard. After removing the bottle from the chamber, he places it in a box and wraps it with happy-birthday gift paper, a pretty irony.

He sterilizes his equipment, destroying all trace of *b. Dragonum*. It's far too deadly to risk being accidentally loosed upon his clan while he's gone, and the thermos of spores is all he needs now.

True, Vixen and Gabe are infected, but he can't count on either of them to spread *b. Dragonum*. It will die out when Gabe succumbs. He expects Vixen to heal herself and then work on Gabe ... who, by now, has little time left to live.

Carrying the box, he leaves the lab and locks the forecastle door. The sun has almost reached the horizon, and lights are coming on in the ships of his clan. He goes to the rail and surveys the meadow. His clan. His people. Morna gardens on her deck, taking special care with her marijuana plants. He smiles at a memory of her doing much the same thing with roses, hundreds of years ago, when the clan crossed the ocean to the new world.

A cluster of children puts finishing touches on yet another snowman. One of them is Alexandra, the green-eyed child that Vixen brought to her first use of *lledri*. The girl and the children with her are the future of Clan Bleddyn. And they are vulnerable to his cure because they have not discovered their *keys*. He thinks a healer can control the disease, but his healer is not here. He can't take any chance his clan will be exposed.

He unlocks the forecastle door and gets his emergency cell phone from the cabinet. Drago dials the Clans' central message number. He gets a voicemail recorder.

He says, "This is Clanmaster Drago of Clan Bleddyn. Be advised that the ..." He smiles. "... the difficulty about to be visited on the *lessi* is highly contagious. If ye are affected, use your *key* immediately. All clan members who have not found their *keys* should be absolutely quarantined from the *lessi* world for at least two months. Starting immediately." He can't resist adding, "After that time, the *lessi* will plague us no more."

When he leaves, he stops to think about the door's vulnerability. He doesn't want anyone forcing the lock as Vixen had, so he focuses *lledri* on the lock's metal parts. They heat until they soften and fuse.

Whistling a jaunty jig from his childhood, he goes to his quarters and packs a bag. In a few hours he'll be on his way to the rainy season in the Northwest, so he makes sure he has his rain gear. He wraps the thermal bottle "present" in his slicker to cushion it. He'll check his bag, and his cure will arrive at baggage claim unseen, unsuspected.

A tap on his door sounds and Emmaline pokes her head in. "What's all the whistlin'—" She pauses. "Goin' on a wee journey, are we?"

"Just for a day or so."

"Where to?"

"The place of my dreams."

She turns to leave, and he stops her. "I'm not the only one who is going somewhere. Here's what I want ye to do while I'm gone ..."

27

I rouse from my bed to check on my patients. Although paleness to the east signals the coming of dawn, I turn on a lamp in the living room so that enough light spills into their rooms for me to see without wakening them.

Vixen lies in the comatose state of rejuvenation, the fan of her red hair framing her wan face. So like a child in appearance, yet so strong. Touching her brow, I find the expected fever, the normal high body heat produced as *lledri* spreads through her system and eliminates toxins, sick cells such as cancer, bacteria and, now, those awful prions that Drago's bacteria churned out. Vixen will be unconscious for a few more hours, but then she will wake rested and well.

Her courage and stamina surprise me. And the hue of genuine affection for Gabe that suffused her colors had been another revelation from a woman with a reputation for casual wantonness.

Gabe sleeps peacefully in his bedroom, drawing deep, clean breaths, his cough gone. When Vixen and I finally conquered the disease in his body, he was almost as drained by the illness as Vixen was with the struggle to eliminate it, and she was as near death as I have ever seen a clansman come. I go to Gabe and ease my *sight* into him to explore his brain and bloodstream. No sign of the disease. I take a moment to infuse a little extra *lledri* into his system, more energy for healing.

He shifts in his bed and then opens his eyes. "How is she?" I *see* threads of rosy gold in his colors; he cares for Vixen. I also *see* a color that Vixen has evoked in all the men I have observed her with, the amber of lust. Just as Vixen used men, they used her. But I can't recall having seen affection before.

"She sleeps. She will be fully recovered when she wakes." I stroke his brow. I like this caring, gentle man. "Don't worry. Rest now."

He nods and closes his eyes.

My mind churning, I go to the picture window that looks out on the city. Chicago's night lights glow undimmed by the new dawn. Cities at night look so marvelous, with their myriad points of light, seemingly peaceful. But I have roamed *lessi* cities at night; violence prowls under the thin skin of darkness.

None of it compares to the biological violence Drago seeks to unleash on humanity, on his kin as well as the *lessi*. The presence of prions in Gabe's and Vixen's brains had shocked me. They were identical to the mad cow disease I have studied. But this disease takes only hours instead of years to reach full potency.

I could not have cleaned it from Gabe without Vixen's help. Nor would much have been left of him had Vixen not held it off until I got here. If this plague strikes the Clans, I fear that most healers will not be able to protect their young who cannot turn their *keys*. I think Drago is truly insane.

Before Gabe slipped into sleep, he had gripped my hand and said, "What about Berry? And Bonnie?"

I didn't have an answer. The *lessi* world will be defenseless against this horror. Perhaps I can take Berry and Gabe to my clan and keep them quarantined until the pandemic passes. But that would leave Berry's mother and so many other worthy *lessi* to truly horrible deaths.

There is only one answer, and it cannot wait for action by the Grand Council. I know Drago, and his arrogance and lust for revenge will drive him to unleash his pestilence as soon as possible. I must stop him. Now.

I take a skimmer from a storage closet. Launching from the top of the building will be simple and safe in the predawn dark. I go to the door that opens on a hidden escape route to the roof.

"Where are you going?" Gabe stands in his doorway, scratching at his black beard. He is dressed.

"To find Drago."

"To stop him?"

"Yes."

He crosses the room to me. "I'm coming."

I shake my head. "You have no defenses, and you need rest."

"I know where he is."

I had planned to circle high above the city, searching for the concentration of *lledri* that attends a clan's gathering place. Gabe could save me critical hours. "Then tell me, but stay here. Berry will need you."

He shakes his head. "If we don't stop Drago, nobody can help Berry. This is how I fight for my daughter."

He has me there. "Can you warm yourself?"

Gabe shrugs. "Some."

I need to preserve my energy to lift us, and later to deal with Drago. There will be no spare strength to warm Gabe.

Or myself, come to think of it. I point to a closet. "There are coats in there."

The Clan Bleddyn location Gabe guides me to is familiar. The forest preserve is a popular spot among the Clans that roam America, with deep meadows sufficiently hidden from roads and flight paths and hikers, yet convenient to the entertainments afforded by the city. Graeme and I used to relish the food in Greek Town restaurants despite the hassle of trying to find a place to park on Halstead Street. We Magians are such hypocrites, denigrating the *lessi* yet enjoying their good works at the same time.

The sun is up when we reach the meadow. A dozen clansmen and women stroll through the area, gazes fastened on the ground. Occasionally one stoops, picks something up, and puts it into a sack. There can be only one reason for policing the area. "They're leaving."

Frost is thick on the deck of Drago's galleon. Gabe leads me to the forecastle door. "His lab and the sick animals are in here." He tries the door. "Locked." He looks to me. "Vixen unlocked it with her *lledri.*"

I probe with *lledri* through the keyhole and find a mass of metal. "Drago has fused the lock."

"Step to the side."

Gabe studies the door, then rears back on one leg and gives it a powerful kick right where the door latch is. The door slams open, and Gabe gives me a satisfied grin. "I've always wondered if that really worked like it does on TV."

Inside the first room, animals hunker in cages. I *see* hunger in their auras. Now that the door is open, Emmaline can feed them if it's safe.

I sweep the room with my *sight,* alert for the black color radiated by Drago's germ. It's clean. Motioning for Gabe to stand behind me, I open the door to the lab, take a step inside, and search again. "Drago has sterilized the place."

Going to the glass box on the counter, I find the two monkeys Gabe had described. *Lledri* cannot penetrate the glass so I can *see* the disease, but there's little doubt that is there. One monkey is not breathing, the other in a coma, its chest hardly moving. Its suffering will soon end. I would open the box and give it relief, but I don't want to release more of Drago's disease.

Gabe calls, "Look at this." He stands before a computer on the counter. When I go to him, I see a photo of the Seattle Space Needle on the screen. Gabe clicks an icon on the task bar at the bottom of the screen and a browser comes to life.

A screen from u-travel.com appears with a confirmation of Drago's flight reservation. I say, "Seattle? Why?"

"Maybe there's something else." Gabe clicks the back button until he comes to a screen from the weather channel. A map of the United States with the jet stream superimposed appears. It curves over Seattle and sweeps across America, straight for Chicago and then onto the east.

Gabe minimizes the window and the photo of the Space Needle reappears. He looks to me. "Do you think—"

"We've got to get to the airport." I hurry out, and Gabe trails me. I'm now glad for his company. I might need his strength. And his bravery.

"Do you think we can catch a flight?"

"I have a plane."

Emmaline's voice sounds behind us. "Oh, it's you."

We turn to face her. She stands in the doorway to belowdecks, a cast iron skillet in her hand. "I heard a crash."

Emmaline has been a friend for decades, and I go to her. "I'm sorry to have alarmed you. But there was no time."

"Drago's not here. If you'd come tonight, nobody'd have been here. I don't know why the rush, but those are his orders."

"Where are you off too?"

"To join the rest of the clan in Louisiana."

I look to Gabe. "To get them away from contagion."

Emmaline's brows rise. "Contagion?"

"I'm afraid Drago has finally found his 'cure' for the *lessi*."

Emmaline is one of the most intelligent women I know, and it takes her only seconds to say, "Oh, that evil little man. Lord save us all."

"We're going to try to stop him, but I need you to help here." Rhianna points at the monkeys in the glass box. "These animals are infected with Drago's disease. As soon as the second one dies, their bodies need to be cremated and the box sterilized. You have to make sure that not a single bacterium remains."

Emmaline peers at the monkeys. "Poor things."

"You have to be extremely careful, wear a mask and gloves. The bacteria are easy to *see*—they're black as death."

Emmaline nods, her lips set tight in a determined expression. "It will be done." She gives me a hard look. "And find that little bastard."

~

America the Beautiful, the ringtone on KB's agency cell phone, jerks her from sleep. Only someone from Homeland Security could be calling that phone. Her alarm clock glows the time: seven in the morning. She's overslept. She snatches up the phone—the screen shows Kurt Swilly's name. Oh, please let Electronic Surveillance have something good. "Yeah?"

"Hey, KB, we got a hit on one of your suspected Artisans. The little guy."

Schultz's murderer? She wants him most of all. "Tell me."

"Facial recognition program at O'Hare caught him checking in for a flight to Seattle. He's probably halfway there by now. United flight 535."

"God, that's great. Nothing on the other man or the woman?"

"You'll be the first to know."

She swings her legs out of bed. "Thanks, Kurt. I owe you."

"I'll settle for a ticket to a Cubs game."

"It's yours." She dials headquarters, gets a reservation on the next flight to Seattle, and then has pics from the surveillance camera of the little killer sent to the Seattle office. She adds shots of the other two, just in case. Then she paces while she connects with Seattle.

She describes the perp to the officer on duty. "I'm beaming you photos. The guy looks harmless, kind of like your neighborhood pharmacist, but he killed one of our people. Got it on video." Well, sort of. "I'm sending photos of two other suspects to watch out for."

"You think he's one of the terrorists we've been hunting?"

"I know he is. Grab him at the airport and hold him, but be careful. These people can fool you, they, uh, well, they disguise themselves. You have a thermal camera?"

"There's a unit on museum surveillance that has them."

"Get one to the airport if you can and check passengers from that flight with it. I'm on my way."

~

While Rhianna is forward with her charter pilot, Gabe buckles into a leather seat on the Gulfstream jet. The Clans are really something. On the way to O'Hare, Rhianna revealed that, with centuries to guide investments, they are unimaginably wealthy. Yet they prefer to live apart in their old wooden ships, wandering like gypsies.

He glances at his watch. Almost eight o'clock. Digging out his cell phone, he hits the keys for Bonnie. When he gets her, he says, "I just wanted to let you know that I have to go out of town for a few days. I'd like to say goodbye to Berry."

"Make it quick. I've got an open house today and I need to get her to day care."

"Mrs. Fleister's?"

"Yes. She's good with her."

Berry likes Mrs. Fleister. "Listen, I'll be taking off soon, and I'll have to shut my phone off."

"I'll get Berry."

Rhianna returns and sits next to him. When she raises her eyebrows, Gabe covers the phone. "Calling Berry."

She smiles and nods.

After a wait, Berry's voice comes on. "Daddy?"

Oh, man, the sweet sound of his daughter. Gabe chokes up, then pushes through it. His voice needs to sound normal.

"Hey, my girl, I just wanted to tell you that I love you."

There's no response. There never is to that statement. Berry just doesn't seem to know how to handle it. But that's okay. "You do what Mrs. Fleister tells you today, okay?"

After a pause, Berry says, "Nice lady."

"Yes, she is."

"Rhianna?"

Oh, God, she still thinks of her. If Gabe gets through this, there's hope, there really is hope. He turns to Rhianna. "She's asking about you."

She holds out her hand and he gives her the phone. "Hi, Berry." A pause. "Yes, me too." After another pause, she says, "Here's your Daddy again." When she gives Gabe the phone, she smiles and presses a hand to her heart. "She said 'marshmallows.'" Her eyes are moist.

He says to the phone, "We'll roast all the marshmallows you want."

After a silence, Bonnie's voice comes on. "We've got to go. How long will you be away?"

"Maybe a couple days."

Maybe forever.

~

In a cab on the way to the airport, KB's cell phone rings. Bailey says, "Picked up another call from Gabe River's cell phone. He's going out of town."

"Where?"

"Didn't say."

To Seattle? "Patch it through to me."

She listens, and then says, "Damn." River could just disappear. Maybe he'll call the kid again after he gets where he's going. But maybe not. She'll lose him.

Hold it. Clearly, River is mushy about the kid. That's the bait she needs. "Bailey, find me an address for that day care center." It takes two very long minutes for Bailey to come back with an address in Glen Ellyn, a town south of Palatine.

Does KB have enough time before her flight leaves? What the hell, even though the RAC doesn't like them to flex Homeland Security's muscle, she can hold the plane if she runs late.

After giving the driver a new destination, she gazes out the cab window and up at blue sky. Jeremy is up there, watching from heaven. Don't you worry, little brother, there aren't gonna be any terror attacks on my watch.

An hour and a half later, she's seated on American flight 687 to Seattle. Next to her, Berry River stares at the seatback in front of her. Weird little kid. Doesn't like to look you in the face, never says a word. KB tried to be nice, but had given up after getting nothing but stony silence. She started to feel sorry for the kid, but then remembered that her father is a terrorist.

Thank God for the Patriot Act. She'd only had to flash her ID and then explain to Mrs. Fleister how she could be taken into custody immediately and held incommunicado for as long as KB wanted if she didn't release the kid into her care. The threat of shutting down her little business indefinitely had gotten the old biddy to swear to keep her mouth shut and, most important, not to alert the terrorists by calling the girl's mother. KB takes out her cell phone.

A flight attendant hurries to her. "I'm sorry, but you can't—"

KB flashes her ID "Thanks for your alertness, but this is official business." The attendant nods and leaves, and KB calls Gabe River's phone. Damn, she gets his voice mail. "This is Agent Volmer. I have your daughter. If you want to ever see her again, do not, I repeat, do not tell your cell members. Call me immediately. Make it a video call and you can say hi to your kid."

That ought to get a response. Wherever he is, he'll call.

28

Drago ambles off his plane and into a United Airlines gate area at SeaTac International Airport. Damned if he doesn't feel good. Chipper, almost. He eyes the *lessi* thronging around him, seeing the vapid colors of their mundane little lives.

Good riddance.

Then he comes upon a pair of men who stand out because of their stillness in the flow of people. Unlike the casual dress of virtually everyone else, both wear dark suits. One aims a small video camera Drago's way. The man lowers it and shakes his head as he says something to his companion. The other man takes a piece of paper from an inside coat pocket. They study it, and then they watch him.

Drago's mood chills. They start his way. He thinks of Rhianna's warning that the *lessi* have discovered *lledri* and that they, what was it ... that they have a camera that detects it. But he's *truself* and not utilizing *lledri*, so they won't see anything out of the ordinary. Still, here they come. He heads down the concourse to find baggage claim.

The larger of the two men takes an angle to intercept him. Concerned, but not worried, Drago decides to let things happen. This is interesting.

The intercepting man steps in front of Drago. "If I could have a minute, sir?" His colors radiate the burgundy of hostility.

Drago stops and puts on a smile. "What is it?"

The man produces a wallet and shows his credentials. Nelson Biddle, Homeland Security.

Drago glances back and sees that the other man has come up behind him and stands there, his body tense. His colors include animosity as well.

When Drago turns back to the agent, he begins gathering *lledri,* though he doesn't know what he'll do with it yet.

Biddle says, "May I see your ticket, sir?"

Drago hands over his ticket jacket. The name on it is Franklin Andrews, and he has a fake ID to match. He continues to gather *lledri* into a swirling globe of energy just above his head.

Biddle examines the ticket, then hands it back. He takes a piece of paper from his inside coat pocket and holds it up. After glancing from the paper to Drago and back, he turns it to Drago. "Is this you, Mr. Andrews?"

It's a grainy, black-and-white image of him. He recognizes the hallway in the building where Rhianna and the *elessi* were imprisoned. Drago smiles. "No, that's not me. I can see why ye might think so, but I've never been in that place."

Biddle puts the paper away. "Will you come with me, sir? We just need to check on a few things. I'm sure you'll quickly be on your way."

Drago is tempted to go along with them, to play with their primitive suspicions, but he's hungry, and he promised himself a brunch at the Edgewater Hotel. "I don't see why. I haven't done anything."

Biddle slips a hand inside his coat. Reaching for a gun? "We're not so sure of that, Mr. Andrews."

A hand grips Drago's arm from behind, and the other agent says, "If you don't mind?"

Drago hates the touch of a *lessi*. He whirls. "Unhand me, ape!" He propels a beam of his gathered *lledri* at the second agent's forehead. The man's head snaps back, then he staggers backward, releasing his grip on Drago's arm. He slams into a young mother holding a baby and they go down in a tangle.

Drago spins. Agent Biddle has his pistol drawn and aimed at Drago's chest. Insolent insect! Drago punches the man in the gut with a blast of *lledri*.

Biddle triggers a shot as he doubles over. The bullet creases the outside of Drago's thigh. The pain is immediate, hot, and immense. Fury rules. Drago *reaches* into the agent's chest and incinerates the man's heart with *lledri*. The lifeless body sprawls on the floor.

People stop and stare. The other agent lies unconscious while a pair of teenage girls helps the fallen mother stand. Drago shouts, "Police! Where are the police?"

A man in a pilot's uniform points up the concourse. "There's security at the gate right up that way."

"Watch these guys." He runs down the corridor as if going to get help. The second he turns a corner he slows to a walk and projects a *glamère*, choosing the image of the agent he'd accidentally killed in Chicago. His thigh hurts. Glancing back, he sees a trail of blood drops. There aren't many, and he can only hope that the swarming *lessi* won't notice. He expands his *glamère* to prevent the blood on his trousers from showing.

After fetching his bag, he takes a cab to the Edgewater. He returns to his truface appearance, but still conceals the blood on his pants with illusion. Trying not to limp, he makes his way to his room.

In the bathroom, he washes the wound, a three-inch furrow across the flesh of his thigh. It bleeds enough to be troublesome so, gritting his teeth, he struggles to focus his *lledri* enough to cauterize the wound. Despite the clumsiness of his *touch,* he succeeds, along with a little bruising. He streams *lledri* into his mind to ease the pain.

Taking the birthday-wrapped package from his bag, Drago removes the thermal bottle and sets it on a nightstand. A quick examination with his *sight* shows no leakage of the spores.

He puts on clean pants. Now for a nice brunch—he'll be damned if interference from the *lessi* will make him change his plan. And then a quick visit to the Seattle safe house to get a skimmer.

His leg still hurts, but he's angry, and he can ignore the pain. The encounter has not been all bad, though. His reasons for wiping out the *lessi* have been confirmed. And now his mission is even more personal.

~

Gabe strides alongside Rhianna on the way to the ground transportation area at SeaTac Airport. He takes out his cell phone and turns it on. The message light flashes. Keying up his voice mail, he gets KB Volmer telling him that she has Berry. It hits him like a punch, and he stops.

Rhianna goes on a few more steps, then halts and turns back to him. "Something the matter?"

He holds up the phone and works at keeping his voice normal. "Got a voice mail. I need to answer it."

She points to a shop that displays clothing. "I need some rain gear. *Lledri* can keep you warm, but it's not so good at keeping you dry." She glances above his head. "Is anything wrong?"

She probably sees his fear there. He can't lie. "I don't exactly know."

"Good luck." She goes into the store.

Getting KB's number from the recent calls screen, he launches his video call app and dials her. When her face appears on his phone, he says, "What do you mean, you have my daughter?"

KB says, "Why, hello, Mr. River. Yep, right here next to me. I thought it might help you see your way to cooperating."

How can she have gotten Berry? She can't. It's a bluff.

"You're probably wondering if I really have her. Say hi, Berry."

The image shifts to Berry, slumped in an airliner seat, buckled in. The bottom drops out of Gabe's world. Then the picture shifts to one of agent Volmer next to Berry.

It takes a moment to find his voice. "Where are you taking her?"

"First to catch one of you murdering bastards in Seattle, and then to bring you in."

Gabe almost blurts, "Don't bring her here!" but he stifles it. He glances at the store. Rhianna is toward the back, holding up something yellow. Heading for a quiet corner by a vacant gate, he says, "You don't know what you're getting into."

"I'm listening."

What's he going to tell her? That there's a bioterrorism attack? A plague? "Just don't take Berry to Seattle."

She says, "You're there, aren't you? Meeting up with your partner who killed Schultz. And that woman too, I bet."

Who is Schultz? Then Gabe remembers the man slumped over the desk when Drago helped him escape. He'd been dead? "Please. Berry's just a child."

There's a pause. "She's an odd little girl. Not too sociable."

"She's ... she's got a problem. With people."

"Don't we all. You know, I think I'll just let her go."

Thank God.

"Down by the docks. At, let's say, midnight."

He sags against a wall. Fingers of nausea curl in his stomach. "You can't do that."

"I will."

It hits Gabe that maybe this attack dog of an agent could help them stop Drago. And she'll be bringing Berry to him. "You want me and the man you're looking for, I'll tell you where. But you've got to let Berry go."

Silence stretches. Then, "Deal. I land in a half hour. Meet me at the American Airlines terminal."

"No. The Space Needle. As soon as you can."

"That's crazy. I'm not gonna—"

He sees Rhianna emerge from the shop and ends the call. He shoves the phone in his pocket and goes to meet her.

She shows him a yellow poncho with a Seattle logo on it and smiles. "I know it's not terribly fashionable, but it has a hood." She examines him, no doubt reading his colors. What does she see? She says, "What's wrong?"

"There's a problem with Berry." She frowns, and he glimpses a pale yellow-gray in her colors. Worry?

Rhianna says, "Does she need help? Maybe Vixen—"

"She's okay for now."

She glances over his head, probably checking his colors. "But you're still worried."

"Yeah. Can't help it."

"Then we'd better get going so you can get back to her."

~

KB smiles. She has a lead on the terrorists, and the guy is clearly scared. They'll make mistakes.

Her tattoo itches. She pulls her sleeve up and runs her fingers across its spreading wings, but not to scratch. The soreness is mostly gone. She takes a little jar of tattoo balm from her purse and spreads it on the tattoo. Relief is quick, and the colors look vibrant. All she has left of her little brother.

She glances at the girl—Berry gazes at the tattoo. KB holds her arm out to display it and says, "Pretty, isn't it?"

Berry turns her gaze up, and KB almost flinches at the fear she sees in the child's wide eyes. Wide, innocent eyes.

KB looks away. She's seen that expression before, on the face of her little brother at about the same age when they'd gotten separated from their mother at a parade in downtown Chicago.

Feelings rise in her—sympathy, pity, guilt... moisture gathers in her eyes ...

No! She hardens her heart. The kid will be okay after this is all over and KB will have saved lives by catching the terrorists. And she would avenge her brother, at least a little. It's all good.

But she can't look at Berry.

29

Wind gusts whip me and Gabe with rain when we run from the cab to the Space Needle. I'm glad for my poncho—I wish *lledri* was as good for keeping flying water out as it is for keeping heat in.

When the cashier sells us tickets, she says, "You're our first customers this morning. People don't usually like to go up when it's stormy like this."

Gabe says, "We don't either, but we're researching for a novel. Want it to be authentic."

After we head for the elevator, I give him a little shake of my head for his lie. He shrugs and says, "Hey, it's the truth. I'm a writer. Everything is research."

In the elevator, I watch Seattle through the glass front as we rise. Gabe stands against the back wall and averts his gaze from the view. I say, "Either Drago hasn't come here yet, or he's taken another way up."

"Another way up?"

I give him a look.

"Oh." His eyebrows rise. "Or we're wrong on the location."

I don't want to think about that possibility. That picture on his computer *has* to mean we're right.

The observation area at the top of the Space Needle seems deserted, then a security guard ambles around a curved wall and comes our way. "Good morning," he says. "Adventurers, I see."

We can't have him wondering where we are when we go to the roof. I smile and walk to him, at the same time *reaching* inside his neck to apply pressure to his carotid artery with *lledri*.

He collapses just when I get to him, and I ease his fall to the floor.

Gabe says, "What did you do?"

"Just rendered him unconscious. It's like a choke hold, only from the inside. He'll be out for a while, and then he'll be fine." Gabe's mouth twists with emotion, and I say, "I'm sorry. It was necessary."

We drag the guard to a chair and arrange him in it. He looks as if he's napping. I point to a large waste can by the railing. "Move that over, if you will."

Gabe muscles the container aside to reveal a trap door in the floor. He examines it and says, "How do you know about this?"

"That leads to the roof access through service tunnels. It seems juvenile to me now, but clansmen like to come here for the view and the restaurant, but don't like to pay the elevator fare. So we fly skimmers up, park on the roof, and enter this way." Drago is coming here, I know it. I just know it. "It will be the way Drago comes. On top in the wind is the best place for him to release his disease."

Gabe opens the trap door and I lead the way. We wend through machinery—heating and air conditioning equipment, gears and motors for rotating the restaurant—and then up stairs to the exit to the top.

I climb up and out the trap door to the flat roof above the equipment and Gabe follows me. It's about forty feet wide,

and rising from the center is the antenna, the topmost structure on the Needle. Just below is the wide, sloping roof that
covers the observation area and, below that, the rotating restaurant.

The wind has died down, but the rain keeps up its relentless
drumming. "Follow me." I circle the antennae with Gabe close
behind, but there's no sign of Drago. I lead Gabe to a leeward
spot. "We can wait here for him."

I see thin yellow in his colors, and he's pale. "Are you
okay?"

"Heights scare me." I raise my eyebrows, and he says, "A
lot."

He keeps focused on me and doesn't look out at Seattle,
sprawled out beyond the Needle. Sometimes there's a safety
rail around this structure, usually when they repaint the surface. But not today, poor Gabe. And yet the color of courage
shines brighter than that of the fear in his aura.

When we sit, backs to a wall, I generate warmth with *lledri*.
Gabe wraps his arms around himself and shivers, so I bend
his escaping energy to flow around his body and contain his
warmth. He says, "Thanks. I think I can keep it going. It's still
hard for me to work with *lledri*." He grins. "Especially when
I'm scared shitless."

I smile. "You'll get there."

And then I stare into the rain and will Drago to appear.

~

With Berry River in tow, KB stands just inside a police tape
in the United Airlines concourse with the lead Homeland

Security agent. He's a squared-off, powerful-looking guy named Warren. Cops are putting a dead agent into a body bag, and EMTs lift an unconscious one onto a gurney.

"What's the doc say about him?"

"Skull fracture. Don't know how bad."

She indicates the body bag. "What happened?"

Warren looks puzzled. "Don't know yet. No apparent wounds, witnesses saw no weapons or heard anything unusual."

"Just like our guy in Chicago. The Artisans make it look natural, but I'm sure it isn't." She takes out her phone and dials River, but the call goes to voicemail. Still, she knows where he is, as crazy as it sounds.

She draws Warren aside, out of earshot of the forensics guys and onlookers. "Listen, I have a tip from an informant. I know where the perp is."

"What are we waiting for?"

"We need a chopper."

Warren raises his eyebrows at her.

"My information is solid." She lifts Berry's hand. "I have leverage."

"The kid got to go with us?"

"She's the leverage."

Warren pulls out a phone. While he calls for a helicopter, KB eases her hand inside her coat and grips the butt of her gun. Her palm is sweaty. She wipes it on her slacks.

When he finishes his call, she pulls out her thermal camera. "I'm gonna nail these guys this time."

~

After an hour of sitting in the rain, Gabe's coat is soaked through. His hair and beard drip water—Rhianna's choice of a poncho was a good one; the rain just rolls off her hood.

The wind picks up, and a scrape sounds around the curve of the antenna's base. Rhianna stands and he gets up with her. She edges forward, and a few feet around the shaft they come to Drago, standing beside a skimmer. He gazes up at the storm clouds overhead, steadily pushing east. One hand grips a red and yellow thermos bottle. Rhianna says, "That must be it."

He whirls to face them, surprise clear on his face, and there's a white spike in the colors of his aura. But he recovers quickly. "Rhianna. And her pet *elessi.*"

"We're not going to let you do it, Drago."

She walks toward him. Gabe does too, but widens the distance between him and Rhianna to make it harder for Drago to attack them both. Unfortunately, his move takes him toward the edge of the roof. He glances out and wishes he hadn't. Even though he's thirty or so feet from the drop to the lower sloping roof below, his legs weaken at the sight of the empty space beyond it.

He jerks his gaze back to Drago. Rhianna stops fifteen feet from the little man. Gabe does the same, careful to keep his eyes focused only on Drago and not the long fall.

Rhianna spreads her arms. "This is not sane, Drago. You'll kill hundreds of millions of people."

"Ye are wrong. I'll kill billions." He holds up the thermos. "Nothing can stop this." He glances at Gabe. "Well, almost nothing. I'm surprised to see him alive. Ye are an incredibly skilled healer, Rhianna. What of the little tramp?"

"Vixen is the main reason Gabe is alive, and she's recovering now."

He twists the cap off the red thermos and tosses it up. The wind sends it careening eastward. Only the threaded top remains to contain the plague inside the thermos.

Rhianna says, "Don't. You'll kill clansmen, too."

"I don't think so. Ye have proved that the infection can be beaten with *lledri*, and I've warned the Clans that this is coming. As soon as the *lessi* report the beginnings of a pandemic, the Clans will go into hiding." He smiles. "And when they come out, the world will be ours."

Gabe says, "How can you kill innocent people, children?"

The little man laughs. "Innocent? The *lessi* have raped and polluted the planet, and now doom it to vast flooding as they warm the globe beyond its natural bounds. And they don't learn—their children will only grow up to do more of the same." He puts his hand on the thermos top. "They killed my son."

Rhianna says, "I'll kill you if I have to."

Drago winces and glowers at her. "Release my heart."

"Not until you give that thing to me."

Gabe starts forward. "I'll get it."

Drago trains his gaze on Gabe and sudden pressure on Gabe's chest slows and then stops him. And then pushes him back. He staggers and then drops to the rain-slick surface. He slides, pushed by Drago's *lledri* toward the edge, and there's nothing he can do about it.

He cries, "Rhianna!"

She glances at Gabe and then shouts, "Stop, Drago!"

"Or what, Rhianna? You can incinerate my heart, but then I'll drop this, and I can assure you that it's not sturdy enough to survive a six-hundred-foot fall."

With a fluttering roar, a black helicopter descends from the sky. As it hovers over them, a shaft of light, bright even in the gray daytime, strikes from above and illuminates Drago.

Drago looks up; the push against Gabe's body ends and he stops sliding. KB Volmer stands in the open side door of the chopper, flanked by a man aiming one of those damned thermal cameras at them. She aims a pistol at Gabe, then reaches out and pulls into view next to her ... oh, God, it's Berry.

The male agent lifts a bullhorn and his voice booms above the chopper's noise. "This is Homeland Security. Drop your weapons and lie down. I repeat, this is Homeland Security. Drop your weapons."

Gabe scrambles to his feet.

Rhianna whirls and faces him. "You betrayed us!" He feels a grip on his heart.

He points at Drago. "No, not you. Him. To stop him."

Agent Volmer shouts, "Lie down. Now."

The pressure grows in Gabe's chest. He struggles and lifts his hand to point at the helicopter. "She had Berry. I did it to get help. For Berry. For my daughter."

Rhianna looks up at the chopper and then back to Gabe. Sorrow is on her face, and gray-violet flickers in her colors. The pressure on his heart lifts.

A bright whirl of *lledri* coalesces above Drago's head. He points at the helicopter and a shaft of the *lledri* slams into the fuselage near the tail, twisting the chopper in the air. Berry lurches toward the open doorway, but Volmer grabs her and throws her back into the interior.

When the chopper steadies, she pulls out a pistol and fires at Drago, her bullets pockmark the roof near him.

If she hits him or that thermos ... Gabe sprints toward Drago. Drago hurls a spear of *lledri* at the chopper. It strikes the tail rotor and sends the helicopter spinning away, and the chopper spirals down and out of sight.

Gabe yells, "You bastard!"

Drago twists to face Gabe, and then sends *lledri* hurtling at him. But a beam from Rhianna deflects it wide.

Drago cocks his arm and arcs the thermos into the air.

Gabe pivots and runs with all his strength. As the thermos falls, Gabe leaps and lays out, his arm stretching.

He grabs the thermos and twists, flinging it back toward Rhianna. The last thing he sees before he plummets below the edge of the roof is the thermos inches from slapping into her hand.

He falls twenty feet and lands on the white roof below, bounces, and rolls down the curving slope. His hands flail against the rain-slick roof, but his fingers slip. The roof ends. He falls.

He strikes the protective cables that fence the observation deck to keep jumpers from leaping. He grasps a cable with one hand, but the force of his momentum tears him away.

Gabe drops ... and hits the rings of the "halo" that flares out from beneath the restaurant. And then he plunges, nothing beneath him but hundreds of feet of air.

The helicopter sits on the concrete below, safely landed near a merry-go-round in a children's play area. Figures run from it ... the agent tows Berry by the arm!

Gabe works to gather *lledri* the way Vixen showed him. If he can push up ... but his fear overwhelms his feeble efforts. He twists to look at Berry, and his love fills him.

Pressure builds underneath him, against his belly. Something clutches at the back of his jacket, and then pulls up.

The push from under him grows, and the ground stops coming up so fast.

Rhianna appears beside him. She grips his jacket.

He swings upright, and they settle onto the pavement. The fear that floods through him turns into immense joy.

Agent Volmer's shout comes. "Drop it."

He and Rhianna turn. The agent stands with her feet spread wide, her pistol gripped in both hands. Berry huddles beside her.

Volmer shouts again. "Drop the bomb. Drop it or I'll shoot." Her expression is fierce, almost crazy.

Gabe glances at Rhianna. She holds the yellow thermos. He raises his hands and shouts, "It's not a bomb. Don't shoot."

"Drop it now!"

Rhianna raises the thermos. "It's not a—"

Volmer fires.

~

My reflexes take over and I hurl *lledri* at the agent. It slams into her and knocks her backward. Her gun flies from her hand and she falls on her back. She lies still, unconscious, but a red-orange spike of pain shows in her colors. Good, I hope I've broken the bitch's bones.

Gabe shouts, "Berry" and runs for his daughter. Poor Berry, she stands frozen, no doubt overwhelmed. But she's of tougher stuff than I think—at first shuffling and then running, she races toward her father.

A sense that something is badly wrong troubles me. When the woman fired, there'd been a shock in the hand that grips the thermos. I hold the bottle in front of me. The agent's bullet has scored the side. Black spores seep from a breach. The spores can last for years, and, in a city like this, just one will be enough to launch the plague.

I widen my *sight* and *see* the dark cloud of more spores' muted life spreading away from me, the leading edge just a foot away. Loosing a wave of *lledri*, I destroy them. I encircle myself with a sphere of *lledri* to contain the spores, but I know the wind and rain will defeat me.

Gabe reaches Berry and holds her in his arms. The red-gold of love fills their colors ... I can't let that be killed.

There is only one answer.

Lledri flows free and thick in a city such as this. I locate my *key* deep within me and stream *lledri* into it, at the same time confining the energy there. My Final Fire will destroy the spores.

"Gabe!"

He turns to me and his eyes widen. He must be *seeing* the *lledri* pour into me. I yell, "Take cover."

With Berry in his arms, he sprints for the merry-go-round.

Motion to my side catches my eye at the same time invisible *lledri* fingers clutch my heart. Drago descends on his skimmer, his face twisted and fierce, and hatred dominates his colors. I divert *lledri* and flip his skimmer twenty feet above the pavement. He topples, and his grip on my heart vanishes as he saves himself from a fall.

Heat builds inside me. The energy of the *lledri* is close to breaching my ability to hold it. Searching for Gabe, I find him making Berry lie down on a colorful unicorn bench on the carousel. He straightens and turns to me.

Oh, Gabe. There is so much I want to teach you and Berry.

I hope you will somehow make contact with my clan. Mary Fay will bring you in.

I wish I could see Berry better.

I clutch the bottle to my chest. The force inside me is too much. Now it spreads in a widening sphere. It isn't painful, more of a delicious warming. It gathers speed, I *see* streams of *lledri* sucked toward me from outside as if into the vortex of a whirlpool. My Final Fire grows, multiplied beyond my control ...

Survive, Gabe. Love your daughter as I have my son. Teach her, and share a long, long life with her. I send a tendril of *lledri* that reaches Gabe for a last *touch,* my last contact with a human being.

My *touch* reaches Gabe.

I don't want to die.

Light bursts from my chest—

30

Drago gets to his knees and staggers to his feet. The shock wave of lledri from Rhianna's Final Fire had passed over him, but he'd sensed its force. In all of clan history, a Fire's energy has always gone up. But, impossibly, a great beam of her lledri went into the elessi who now lies stunned on the ground next to the merry-go-round. Or dead.

There is no Rhianna, no thermos, only a circular scorched place on the pavement. He peers with his *sight*. No spores of *b. Dragonum*.

The little girl scrambles from a bench and runs to her father. The child throws her arms around Gabe and cries, "Daddy."

Rhianna and the *elessi* half-breed have destroyed years of work, his cure consumed by Rhianna's Fire. Well, now it's his turn to destroy. He strides toward the downed man, gathering *lledri* to send it smashing into Gabe's heart.

A shout comes from the direction of the downed helicopter. "Hey!" A burly man limps toward Drago, blood staining one pants leg. He holds a pistol high. "Drop to the ground."

Maybe there's a better way to punish Gabe. These Homeland Security agents have a taste for torture. And now they'll have the little girl to use. Yes, Gabe River will suffer a great deal more if Drago leaves him here alive.

Drago hurls a fist of *lledri* at the man, but pulls his punch. The force strikes the man's solar plexus; he falls to the pavement and doubles over, struggling to breathe.

Drago heads for his skimmer. After he dries off at the safe house, he'll charter a jet for the trip back to Chicago. He's had all of the *lessi* that he can stand.

He raises his gaze to the top of the Space Needle. "I'm not done. No, I'm not done."

~

The solid beat of her father's heart against Berry's chest helps slow her own racing heartbeat. Daddy is alive. Berry sits up and searches for Rhianna. She can't see her ... but it feels like she's here, somewhere.

Movement catches her eye, and Berry watches a small man with angry colors flashing above his head rise into the air on something that looks like a big spoon without a handle.

A moan slips through the patter of rain, and a lump on the pavement stirs. The man who was in the helicopter with her and the angry woman lies there, a pistol in his hand. The man raises his head and looks at Berry, then struggles to his feet and limps toward them.

Berry shoves her dad's side. "Daddy! Wake up." Her father's head wobbles, rain splashes on his face, but he doesn't open his eyes. The colors around his head show the waves of reddish orange that Berry has learned means hurting—she'd seen it when Rusty fell. And Rhianna had fixed him.

What did Rhianna do then? Can she do it now?

The man with the gun limps closer, and the color of pain is around his head, too. But so is the scary purple-red that means he's really mad. Mad enough to hurt Daddy?

Berry shakes her father again, but he doesn't wake up.

Closing her eyes, Berry thinks hard about when Rhianna helped her horse. She'd put her hands on him. She leans forward and puts one hand on her daddy's heart, the other on his forehead. Now what?

Rhianna had moved the sparky stuff into Rusty, taking it from Berry and the swirls of dots in the air. Berry doesn't know how to take it from the air, but she's been playing with the sparks that come from inside her for almost a year, drawing designs in the air and sometimes using it to give her mom's cheek an "air kiss."

The man raises his gun and aims it at Daddy. He says, "Hands above your head."

But Daddy can't move. Berry grasps the sparks and sends them down her arms to where her fingers touch her father. It takes just a little *push* to send it inside, toward her daddy's heart and into his head. But is that enough?

Daddy tosses his head side to side, but doesn't open his eyes. "Mmmmm."

"Daddy! Wake up!"

The man with the gun stops a few feet away. "I'll shoot."

Berry pushes the sparks into her father faster. Oh, please, please ...

Daddy's eyes open. Blinking against the rain, he looks at Berry. "Berry?"

Then Daddy sits up and hugs Berry against him. Things will be okay now.

~

Gabe crushes his daughter to his chest. Joy swells in his throat and tears well up to mix with the rain—he never, never wants to let go. Berry wriggles and Gabe gives her a kiss on her head, and then grips her shoulders.

He *sees* the blaze of Berry's aura—it's mostly the buttery yellow of happiness. How ...?

Berry looks into his eyes. "Daddy." Then she moves her hand through the air above Gabe's head and says, "Rhianna."

The image of Rhianna vanishing in a blaze of *lledri* explodes into Gabe's mind ... a shaft of her living energy, a cylinder of brilliant light, had slammed him ... and then there'd been blackness.

Rhianna ... Gabe knows she's gone, but there's a flavor, an essence of her in his mind—intelligent, aloof, caring, warm. It feels like he can ask her a question and get an answer.

The plague. Did she stop the plague?

A man's voice comes, heavy with menace. "On your stomach. Now."

Gabe turns his head toward the voice. His gaze passes Agent Volmer, still on the ground where Rhianna zapped her. He comes to a heavyset man aiming a pistol at him.

He eases Berry around behind him. The man's colors—how come Gabe sees them so clearly now?—are angry and hurt-looking. Keeping his voice low and soft, Gabe says, "I haven't done anything."

"I see one of our agents on the ground, maybe dead, and you're the only one around. Your accomplice got away after he hit me with something."

Accomplice? Drago? "Sir, I was unconscious. I don't know what happened." Well, that isn't the complete truth, but it's close enough. He sure as hell doesn't understand what's going on now, other than that he and Berry are in deep shit.

The man gestures with the gun. "I don't want to hurt the girl. Lie face down and put your hands behind your back."

"Who are you?"

"Homeland Security. I'm giving you five seconds, and then I'll fire."

No way is Gabe returning to that torture chamber. But what can ... Berry leans close and whispers, "Can you hit him with the sparky stuff?"

He isn't good enough to ... then he realizes he now sees *lledri* clearly. He tries reaching with his thoughts the way Vixen showed him, and somehow it's easy to round up a handful of swirling energy. He sends it flying at the agent.

The agent brushes a hand at his chest. "Lie down!"

Okay, more. Gabe gathers a larger collection and "throws" it harder.

This time the agent staggers back. He straightens, and then his gun booms. The bullet *spangs* off the pavement only a foot from Gabe. The fucker's going to hit Berry! His instincts take over and a shaft of *lledri* zooms at the agent.

It hits the man's chest straight on—he flies back two yards and then falls on his back. The gun skitters across the pavement. The agent lies still. Colors radiate from him, mostly a red-violet, so he's alive.

Sirens howl in the distance, moving closer. Cops and fire fighters will be all over the scene. Gabe gets to his feet, takes Berry's hand, and leads her away.

A few minutes later, he pulls Berry into the doorway of the Experience Music Project rock and roll museum and peers back the way they'd come. There's no sign of pursuit. Berry's hand shakes, and Gabe kneels beside her. Berry shivers, and her skin is pale. Have to get her warm and dry. He bends Berry's *lledri* and sends it wrapping around her body, and then wonders how the hell he did that so easily. But Berry's shivering stops.

Gabe uses the Uber app to get a car to the nearest hotel. Safe from the rain and pursuit, he pulls Berry close to help warm her. "We're gonna be okay, we're gonna be fine." And then it hits him that Bonnie must be terrified. He fishes out his cell phone to call her and then book a flight home.

Home.

His gaze settles on Berry. He isn't going to live apart from his daughter any longer.

31

KB can't find anything good on the hospital TV. She'd like to throw the remote at it, but that would hurt too much. Bandages wrap her ribs, six of them broken, they told her. Lying helpless in a hospital bed sucks bigtime. She eases a breath in and tries a relaxing exhale, but that hurts too. A wrist-to-shoulder cast encases her left arm, broken in two places. Her right knee, the kneecap split, is locked in a brace. She doesn't understand what the Artisan hit her with, but it sure hurts.

What happened to the Artisans? And the kid? When Warren left the helicopter and reached the area, he hadn't spotted any sign of the woman and her bomb, though he had seen a big flare of light. Something knocked the wind out of him and, when he recovered, he'd gotten his gun on Gabe River and his daughter, and then something hit him again. When he came around, they were gone, and so were the little man who killed Schultz and the woman with the bomb. There was a scorch mark on the concrete that forensics can't figure out—what was that about?

But the Artisans had stopped doing whatever they were doing. By God, she'd done it.

Her cell phone rings on the bedside tray and she shoots her hand out for it. Pain rips up her chest and she has to stop, then she edges closer to the tray to get the phone.

It's the RAC. "Agent Volmer?"

"Yes, sir."

"How are you feeling?"

Like shit, basically. "All right, sir."

"I understand that it won't be easy for you to get a report out, but I need one as soon as possible. You have some things to explain."

She looks to the thermal camera sitting on a chair, its lens shattered and body dented in the helicopter crash. But the memory card could still be good. She brightens at that thought; and she also has footage from the woman's escape from her the cell at headquarters.

Yes! She might finally have the goods on the Artisans. And then she'll round them up. She knows where River's kid lives, and he won't cut that tie. "Yessir, I'll do what I can as soon as I'm back in Chicago. You'll see—"

The RAC says, "You should know that I've cancelled the order for the arrest of Gabriel River."

She jerks upward, then moans when pain tears through her rib cage. It takes a moment to get her breath. "No. Please, sir, you can't—"

"Bailey came to me with the results of a most thorough investigation, and there's absolutely nothing suspicious in his background. He's an innocent bystander."

"But he went with the Artisans. He was—"

"He may have been coerced, and there wasn't any concrete evidence that the other people you suspect are what you say they are."

Why can't he believe her?

He says, "Mr. River is not a target of this agency. Is that clear?"

Crystal. "The little man? The woman?"

"We're watching for them, but more to clear up your allegations than because they've done anything." He pauses. "It seems to me that it's you who's done all the doing."

"Sir, I acted on good information." And good instincts.

"Well, let's see that report. Goodbye."

She ends the call. But this is not the end. She gazes out the window. The fucking rain is still falling. She'll get them. And Gabe River is not going to disappear. There will be nothing in his life that she won't know.

One day he'll pay. He'll be hers. Behind bars.

She shifts her hurt knee and a bolt of pain wracks her. The doc thinks she'll end up with a limp. She buzzes the nurse in hopes of getting another hit of OxyContin.

An itch on her forearm catches her mind. She pulls her sleeve up and gazes at her tattoo. She whispers, "I'm sorry, little brother." She gazes at the rain out the window. "But Gabe River hasn't seen the last of me."

~

Drago lowers his skimmer through the low light of dusk to the deck of his galleon. His ship and the other two he'd left in the forest preserve clearing had not gone to where they were supposed to, as he'd instructed Emmaline, to their refuge in the swamps of Louisiana

He makes no effort to still his rage; she will suffer the full force of it. He slams open the door to belowdecks and descends with a thunder of bootheels. He shouts, "Emmaline! Where the cursed gods are—" He stops midway down the stairs.

In the room, a black woman stands, followed by the other four members of the North American Grand Council, from where they lounge on couches and chairs in his living room. The woman is that embarrassment of an *elessi*, Mary Fay, the "clanmaster" of Rhianna's clan.

They must have been mad to name the woman to a position of authority, not only a half-breed and not only a female, but black-skinned as well. What an abomination.

The men and women face him as he steps from the stairs. He looks to Owain, clanmaster of the Pacific coast Magian clans, for a smile from his old friend. He encounters a glare and a thin-lipped mouth turned down at the corners. The expressions of Morgan and Bronwen, from the Canadian and Mexican clans, are equally hostile. Kendrick of the Colorado clan won't even look his way.

No matter, he has done no harm. He smiles and holds his arms out as if to embrace them. "Greetings, my friends." He holds up his hands, palms out. "If ye are here about the final cure I attempted to unleash on the *lessi*, ye can rest easy. It came to be no more than an attempt, unfortunately foiled by that traitoress Rhianna."

Owain says, "So it is true that you were releasing a plague to create a mass slaughter of human beings?"

Drago shrugs. "I wouldn't classify the *lessi* as human beings, but yes, I tried to do that. But my creation was eliminated by Rhianna in her Final Fire."

A gasp bursts from Mary Fay. "Her Final Fire? Oh, no." She clenches her fists. "What did you—"

"I did nothing to harm her. She gave up her life in her misguided attempt to, sadly, save the *lessi*." He claps his hands together. "Now let's let bygones be bygones. Would ye care for a glass of wine? Or I have a delightful sherry that ye might enjoy." He raises his voice. "Emmaline? Where are ye!"

She steps from the galley. "I'm here, and I won't be servin' the likes of you."

He scowls at her. "Why ye—"

"No one will be serving you, Drago." Mary Fay steps forward. "You are shunned. No Magian may have congress with you or assist you in any way. Your crime was unspeakable."

His anger builds, and he strides toward Mary Fay, his fist raised to pummel her. But his feet stop moving as if stuck to the floor. "Who dares use *lledri* against me! I will strike you all dow—"

Pain takes him over as his testicles are gripped by an invisible hand. Mary Fay's expression becomes a fierce smile with sharp teeth in it. He swings an arm to point at her, ready to deliver a massive blow of *lledri*, but increased pressure crushes his balls, multiplying the pain tenfold. He collapses to the floor, writhing, gripping himself, the agony more than he could have imagined.

Owain glances at Mary Fay and nods. He says to Drago, "You will leave here with no more than what you are wearing and have in your pockets. You will go afoot, skimmers and anything else of the Clans is denied you."

The pain lowers by half as unseen pressure formed of *lledri* lifts him to his feet and elevates him to the open doorway to the deck. He shouts, "I was unable to eliminate the *lessi*, but I will scrub the earth clean of ye for your betrayal!"

Mary Kay says, "Begone." The grip on his testicles releases and an invisible force pushes and sends him sprawling on the galleon's deck. The door slams shut behind him.

Dozens of the members of his clan surround his ship. As if given a silent command, as one they turn their backs to him and walk away, toward their ships.

"Damn ye! Damn ye all!" He grabs the skimmer he'd ridden from the Chicago safe house, but it is as if it were glued to the deck.

There is nothing left but for him to leave.

He stops at the edge of the meadow and faces the darkened ships. "Ye will suffer. I will bring down my wrath upon ye, and ye will suffer."

32

It's cold and clear in Palatine, but the crisp air feels good to Gabe after being soaked by bone-chilling rain in Seattle. When Bonnie opens the door to greet Berry and him, her smile is wide and her cheeks are wet with tears. She pulls Berry from Gabe's arms and holds her, burying her face in her hair.

After a long moment, she looks up at Gabe. Her colors are pure happiness. "I'm glad to see you, too."

He's glad to see her. The romance is dead and gone, but he likes this woman who's been such a big part of his life and an incredible mother for Berry. If she'll go for it, coming back to live here long enough to see Berry through growing up will be okay. And then ... well, after finding his *key* cell during the flight back, he figures he'll have a long time to discover things. And there will be lots of time to spend with Rhianna's clan, to learn, to grow what he can do now. To teach Berry.

He looks at Bonnie with one of the many abilities that he's been discovering since Rhianna's *lledri* poured into him, including knowing what a *key* cell is and what to do with it. He sees that Bonnie's brain shows none of the abilities Berry and he have. But he also sees her honesty, strength, and warmth. "I want to come back."

She nods. "I've been thinking about that."

Good old Bonnie. It has to be her way, and that's okay with him.

She says, "This has been a real scary time" and gives Berry a kiss on the cheek. "Whatever happens with you and me, I'd like you here for Berry."

She has always been wise, Bonnie has. He should have known that she sees "us" clearly. He wishes he still felt the love for her that he once had, but it just isn't there. He likes her a helluva lot, though, and partnering will be okay. Better than okay.

"I'm gonna go get my stuff. Be back by, oh, four o'clock."

"What about work?"

"I don't need to go in today." He'll have to bite that bullet later.

He takes a cab to the parking lot where he left his truck the day Homeland Security snatched Rhianna and him, and he's glad to see that it hasn't been stripped or towed.

Fat snowflakes flutter down when he gets to his apartment. He stands in the backyard for a moment, just to take in the easy settling of the snow. He plans to enjoy every moment for the rest of his life. Falling off the Space Needle gives you a new perspective about the value of moments.

A blue jay swoops overhead, and he wonders what it's doing out in the winter. And he wonders if he can reach out and connect with it the way Rhianna did his horse. Before he can try, the jay takes off, gaining altitude and heading west.

Inside his apartment, he finds the dirty cups in the kitchen sink. Funny, there are four. He remembers the first amazing opening Rhianna caused in Berry. If only she could see her now.

When he picks up the phone to cancel the land line, he finds the voice mail signal beeping. Four messages. The first two are old ones from Bonnie, and he cringes at the fright in her voice.

Then Lawrence's voice oozes out of the receiver.

"Gabe, I'm calling to ask you to come back in and talk about what, er, happened. I realize I might have been hasty. Guess I was having a bad day. Anyway, no hard feelings, so let's talk, okay?"

Gabe doesn't think so. It isn't worth it.

The next message is the voice of Phil Esterhaus, his former Allied Hardware client.

"Gabe, I don't know why you had to leave our meeting the other day, but I hope we can get together. I really want to do your campaign, the funny take-off on a sitcom. Liz told me that you're not with the agency any more, but maybe that's a good thing. We can work together directly, if you're willing. Give me a call?"

Gabe thinks back to the meeting where he'd *seen* Phil lie. Phil must have been lying to Lawrence, not to him, saying nice things about Lawrence's campaign before he got to the one he really liked. This is very cool. Gabe can make enough on the creative fee for a twenty-million-dollar account to do whatever he wants, including work at home in his pajamas. He makes a mental note to go shopping for pajamas.

He's packing bathroom stuff when the door buzzer sounds. He opens his door a crack and peeks down the half-flight of stairs to the foyer. It's Vixen. A blue jay perches on one hand.

A lump of joy hits his throat, and he buzzes her in. She goes to the front door, sends the jay flying, and then trots up the stairs, looking just as she had when he first met her, like a tiny, gorgeous nineteen-year-old with bushy red hair flaring over her shoulders.

She stops when she reaches his landing, and her eyes glitter above her smile. In her colors he sees warm yellow and rosy gold. She says, "Hey. I was just in the neighborhood—"

He slips his arms around her, enfolds her, and pulls her close. Her arms reach up and around his neck and return his embrace. There's so much he wants to say, including thank you for teaching him *lledri* and thank you for saving his life. But right now, all he wants to do is hold her.

She leans back, and laughter flavors her words. "What, you're not going to invite me in?"

He laughs, takes her hand, and pulls her inside. She looks up at him with those amazing blue eyes, and he sees the woman of many years and huge spirit that lives under her teenage surface. He isn't usually short of words, but he feels like a high school kid talking to a girl he has a secret crush on. The best he can manage is, "I'm moving out."

She lifts an eyebrow.

"I'm going back to live with Berry. I have to help her grow up with this ..." he twirls his finger at his head. "... with this *lledri* thing. I need to be there full time."

Vixen studies Gabe, and he wonders what she sees in his colors. He knows what he feels, and right now it's all about her. But he says again, "I have to."

She sighs and then nods. "I know. It's the right thing." She raises her brows again. Her aura darkens with a grayish yellow—somehow he knows it's the color of worry—and her voice is tight. "It's ... just for now?"

He puts his hands on her shoulders. "For now. For a while." He traces the fingertips of one hand down her cheek and then through the tumbling copper of her hair. "Just for a while. Promise."

The gray-yellow vanishes and her smile returns. "I can live with that. We have time." An amber color takes over her aura; he feels her *touch* on his belly, and then it heads south. She peers into the apartment. "Have you packed your sheets yet?"

Gabe pulls her to him for a kiss and sends his touch gliding over her body.

A woman's voice whispers from a back corner of his mind. *Life is good.*

Rhianna?

Epilogue

A smile comes to Gabe when the blue braided rug in his mother's room tugs at childhood memories of playing on it. He gazes down at her lying on her bed, and the feeling of a smile shrinks to one of loss. She looks like an elderly angel, dozing, at peace. He thinks her mouth holds a small smile, but he knows she has been unconscious for days. During KB Volmer's "visit," she'd suffered a hemorrhagic stroke, the bleeding in her brain sending her into unconsciousness.

Pulling a chair close, he reaches out to brush a strand of gray hair from her face. He has no intention of saying good-bye to the lively woman who has given him a lifetime of love. He is here to save her. To restore her.

If he can.

"I don't even know how to start, Rhianna."

I do.

He still isn't used to hearing her voice in his head, but he doesn't mind it. She thinks much of her essence filled a part of his brain rather than dissipate the way it should have during her Final Fire. She'd said there was no record of anything like it happening in the history of the Magian clans.

You have the touch, *Gabe, and I have the knowledge from studying human anatomy as a healer for a century. We have* lledri. *We can do it.*

After checking to be sure the door to the room is closed, he closes his eyes to aid in focusing. His mind's eye sees streams of living *lledri* radiating from himself and his mother. But when he pushes closer with his awareness, a dark area in her brain becomes clear.

Rhianna's voice comes. *There it is. We need to dissolve the clot. I will direct your touch.*

He loosens his control and Rhianna's guiding will joins his. Cell by cell, they use *lledri* to break the clot into harmless fragments that drift away to be cleaned by his mother's kidneys.

Once the fragments are all gone, blood flows freely into the starved cells of her brain. He pours *lledri* into them, and healthy *lledri* streams back out.

"Gabe?"

It's his mother's voice. He opens his eyes and smiles. "Yes, Mom. I'm here."

She smiles, and it warms him.

Rhianna's thought comes. *Ahhhh.* Apparently it warms her, too.

His mom frowns. "I had the most terrible dream. A very nasty young woman was yelling at me, and then everything went dark."

He strokes her cheek. "That's all over with."

Her smile comes back. "Good." She takes his hand and wraps hers around it.

"I love you, Mom."

She nods, and then her eyes drift closed.

You know, Rhianna, I like doing this. I wonder if...

Yes, Gabe, you can most certainly become a doctor.

He senses an internal smile along with her thought. *With a ghost beside you. Actually,* inside *you, I guess.*

Yeah." He chuckles. *"Welcome home. Pardon the mess.*

Soft laughter echoes in his mind.

The Colors of Emotions

Human caring, affection: rosy gold, a rich hue
Wonder: airy sky blue
Surprise: blue-white
Happiness: buttery
Amazement: white flash
Amusement: pink
Hope: gold
Courage: red-brown
Contentment: pale orange
Battle, fighting: bloody red
Lust: amber
Lies: bile, bilious, yellow-green
Enmity: burgundy
Anger: purple-red, bruised red
Malice: red-black
Madness: acrid, bloody tornado of colors
Pain: jagged bursts of red-orange
Fear: acid yellow
Combat: burnt orange
Hunger: gray
Suspicion: murky gray
Depression: ash-violet
Worry: pale, yellow-gray
Sadness: ash color

Novels by me I think you will enjoy

In small-town Bloomsburg Illinois, newbie vampires Patch, a calico tomcat, and Meg, a pinkish human being, are targets for vigilante vampire hunters. Patch and Meg come out of the coffin to campaign for sheriff so they can stop the vampire killers.

On the way to election day, Patch is kidnapped, tried for murder (hey, it was one of those yappy little dogs), there's betrayal at the American Vampire Association, a bloodthirsty preacher has vampicide on his mind, and Patch and Meg are hit with a deadly double-cross.

Support Your Local Vampire Kitty-Cat is serious fun in the way only satire can be. More than that, it's the story of a cat and a young woman who struggle with a curse that is destroying their lives.

Join Patch in a tale rife with action, humor, and what vampire life, so to speak, is really like.

The old vampire saying, "Life doesn't get any easier after you're dead," nails it for vampire kitty-cat Patch when Meg, his vampire partner, is arrested for murder. When the sun comes up, innocent Meg, locked in a jail cell, will be toast.

Worse, her incarceration means curtains for Patch. Trapped in their apartment, he can't open the refrigerator to get to their V1 Juice (blood), much less open the bottles.

Opposable thumbs are so handy.

Meg begs Nick, the cop who nabbed her, to help Patch, but he's down on cats. Reciprocally, Meg hates Nick for sending them to their doom.

And Nick is the only one who can save them.

The air was as still as it was hot—only the whir of a grasshopper's flight troubled the quiet. Jesse felt like an overcooked chicken, his meat darn near ready to fall off his bones. Mouth so dry he didn't have enough spit left to swallow, Jesse croaked, "That guy tryin' to kill us?"

Turns out the answer is "not yet." A ranch hand is murdered and bad things start happening to Jesse, just an average kid working on a ranch the summer of 1958.

And then there's Lola ... the boss's daughter is a firecracker of a girl, and her bold ways send death their way.

It will take all of their heart and courage to survive.

Paperback and Kindle available on Amazon.

In the time it takes an average person to read this novel, three Americans will die from a handgun bullet.

In today's America there is no hope of preventing those killings. Dealing with gun violence is mired in a cultural logjam—as things are, nothing will change.

But what if gun makers could make billions if s lethal firearms were illegal? They'd make it happen.

What if we could defend ourselves without using lethal firearms? We'd make it happen.

In *Gundown*, guns are still everyday killers. Ordinary people have no defense—except in Oregon, where reforms have self-defense on the rise and guns that kill are banned.

But gun advocates fear losing their rights. Hank Soldado, Army veteran and ex-cop, is a good guy with a gun. He accepts an assignment to stop the gun-reform leader.

Going undercover to get close to his target—the closer he gets the more he's drawn to the man's vision for a way to turn America's murderous gun impasse into gun-free self-defense, security, and safety.

Then treachery strikes to destroy that vision, and Hank becomes the only one who can save it—a man who has a lifetime of guns in his blood.

Paperback and Kindle editions of these novels are available on Amazon and through your local bookstore. I hope you'll give them a look.

Thanks for reading.

About the Author

Ray Rhamey has been a writer for all of his professional career, beginning with writing programmed instruction training manuals for an insurance company (mind-numbing). He moved on to advertising and had a terrific time doing that. During those decades of creativity, storytelling crept into the ads he wrote, and he started working on screenplays.

Screenwriting lured him out of advertising and to Hollywood. Although he mastered the art of crafting a professional script and had an agent, he didn't concoct a story that anyone was interested in spending millions of dollars to produce. Ah, well. (Although, on the kid side, you can still see his film adaptation of *The Little Engine that Could.*)

So he moved on to freelance editing of fiction and writing novels. He also writes a blog about the art and craft of storytelling, *Flogging the Quill.* It is the source of his highly recommended book on writing craft, *Mastering the Craft of Compelling Storytelling.*

In addition to writing and editing novels, Ray's scope of services includes book design and production for self-publishers and Indie publishers. You can see samples at www.crrreative.com.

Ray grew up in Dallas, Texas, but has since lived, as his grandmother would have said, all over hell and half of Georgia (but not actually in Georgia). As of this writing, the places he's called home are Dallas, Texas; Bloomington and Chicago, Illinois; St. Louis, Missouri; Studio City and Van Nuys, California; Ashland, Oregon; Cincinnati, Ohio; Salt Lake City, Utah; Louisville, Kentucky; Seattle, Colfax, and Pullman, Washington.

His four amazing kids live in North Carolina, Oregon, Illinois, and Missouri. They make the world a better place.

He has three websites that serve readers and writers:

rayrhamey.com features his fiction and non-fiction

crrreative.com, book cover and interior design, editing

floggingthequill.com is his blog on storytelling where writers can get critiques of their opening pages as well as coaching in fiction craft.

Hey, if you enjoyed *Final Fire*, I hope you'll post a review and rating on Amazon.com. It will be a huge favor.

All best,

Ray